CH

DEADLY CREED

THE RED TEAM, BOOK 11

ELAINE LEVINE

D1707298

Published by Elaine Levine
Copyright © 2017 Elaine Levine
Last Updated: February 12, 1018
Cover art by The Killion Group, Inc.
Cover image featuring Jordan Martinez © Luis Rafael Photos
Editing by Arran McNicol @ editing720
Proofing by Carol Agnew @ Attention to Detail Proofreading

Print ISBNs:
ISBN-13: 978-1985830424
ISBN-10: 1985830426

The dead just don't seem to stay dead...

A recent grad with a degree in gifted ed, Wynn Ratcliff jumped at the chance to be a young linguistic savant's private tutor. The job let her stay near her grandmother while she was recovering from her stroke. Unfortunately, the terrific opportunity came with some horrific negatives...namely catching the eye of her employer's enemies. After her grandmother's murder, Wynn fled back to the safety of the real world and her life as it was before she met Angel Cordova and his team of terrorist hunters.

She soon discovers the reality she thought she was returning to is gone...or perhaps it never existed. Former spec ops soldier Angel Cordova has no choice but to retrieve Wynn when he learns she's being stalked by the enemy his team is fighting. It's not entirely against her will that he brings her back to the team's headquarters, but it is under duress. Keeping her safe means steamrolling the life of her dreams. Setting her free means handing her over to their enemies, all wrapped up in a sparkly bow.

It's a choice no man should ever have to make about the woman he loves...one he knows she will not quietly accept.

～

Length: Approximately 381 pages
Ages: 18 & up (story contains sex, profanity, and violence)

Deadly Creed (The Red Team, Book 11) is part of a serialized story that includes nine full-length novels and nine wedding novellas. This series is best read in order, starting with The Edge of Courage.

Join the conversation on Facebook: Visit Elaine Levine's War Room - http://geni.us/hxFk to talk about this book and all of her suspenseful stories!

OTHER BOOKS BY ELAINE LEVINE

DEDICATION

I asked you, Barry, how it was that Grandpa Louie lived such a long and healthy life. Simple, you said. He laughed every day. And not just chuckles. No, his were belly laughs that shook his shoulders and made his eyes tear. Each one bought him another day.

I can still hear that laugh and the infectious way it rippled through anyone nearby. Thank you, B, for following his example and making us rich with so many extra days.

And thank you, Grandpa Louie, for showing us that laughter matters.

A NOTE FROM THE AUTHOR

We begin *Deadly Creed* at the point where *Razed Glory* left off. To maximize your enjoyment of this serialized story, I highly recommend reading the series in order, starting with *The Edge of Courage* and including the Red Team wedding novellas, before beginning this book!

And make sure you never miss a book from me by signing up for my new release announcements at http://geni.us/GAlUjx.

—Elaine

WHEN WE LAST VISITED THE RED TEAM…

Here's a refresher for those of you who have read the previous Red Team books (skip this and go read them if you haven't yet!). This is where we left our heroes…

***** **Spoilers!** *****

- It's late October, and the team is in their fifth month of investigation.
- Ace was a photographer at Rocco and Mandy's wedding, where she dropped a bombshell on the team regarding Owen's past love.
- Owen has gone AWOL.
- Lion and his pride of watchers are still missing.

- Wynn has returned to the life she had before working for the Silases.
- Grams was buried in Wolf Creek Bend.
- Mandy and Ivy are both pregnant.
- The Friendship Community continues under quarantine for the smallpox outbreak there.
- Yusef Sayed is still acting as the team's eyes and ears from his motel in Cheyenne.

And now, we continue with Angel Cordova and Wynn Ratcliff's story in ***Deadly Creed***...

1

He let her go, just let her walk right out of his life, the only woman he'd ever met who could have been the One.

Angel Cordova closed his eyes and saw Wynn Ratcliff standing alone in the cold wind next to the fresh dirt mounded over her grandmother's grave. It was for the best that she was gone. A woman like her didn't belong in his world. She was too soft, too fragile. Too kind.

Angel shoved those memories from his mind. His team lead, Kit Bolanger, had given the group the afternoon off. None of them had their heads on straight after the funeral earlier that day. Wynn's grandmother had made everyone fall in love with her, and they all were wounded by her death.

He wandered into the living room. Ace was sitting on the sofa with her laptop. "What are you working on?" he asked, hoping Val had told her the war room was the place for any of the team's work.

"I'm putting together a photo album for Rocco and Mandy from the pics I took of their wedding." She smiled at him. "I wanted to do it sooner, but things got crazy."

Angel sat next to her, careful not to bump against her and jostle her broken arm. He wondered if she'd taken some pics of Wynn. Crazy how he craved the sight of her. She was gone. Long gone. He had to let her go.

But really, would it hurt anyone if he just looked at some pictures of her?

"I'll start it over at the beginning." Ace reset the photo album, then handed him her laptop.

The pictures were more than 2-D images; they were multidimensional vignettes of emotion and light. Ace had an eye for life. He watched the photos, trying to focus long enough to do each image justice, though he just wanted to jump forward to pics of Wynn. He remembered she'd been busy that day with Zavi and Casey. Doing her job. Letting Mandy have her day and giving Ivy the chance to do the things a friend does at her bestie's wedding.

He flipped to the next digital page, and there she was...in a collage that filled the page. Laughing with Zavi, pulling him into a hug, doing some flower project with Casey as Zavi watched.

"She looks happy there. Look at her eyes." Ace pointed to one of the pics.

Angel nodded. "She does."

"Not like she did in these." Ace clicked to a different grouping of Wynn's pictures, the motion a little awkward since she was using her left hand, sparing her injured right arm. All of the pics that slowly slid across the screen were candid shots. "She looks scared in these. I'm not sure if I should include them in the album." She looked up at him. "I want this collection to be a tribute to happiness, not fear."

Angel clicked on each picture, bringing it to full size. He went through a whole bunch of them. How scared Wynn must have been just about the whole time she was here. He felt Ace's eyes on him.

"You're in love with her," she said.

A wave of frustration came over him before he gave a harsh laugh. "Not that it matters now."

Ace linked her good arm through his and looked up at him. "It matters. Love always matters." Her eyes held his. "Val showed me that."

"He didn't keep you here when you wanted to go. I can't do that to her, either."

"What matters most to you? Your heart or your life?"

Jesus. Ace was relentless. Both were lost without Wynn in his life. He eased himself away from her then got up and walked over to the patio doors. Tomorrow they'd be clearing the silos and those connector tunnels that Ace had discovered. At least the next few days would be busy and exhausting. Maybe by the time they finished that task, he would have purged his craving for Wynn.

Then again, maybe not.

"Send me the pics of her, when you get a chance. My email's just like Val's but ACordova."

~

ANGEL AND MAX CAMERON were about to enter the last tunnel in their section of the vast underground network of decommissioned missile silos along the Colorado Front Range east of Denver.

Max was pissed, his movements jerky as he set up a couple of eyes on either side of the tunnel entrance. "We should have cleared these tunnels after Kelan discovered King's Warren."

"Maybe."

"Maybe nothing. We gave the Omnis time to bug out."

"We didn't know the tunnels were interconnected until Ace told us. We got here as soon as we could."

Angel was disgusted as he thought about Ace Myers being kidnapped from her crib and brought to live in the tunnels and abandoned silos. The northernmost silo complex in the system had been called King's Warren. It was a fitting name. The tunnels there like subterranean rodent works, always evolving. She knew

4

them as only a Warren native could, but they'd continued to change in the six years since she left them. The team had mapped more corridors and levels than were ever documented in the official Department of Defense blueprints—or in the maps Ace had drawn for them.

Each of the Titan I complexes they were clearing had three missile silos, a power dome, and a control dome. A few of the original complexes had been somewhat modernized, but most were crumbling heaps of concrete and rusty steel melting into pools of unknown chemicals. Water made a constant dripping sound, echoing in the dark space, giving the jungle of tangled metal a whisper of nature.

Ace had been right that the missile complexes were connected by newer tunnels that didn't exist on the official government schema. King's Warren, where Ace had lived and Fiona had been stashed, had been the team's starting point three days ago. They were now halfway through the whole structure. Angel and Max had the lead. Kit and the other guys were following behind, clearing every nook and cranny, mapping their discoveries. Christian Villalobo, their FBI handler, and his team were coming up from the southern end. They were to meet in this silo.

The undocumented levels that had been cut into the ground pulled oxygen from airshafts that went even deeper underground. Angel supposed those nooks were the hidden villages that Ace had told them were where her mentor, Santo, and his followers had hidden from the Omni World Order.

Angel hated to imagine an orphaned Ace navigating an industrial wasteland like this. How she'd survived her childhood, he couldn't comprehend.

He and Max reached the far end of the tunnel and the entrance to the next missile complex. Lobo was there to greet them. "We got something."

This middle complex was so brightly lit that they shoved their night-vision goggles up. This one was the most updated they'd found yet, and it was swarming with Feds, including a couple of dogs and their handlers. Angel came to a sharp stop and looked around. It was as pristine as a newly constructed clean room. Even the persistent drip of water was absent.

"The place was empty when we got here," Lobo told them. "No people, no papers. The control dome's been renovated for staff housing. There's a server farm in the old power dome. At least, the framework for it's in place, but all the hard drives are gone—or not yet installed. But that's not what's interesting."

Lobo led them through a blast gate to the area where the three silos were. They stood in front of a curved wall finished with what looked like white automotive paint. A sign on the side read, "Property of Syadne Tech."

Angel looked at Max, catching his tension. "You've seen something like this before."

Max nodded. "Under the WKB complex. Syadne built it, too."

"Have you gotten in there yet?" Angel asked Lobo.

"No," Lobo said.

"Waiting on a search warrant?" Angel asked.

Lobo shook his head. "No need. This silo is still owned by the government, though it seems to have dropped off the DoD's books. No evidence the government ever leased it. As far as I can tell, Syadne has no business being here. A representative of theirs is on his way over to open it for us."

ANGEL DROPPED his go bag on the floor in his room, then flipped the lights on. He sat on the end of his bed and dropped his head into his hands. The effort of keeping Wynn out of his mind was exhausting when she was his every thought. He shouldn't have let her go. He dug out his phone so he could get his fix of her from the locator app Max had installed. Seeing her location change as she went about her day was a balm to the frayed edges of his soul. She was living the life she chose.

Her freedom to do that was the reason he did what he did.

He never meant to fall in love. Casual sex and occasional female companionship was the best he'd hoped for, given his situation. He remembered all the times his dad had let his mom down, all the times she'd cried. He'd never understood why they stayed together if they made each other so miserable. It wasn't until Greer uncovered the team's ties to the Omnis that he understood his parents' misery wasn't coming from each other but from the Omni World Order's sick influence in their lives.

Wynn was right to leave him. He, by virtue of fighting the Omnis, had their taint all over him. He couldn't bring a woman into that tar pit, which was why he'd always kept it all so casual with women. Was just easier that way. He didn't have to worry about broken expectations.

Until Wynn.

He got up from his bed and paced around his room. He'd thought about her differently before he learned the truth about his heritage. He'd had no qualms exploring their relationship until he realized doing so ran the risk of repeating the hell his parents had lived.

No, the only way he could consider building a life with her was if the Omnis were put down, once and for all. And that wasn't going to happen with him up here in his room sulking.

He went down to the kitchen to make a mug of coffee, then headed to the bunker. His sour mood lingered. Wynn was where she wanted to be. That was all that mattered. He opened one of the team's tablets then tossed up to the screen Greer's 3-D model of the Omni history and associations that Val's dad had compiled. Next to it he opened pics of Owen, Wendell, Adelaide, Lion, and a blanked-out face of King, since they still didn't know who he was or where the others were.

Angel stepped back and braced his weight on the edge of the long conference table. After a minute, he added a dossier of Syadne to the spread. Those fuckers kept showing up—first in the silo under the White Kingdom Brotherhood's place, then renting the home where Grams was held hostage, and now in the Omnis' underground compound.

He glared at the big screen. The answer was there, in front of him, just all jumbled, like the pieces of a gigantic puzzle tossed out of its box, face-up, facedown, and every which way. He added pics for the rest of their team. They were all connected to the Omni puzzle. He stared at images a long while before adding Jason Parker and Nick Tremaine, Val's and Owen's dads.

After a minute, he organized the people into groups who were alive, those who were considered to be dead, and a final grouping for those who were confirmed dead.

He was vaguely aware of the team coming into the room and settling in around him. Greer added Hope's pic under Lion, then put Fiona's there, too. In the confirmed dead column, Greer added Senator Whiddon, Jefferson Holbrook, Phillip Bladen, and Ehsan Asir. The screen was getting cluttered and the categories weren't even filled yet. Greer brought up his spider chart that showed all the players they'd encountered in their investigation. He color-coded it to show different categories: friendly, enemy, alive, dead, status unknown.

Angel expanded Greer's 3-D model tracking the history of scientific discoveries through the centuries of the Omni organization. Those advancements had definitely begun to pick up speed over the last couple of centuries—with a sharp increase in the most recent period.

Angel tossed up Wynn's picture.

"What are we doing here, Angel?" Kit asked. He was standing at the end of the conference table, his arms folded, watching the screen.

"The Omnis used the White Kingdom Brotherhood to kill Grams. Why did they do that? What do they know that we don't?" Angel asked.

"There's something missing on your board," Blade said.

Angel gave a dry laugh. "No shit."

"Wynn's parents," Blade said. "They aren't up there. We know now we're all in this shitstorm for a reason. What role did Wynn's parents play?"

Angel shrugged. "Grams was not in the Omni world. And Wynn's parents are dead."

Blade shook his head. "Most of us got into this mess because of our parents. Dead or not, we need to understand who they were, what they were before we rule them out."

Angel nodded. He looked at Greer and Max. "What do we know about them?"

Greer tossed up images of Wynn's parents. "Joyce Ratcliff was a molecular biologist and Nathan Ratcliff was a biochemical engineer. They both worked for a private research lab. They died thirteen years ago when their lab caught on fire."

Angel looked at the guys standing around him, wondering if they were thinking what he was...what column did the elder Ratcliffs belong in—known dead or believed dead? Friendly or enemy?

"What if they aren't dead?" Angel asked the room at large. "What if they were testing some treatment on Grams and it went wrong, causing her stroke? Or what if they tested a cure on her and it went really right? Or maybe she improved markedly after being in Syadne-sponsored care."

"Okay. Suppose she was for real a lab rat. What then?" Kit asked.

"I don't know." Angel frowned at the big screen. "Did Lobo get into those Syadne silos?"

Kit nodded. "He did. They were empty. They clearly had been used at one point, but supposedly only for temporary overflow work on an as-needed basis. Syadne has a deed for the silo and several acres of surface land from the nineties, which is when it disappeared from the DoD's books."

Blade crossed his arms and rocked back on his chair. "I never understood why Jafaar cut Grams loose the way he did. He had to know we'd come for her. He held her in association with Syadne. Did they order her release? Or was Jafaar lone-dogging it?"

"Maybe he was ordered to kill her and thought to take a few of us out at the same time," Kelan suggested. "When that didn't work, King had the WKB finish the deed."

"So, there's still the question, why kill Grams?" Blade's gaze shot over to Angel. "Hypothetically, I could accept that the Omnis may have sucked the Ratcliffs into their world, causing them to fake their deaths. They aren't the first people we've thought were dead who weren't. And they were groundbreaking researchers in their fields at the time of their disappearance. But why kill their lab rat, if indeed they were using Grams in that capacity?"

"It's useless to speculate," Kit said. "If you think they were doing tests on Grams, let's exhume her body. Be a quick way to find out."

Angel straightened and faced the room. The group concurred. "Will do."

"Right. Didn't plan to have this meeting tonight, but since we're all here, give me an update on Owen," Kit said to Greer.

"The number that texted Owen is the same one that Ace called from her burner phone," Greer said.

"I think my handler was Jax." Ace nodded to Wendell's pic as Greer put it up on the big screen. "I've suspected for a while that he and Owen were friends.

Jax was in King's Warren years ago. He's the one who gave me my first camera and told me to record everything. He's the one who sent me here to Wolf Creek Bend and with the picture of Adelaide."

Val nodded. "Jax? Yeah. They are friends." He looked around at the team. "Jax is Wendell Jacobs."

Max's brows lowered in a dark frown. "How do you know?"

"Owen told me when I showed him the video of Adelaide that Ace took before her initiation." Val looked at Ace. "Jax is Adelaide's brother. Wendell Jacobs. Son of Senator Jacobs."

"Oh my God." Ace's face went blank.

Angel could tell she was flipping back through her memories to find the threads that might help them now. "Did you see him in the warren often?" he asked her.

"No. Every now and then. Often not for months."

"If Jax had access to the tunnels, how did he not know his sister was there?" Kelan asked.

"The initiates were kept separate from everyone else," Ace said, looking devastated as she considered her next words. "He was there when Adelaide was there. He'd told me to video everything. Adelaide saw the camera and asked me to turn it off."

"But you didn't," Val said.

"No. I kept recording her. But when it came time to give those recordings to Jax or Santo, I left hers out. It didn't seem right sharing a recording she'd asked me not to do."

Kit sighed and swiped his hand over his flattop. "Okay. I think we can assume Owen's gone after Adelaide. My gut's been telling me that's where he went."

The room was silent a long minute. Angel wasn't happy about Owen's heading out on his own. Nothing in this web of lies and death was disconnected from the rest—it was dangerous to think he could take it on alone. He crossed his arms. "So why go rogue? Why not read us in? Why ditch his own team—the only group he knows for a fact has his back?"

"Maybe he thought it was a personal issue?" Val suggested.

"So say that to us," Angel said. "The man has too many fucking secrets."

"If he'd said that, would you"—Val shot a glance around the room—"would any of you have stood down?"

"No. And we aren't going to now," Angel said.

"We are," Kit said. "We'll give him a few more days. In the meantime, we have our orders. Find Lion and the boys. Find King. And figure what it is the Omnis have in play." He looked over at Angel. "I gotta ask, your head in the game?"

Angel gave a harsh laugh. He spread his arms wide as he faced Kit. "You got something to say, say it."

"Wynn's in the middle of this, feel me? In some way that we don't yet know, she's at the heart of all this."

Angel felt his jaw tense as he glared at his team lead.

"Yeah, she is. And I'm worried as hell about her. That note the WKB left with Grams wasn't some weird, random shit. It meant something, and we have no idea what." He thrust out his bottom jaw. "So yeah, she's on my mind. Just means I'm all in."

Kit nodded. "Okay. Get with Doc Beck. We may not have to exhume Grams if he collected her blood while she was at the clinic, if he still has the samples. Be vague with him. He doesn't need to know what we're looking for. Shit, we don't even know what we're looking for. We'll have Owen's labs run the tests. If the Omnis are developing another virus, we need to get out ahead of it. I don't want to exhume Grams, but I will if we have to."

Angel nodded, hoping they could avoid digging Grams up. Having to bury her twice would kill Wynn. He wished he didn't have to tell her. "Copy that."

"Max," Kit continued, "find out everything you can about any real estate holdings Syadne Tech has and all of the OWO's holdings. If they sold a property, I want to know whom they sold it to, and when, and I want to see what relationships exist in those transactions. Might give us some leads on where Lion and his cubs are being held. And someone owns the property where Adelaide is holed up—wherever that is, it's where Owen and Wendell are headed, so also check out property owned by Senator Jacobs and his son."

"Rocco and I can help with that analysis," Blade said. "It's a lot of data to process."

Kit shook his head. "Rocco and Selena can help with that. Blade, I need you to go back over all of our assumptions. Angel's right. We've missed something big. Kelan can help you. Val, Greer, get back over to the Friends' village and have a chat with Santo when you can. He's more plugged in than we knew. If we can get him to cooperate, we can shorten our learning curve."

"I'm going with Val," Ace said.

"No, you're not," Kit nixed that. "Santo's got some weird hold over you. We can't afford to get sidelined right now. And you're not physically ready to fight him yet. You stay with us. You can give Max a hand."

Ace made a frustrated face, but nodded. "Copy."

Kit nodded toward Ace. "Didn't you have a unique way of getting in touch with your handler? Something about hijacking a review thread?"

"Yeah."

"How long does he usually take to respond after you post?"

"Depends. A day. A week."

"Well, open that channel. I don't like Owen being out of communication."

2

The silence was oppressive. Wynn Ratcliff sat in the living room of Grams' house in Cheyenne, Wyoming. Gramps had built it a few years after he returned from the Korean War. It was just as Grams had left it before her stroke, and yet everything seemed different now that Wynn owned it.

Wynn hadn't been in school yet when Grams redecorated after Gramps died. She couldn't remember what the house had looked like before, but her grandmother had told her that Gramps had had no tolerance for anything but masculine colors and furnishings. It was for that reason that she'd picked uber-feminine colors— pale mauve for the walls, beige and pink tones in the textured sofa fabric, and beige wall-to-wall carpet.

Wynn strolled over to the glass and brass étagère that housed Grams' priceless collection of antique Hummels. When Wynn had moved in after her parents died, they'd spent countless weekends going to nearby estate sales looking for more of the little statues. She remembered each of the ones they'd found together. She and Grams had been more than family; they'd been friends. For a long time.

Wynn missed her terribly.

She pushed those thoughts away as she walked through the entire main floor of the ranch house, remembering other times. She was eleven when she'd come to live here. Grams had helped her get through those dark days—and she'd made sure that the rest of Wynn's childhood had been normal and happy.

And now, Wynn was here again, at another transition point. Grams was gone. Wynn's job was gone. Strange the turning points in life you never saw coming.

Was it wicked of her that she missed Angel Cordova, the man who worked for the same company as her employer, almost as much as Grams? She and Angel hadn't talked much of their families or backgrounds. She thought he was of Puerto Rican descent and that he'd grown up in New York City, but that was all she really knew about him.

A memory of them together flashed through her mind. He was holding her, telling her how their first kiss was going to go...a kiss they never had. He was tall, taller than her five foot nine inches, which was rare. His warm, chocolaty brown eyes had laughed whenever he teased her. He'd given her delightful shivers since the first time they'd met that day she started as Zavi's tutor.

What might have been with Angel, Wynn would never know.

She had no doubts about leaving his dangerous world, but leaving him had felt wrong. That last thought pulled her from her reverie. She had to quit thinking about him. He and his friends weren't regular people; they were fighters in the middle of a hidden war she didn't fully understand. She remembered Angel rushing her to the bunker under the big house one night, remembered the terrible wait for the all-clear to come, remembered Mandy and Ivy chatting as if being stowed away in a bunker was normal.

And she remembered the blood covering all of the fighters when the home invasion was over.

There were secrets the team knew that they didn't share with the civilians in the household...those were the secrets Jafaar Majid, the monster who'd stolen Grams from her palliative care center, had been after. Wynn looked at the palm of her right hand and its healing scar.

If only she'd known what she was getting herself into when she applied for the job the Silases had advertised. There wasn't a day that passed that she wished she'd never learned of that job opening. Grams might still be alive...but Wynn would never have met Angel. Leaving their headquarters in Wolf Creek Bend had been her only shot at a regular life. The longer she stayed in the mess he and his team fought, the more their enemy seemed to focus on her. Even being in the periphery of their world made her a target; it had already cost Grams her life. Wynn wasn't ready to cede her life to that world.

Funny how that reality could coexist with the real one, each without being aware of the other. She sighed. Life was what it was. She was alone now. Fully on her own. And it was for the best.

Her absent-minded stroll around the little house brought her back to the living room. The movers had left her things neatly stacked in the basement. It had only taken them a few hours to clear out her apartment yesterday morning. She'd cleaned her apartment yesterday and turned it over to her landlord. Everything was falling into place.

This little ranch house would be her home—at least until the world calmed down a bit so she could make a plan for her future.

Bright morning sunlight cast a soft glow as it filtered through the white sheers. A man walked down the side-walk in front of Grams' house. Wynn had been a frequent visitor here during her college years; she thought she knew most of Grams' neighbors, but not this guy.

He seemed out of place, which was the first thing that caught her attention. He looked to be in his thirties, well groomed, with short brown hair. He wore a suit. No briefcase. Grams' neighborhood was fully residential, off the beaten track from Cheyenne's business areas, so he couldn't be somebody from a nearby office building out for a stroll. If he were a salesman of some type, he'd have a briefcase. If he was someone who worked at home, he'd be wearing something much more casual. As she watched him, he turned to the house and stared right at her window.

She pulled back, to the side of the window, where she could keep an eye on him. She doubted he could actually see inside the house, not through the sheers when it was so bright outside. After a minute, he resumed his trek down the sidewalk. How odd. She watched until he was out of sight. And then some. Maybe he was a realtor, sizing up Grams' house after her recent obituary.

Wynn's heart was racing. After everything that had happened, she was hyperaware of her environment. Maybe the guy had been from a roofing company, checking houses after the hailstorms that had come through the neighborhood last month. Who knew? He'd moved on; she needed to as well.

She looked at the kitchen, remembering she'd planned to go grocery shopping after she mailed out Grams' death notices. There was so much to do. She had to keep putting one foot in front of the other. She didn't know if it was worth it for her to unpack her things from her apartment—she didn't know how long she'd be staying. How long did it take to make a plan for one's life? She had big choices she needed to consider: continue with her education...enter a research program...get a job now—but where? Stay in

Cheyenne or move somewhere else? Keep Grams' house or sell it?

Life was overwhelming. She wished she still had Grams to turn to for advice. But she didn't. She reminded herself that she'd survived Wolf Creek Bend. She could survive this, too.

She went into the kitchen. She'd given the house-keepers the perishable food that had been in the fridge and cupboards when she thought Grams was going to be in recovery for longer than she hoped. She checked the cabinets for dry goods and paper supplies, taking an inventory.

She opened the fridge, remembering how surprised she'd been last night to find a couple bags of lunchmeats and some veggies in the drawers. The dates on the deli bags indicated they were fresh enough to eat, though she hadn't been to the house in weeks. Unsure of its origin, she threw everything away. Maybe someone from the cleaning service had left them. That had to be the explanation. It was a good reminder to call the service and change their schedule, since she was going to be there a while and didn't need them any longer.

She pulled out a pen and notepad from Grams' junk drawer to jot down a few days' worth of supplies. She didn't want to go grocery shopping. She'd avoided it since she got back to Cheyenne by ordering in, but she couldn't live on pizza forever. Sooner or later, she was going to have to be brave enough to go to the store.

She looked at her list, trying to focus on what she

needed, not what had happened the last time she'd been to the market. The house was so quiet, it was hard to think. There was no Zavi and Casey fighting with each other, no shrieks as they played. Even the constant threat of danger at the team's headquarters had had its own noisy energy.

Here, now, everything was calm. Normal. Wynn smiled, realizing that she was going to have to get used to that all over again. She would be safe venturing out to the store; she wasn't going to run into any crazed assassins waiting to gun her down.

Angel felt a sense of *déjà vu* as he stood in the cool breeze watching Grams' exhumation. At least Wynn wasn't there to see this. He wished Doc Beck had collected blood samples from Grams, but he hadn't. Kit had had to work with Lobo to get the necessary permits to exhume her body instead. When her casket was lifted out of her grave, they put it on a gurney and transferred it to a hearse. Angel stayed with her the whole way to the coroner's office.

The coroner opened the casket, then glanced over at Angel. "I thought you said you wanted me to take blood samples from Mrs. Vaughn's body?"

"I do." Angel stepped closer so he could see inside the casket...where there was no body. His first thought was that Grams wasn't actually dead, but he remembered he'd checked her pulse himself. She was dead on the sidewalk outside the grocery store, dead the whole way to the clinic, and dead on arrival at the clinic. The WKB's bullet had ended her life, and Doc Beck had confirmed it.

No, someone had gotten to her body before they did. A small cedar box sat on the cream-colored satin fabric. The coroner opened it, then showed him the contents. Ashes. Had Wynn ordered Grams' cremation? He didn't remember her mentioning that. Why would she have buried Grams' ashes instead of taking a niche in a columbarium?

"Blood samples won't be possible, son," the coroner said.

"Can we determine whose body this was? Or can we at least determine that these are human remains?"

"Unfortunately, DNA is usually destroyed in the cremation process. If there are some bone or teeth fragments, it might be possible to extract some DNA, but it's unlikely." He looked at Angel as he emphasized *might*. "Take the ashes. Your lab may be able to confirm that these ashes are in fact human. And they can look for the presence of heavy metals, if that might help in any way. I don't have the facilities to do those tests here. If Mrs. Vaughn's body was ever in this casket, you might be able to pull her DNA from it. I know it's not blood samples—it may not hold any of the answers you're looking for."

Angel nodded. "Let's do it. I'll take whatever you can provide."

"Will do."

Angel stood back and let the coroner examine the casket. He found a couple strands of hair, which he put in glass jars. He handed the jars and the box of ashes to Angel. "I hope you find what you're looking for, son. Sorry I couldn't be of more assistance."

Angel rode in the hearse back to Grams' plot in the cemetery. The empty casket was put back in its place and reburied. He put the things the coroner gave him in his SUV, then phoned Kit. "I'm finished with the coroner."

"Good. You got the samples from Grams, then?"

"No. Her body wasn't in the casket. It appears she was cremated. I'm not convinced the ashes are hers. The coroner thought the lab might be able to pull something off them, though the chances are slim." He brought Kit up to speed.

"Son of a bitch. They got there first."

"The coroner did get a couple hair samples from the satin liner. We can have those tested, as well. Before I head down to Cheyenne to meet the courier at the airport, I'm going to stop by the funeral home and see if there's anything interesting on their security cameras. And I'll go talk to the cemetery managers. Maybe something shows up there. I'll keep you posted. I'm out."

Wᴀɴ ɴᴇʀᴠᴏᴜsʟʏ ʟᴏᴏᴋᴇᴅ ᴀʀᴏᴜɴᴅ, trying to remind herself she was safe. It was noon. A few patrons were in the library—she wasn't alone here. She hadn't felt this uptight when she first came back to town, but she'd been numbed by Grams' death. And those first few days had been busy packing to move out of her apartment.

But after seeing that odd man out front of her house this morning, the panic she'd felt each time she'd visited Grams at Jafaar's house slammed right back into her. It wouldn't be hard to become an agoraphobic. But doing so meant she'd caved to Angel's enemies, and that was something she would never do.

She'd visited a notary at the bank, then mailed out Grams' death notices, all without anything scary—or even unusual—occurring. She didn't yet have the internet turned on at the house and there were some things she wanted to research—things that couldn't wait the few days until she had service. She wanted to see what she could find about what she'd just been through up in Wolf Creek Bend. Did anyone else in the world know there was a secret war going on there? And what about the team—was there anything online about them?

She sat in one of the open desks in front of a public computer. For a minute, she watched the reflections on the screen of the dormant computer, observing what was happening behind her until she scolded herself that her paranoia was bordering on psychotic. She had to get herself under control. She reminded herself she was back in the real world. Nothing was going to happen to her here; she wasn't alone, and it was broad daylight.

Still, her hands were shaking as she turned the computer on. After everything that had happened in Wolf Creek Bend with Angel and his merry band of terrorist hunters, she felt as if they might somehow know she was checking up on them. But that didn't matter now. She needed to know more about what she'd just come through so that she wouldn't run the risk of getting mixed up in anything similar in the future.

She tried to research the people who lived in the team's headquarters, but the only people who had any data online were some of the women: Ivy with her diner, Mandy with her hippotherapy center, Eden with her dog-training business, and Remi, who was an assistant professor of sociology at the same university where Wynn had gotten her degree. There was nothing on Hope or Ace. Fiona, however, had full profiles on some of the social media sites, but none of her info was recent. Not one of the guys had any personal information about themselves listed on any social media search, or even through a wider look at the internet. There was a website for Tremaine Industries, but there was nothing extraordinary about it, just a regular webpage describing their services and listing some contact info. The most unusual aspect of it was how little it really said about anything.

She looked up Jafaar Majid and Mr. Edwards. Nothing about them, either. Maybe those were aliases.

The girls had mentioned an organization called the Omnis. Wynn researched that as well, and while there were tons of hits, none of them quite sounded like the lethal organization Angel and his team fought.

There was a huge amount of info on the White Kingdom Brotherhood, some of whose members, she'd learned after coming clean with the team, were working with Jafaar and were who'd beaten her up at the house where he had been holding Grams. Still, none of the pieces she found seemed to fit together.

When she finished her research, she realized she'd spent several hours—and had nothing to show for it. She cleared her search history, then stood. This was all a waste of time. She needed to be looking forward, not back. Her strange interlude with the fierce group of fighters deep in the Medicine Bow Mountains was over.

She was unemployed.

Grams was gone.

Wynn had a future to fill, and looking back wasn't going to do it.

She stepped outside. The day had turned stormy, making the air misty. She looked around at the people in the parking lot. Moms with kids. Elderly patrons. Teenagers. It was all so normal. She smiled, comparing this moment with her paranoia from earlier in the day. The relief she felt ended abruptly when she noticed there was a man in the blue sedan parked next to her car.

She looked back at the library, then around at the

other cars, checking to see if anyone else was watching her. She thought about making a call to 911, but no crime had actually happened. Yet. She really was losing her mind. The man was probably just waiting for someone inside the library. Nonetheless, she kept her thumb on the emergency alert on her key fob.

As she neared her car, the man opened his door. When he stood up, she realized he was the very same man who'd stopped in front of her house earlier. He held his hands up, resting his wrists on the roof of his car. "Please, don't hit that alarm. I'm not here to hurt you."

And that was something no innocent man would ever say.

Wynn unlocked her car and tossed her purse inside from the passenger side, keeping both cars between her and the stranger. She was still debating how to get into the driver's seat and get away when the guy continued talking.

"I need you to hear me out. That's all. I can say what I need to say from here."

"So say it."

"You're in danger."

"Hahaha. That's a good one, considering you've been stalking me all day."

"Your parents sent me."

The air in her lungs locked up for a moment, long enough for panic to start screaming in her ears. "My parents are dead." How many times had Grams told her, as a kid, to run and scream if anyone, especially a stranger, came to her with the news that her parents were hurt and needed her? *Remember, stranger danger, Wynnie.*

"No, they aren't. Not yet, anyway."

"Where are they?" Wynn asked, wondering if stranger danger was still appropriate for adults. Probably.

"Someplace safe."

Why was she standing here talking to this crazy guy? She had to get out of there. "Right. Look, I don't know who you are or what you want, but you have to leave me alone before I call the cops."

"I understand." He held up his hands. "I just want you to be safe. That's why I'm talking to you here, in a public space. Your parents sent me to find you before the Omnis do. Those bastards are coming for you."

The Omnis. Again.

"The men you were with in Wolf Creek Bend will kill your parents. They'll do it without a second thought. I'm your only option."

How did he know where she'd just been?

"That's kinda hard to do when they're already dead." She held up her phone and snapped a pic of him. "If I see you again, I'm going to call the police. Leave me alone." She hurried around the hood of her car and jumped into the driver's seat, quickly locking her doors.

She backed out of her spot and left as fast as she could. Drat it all, she still needed to go to the grocery store. Though it was only midafternoon, the sky was already getting dark with the storm looming overhead. Days were short this time of year. She could run in and out of the market and be home before it was fully dark. Or go back home and starve until morning, when it was safe to go out again—there was nothing to eat at the house.

Her nerves tightened as she neared the store. She had to remind herself that what had happened to Grams happened in Wolf Creek Bend, more than an hour and a half away. She'd hoped that, in leaving the team's headquarters and her tutoring job, she'd left that trouble behind her, but it appeared she hadn't. She sat in her car for a bit, calming her nerves. She was in a different world now. The real world. It was time to get on with living.

She forced herself out of her car before she lost even more daylight. Standing inside the protection of her car door, she sent a look around the lot for the blue sedan. It wasn't anywhere that she could see. She locked her car and did a run-walk into the store, keeping an eye out for the mysterious stranger. Of course, he was nowhere to be seen. She made it into the store without incident. Half panicked, she sent a wild look around. Everyone who noticed it looked at her like she was the crazy one. It wasn't until halfway through her shopping that she began to calm down. People were just going about their business. It made her recent experiences in Wolf Creek Bend surreal.

As she shopped, she mulled over the possibility that her parents could still be alive. Of course it wasn't possible. They'd died thirteen years ago. Who was that man? How did he know Angel and his team? Maybe it was some expert-level phishing attempt. Anything was more believable than thinking her parents were still alive. He'd just tied enough facts from her reality into his story to make it something that gave her pause. But why would he do that? That question led her to a terrifying conclusion: they were after her.

Oh, God. She had to get back to her house. She cut her shopping short and immediately went to check out with her groceries. Whatever she'd put in the cart was enough to hold her for a while. She would get home and lock herself up in the house. Grams' place was in a good section of town. The police station wasn't even a mile away. She'd be safe there…if she could just get there.

She asked the grocery clerks for assistance loading her groceries so that she wouldn't have to be alone. The late afternoon was turning to dusk. She couldn't explain why, but the prospect of being out in the dark scared her.

She watched the behavior of the cars in her rearview as she drove home. Sure enough, that blue Ford Taurus picked her up a little ways from the grocery store. It was too far back to see how many people were inside; she counted at least two now. She went past her home, then drove a little farther into her neighborhood, making some random turns to see if the car followed her.

It did.

God, her heart was beating frantically. She pulled over by a house where a man was inside an open garage, working on his car. Putting her car in park, she locked her doors, then got her phone out to record her pursuers. The blue sedan passed her car and went on down the road. She saw the man she'd spoken to at the library, plus two others—one in the front, one in the back. They looked at her as they went past. She hoped her video of them caught their faces and the car's license plate.

She waited a few minutes to make sure they didn't circle back. The man working on his car watched the whole thing. He came over to her. She lowered her window a few inches.

"Everything all right, ma'am?" he asked, clearly worried for her.

Of course he was...because people in the real world were good like that. Still, it was clear the tendrils of the world she'd left had followed her here.

"Yes. Sorry to bother you. Just needed to use my phone and didn't want to be driving while I did it. Thank you."

He nodded at her and waved as she pulled out onto the road. The streetlights had come on. If someone were tailing her again, it would be harder to tell what type of car they were driving now that it was dark. She made her way back to her house. As far as she could tell, no one had followed her here, but she knew that didn't mean she wasn't being watched. She opened her garage door, pulled in, then closed it tight before she got out of her car.

With her house key ready, she unlocked her kitchen door, then locked it behind her and threw the lights on. Her house was quiet. She keyed 911 on her phone but didn't hit send yet, just kept it ready as she went through her house, making sure no one had sneaked in while she was gone. The front and back doors were locked, as were all the windows on the main floor of Grams' house. The closets were clear. She went downstairs and repeated the same checks. The cluttered space in the rec room was eerie. The furniture from her apartment was pushed up against the walls haphazardly. Boxes were stacked upon boxes, throwing hard shadows around the space. There, too, nothing seemed disturbed. Some part of her had thought maybe her parents were hiding in the house. She was buying into that stranger's psychosis.

That thought brought her to a full stop halfway up the stairs. Of course they weren't hiding here. They were *dead*. God, how easily her mind and her heart could be manipulated. She couldn't trust anyone. She had to get away. Leaving Wolf Creek Bend hadn't been enough. She was going to have to go far, far away where no one could find her.

Her heart was still beating double time as she went

back upstairs. She had to go back into the garage to get her groceries. She paused beside the garage door from the kitchen. No one had been in there when she came inside, but could they have forced the garage door open somehow? She checked her phone. 911 was still on the screen. All she had to do was hit send for the call to go through.

She unlocked the door and yanked it open for a quick look. The overhead light was still on. She couldn't see anyone. She made a dash to her trunk. Slipping her phone in her pocket, she grabbed her groceries and hurried back into the house. She set the bags on the ground, then locked the door behind her. Leaning against the door, she took a few calming breaths.

She was safe. For now.

As she put her groceries away, anger slowly replaced terror. How dare those men follow her, intimidate her. Tomorrow, if their nonsense continued, she'd go to the police. She had the video she'd taken as proof. If they tried to interact with her at all between now and then, she'd record them. All of it would strengthen her case. She could get a restraining order against them.

No one was going to make her hide here in Grams' house like a victim. She'd done nothing wrong and didn't deserve their harassment.

She went down the hall to her room. She kicked off her ankle boots and was about to change into pajamas when a knock sounded on her door.

3

----

ngel pulled into the neighborhood where Grams' house was. He was glad Wynn had inherited it—he knew how close she'd been to her grandmother. He was not looking forward to giving her the news that her grandmother's body was missing. Whoever had done it had taken steps to erase their trail. The footage from the funeral home had been corrupted. He'd taken the files anyway on the off chance that Greer could get something from them. The cemetery hadn't noticed anything unusual. The guards patrolling the grounds had reported no disturbances. They didn't have any video surveillance set up, so Angel only had their word to go on.

He stopped at a stop sign catty-corner to Wynn's house. A man was walking up to her front porch. She opened her door to the guy. Angel hoped, given her unique situation, that she wouldn't open the door for just anyone, so maybe she knew the guy. They appeared to be arguing, judging from their hand gestures. The man grabbed her wrist. She yanked herself free, then showed him her phone. He lifted his hands and backed up a step. She retreated inside her house and shut the door. He had the nerve to start knocking on it again.

Angel had had enough. He pulled forward and turned into her driveway. He slammed his door when he got out of his SUV. "Can I help you?" he called out as he moved in on him.

The man, a smallish guy in a suit, spun around to face him. The color slowly drained from his face. "No. You can't." He crossed the porch and jogged down the steps, but he wasn't fast enough. Angel grabbed his wrist and twisted it up behind his back, then caught his Adam's apple, squeezing as he leaned close to growl, "I don't like it when someone touches my woman. And I don't like when she gets angry. It makes me real, real angry. Bad things happen when I get angry. Don't come around here again." He shoved the man free.

The guy stumbled away, walking backward as he held his throat and glared at Angel. "You're going to be the death of her."

"No. I'm going to be the death of you if I see you here again." Angel watched until the man got in his blue Taurus and disappeared. Angel frowned, then texted the guy's license plate to Greer. He went up to Wynn's door and knocked.

She yanked it open, gasped when she saw him.

Everything she wanted and everything she feared danced through her eyes under the dim porch light.

"May I come in?"

She stepped back and let him inside. The feeling of Grams around them caught him up short.

Her living room was pink, mauve, beige, and brass, like the whole space had time-traveled from the nineties. Wynn stood in the center of it, her brown hair soft and long around her shoulders. Her eyes were full of fury. She held her hands in fists by her sides. She wore a wide, knee-length denim skirt with a white tank top and a purple linen shirt. Both were tucked into the skirt, emphasizing her generous curves. Her feet were bare. He stared at them, shocked that they made her seem undressed.

She backed away from him. He shoved the door closed behind him, then slipped his black leather jacket off and tossed it onto the sofa. His eyes held hers as he stalked toward her, carried forward by a hunger unlike any he'd ever experienced. If he didn't touch her skin, taste her lips, feel her body against his *right now*, he didn't know how he'd continue to pull air.

She stepped back until she hit the wall of the kitchen. He told himself she could have gone left or right, rushed down the hallway, zipped around the corner into the kitchen, anything to get away from him...but she didn't.

He lifted his fists against the wall behind her, mostly to keep himself from touching her, but he still melted into the heat in her eyes. How he'd craved this, every hour of every day since she left him. He ordered himself to slow down.

"Wynn, I'm going to kiss you." Their first kiss. Of all the times he'd played it in his mind, none of them had been setup like this.

She flattened her hands against his chest, then slowly moved them down to his sides, where she fisted his tee and pulled him toward her.

Still doing a push-up against the wall, he leaned in, closing the distance between them, inch by inch, until his lips brushed hers. She closed her eyes. He did the same, giving himself over to his sense of touch and taste, memorizing the soft and firm feel of her lips against his, the wetness of her mouth, the tentative way she opened for him, and the ecstasy of his tongue touching hers.

He shivered, stricken by how perfect it felt. Straightening, he wrapped his arms around her and pulled her curvy body to his as he deepened the kiss, letting it say all the words he couldn't. And given the way she responded to him, he could almost believe she'd heard him.

He braced his legs apart to ease the ache between them. His knees brushed against her thighs, tightening the tension in his groin. Her skirt provided no resistance against him and moved as she did. He fisted her long hair, lifting it to his face. It was so goddamned silky.

He rubbed his cheek against hers, against her neck. He nuzzled her skin, so soft and sweet that it was almost sensory overload. Her hands touched his belly, moved up his chest then around his back. He spread her legs wider and ground himself against her core. She moaned. Her breathing was shallow, drawn through parted lips. He set his mouth there, just barely against hers, feeling the air move in cold and warm puffs and imagining her working his cock with those soft lips.

He kissed her chin and ran his teeth over the line of her jaw. "Tell me no, Wynnie. Fucking tell me no."

She caught his face and matched her mouth to his. He thrust his tongue inside, mimicking what he was about to do to her body. He thought he could kiss her for hours...if his body wasn't in such a frenzy to be in hers. He caught her waist and pulled her against him.

"Answer me," he ordered.

"No," she whispered.

He leaned back and looked at her, confused that her body was saying yes but her mouth said no. He dropped his hands from her waist.

She pulled him close again. "Yes."

Her eyes were lowered. He touched her neck, pushing her chin up with the side of his thumb until her eyes met his. "Which is it?"

"I don't take orders from you."

"Yes, you do. When it comes to your safety...and your pleasure. Which is it—yes or no?"

"Yes."

He pulled his wallet from his back pocket and removed a condom, unbuckled his belt, opened his cargos, then pushed them a little way down his hips. She watched him cover himself. He kissed her. Her hands slipped against his cock. Fingers downward, she pressed the wide crown of his dick gently between the heels of her hands. He thrust into the pressure, groaning.

Leaning his head against hers, he started to pull her skirt up in fistfuls, baring her thighs. She wore lacy boy briefs. He stroked between her legs, over her panties. She was damp and hot. He pushed her panties aside and let his fingers caress that sweet, feminine seam, then slip inside her. She sucked in a sharp breath.

"Okay?" he asked, his voice gruff.

She nodded and put her hands on his shoulders. Her eyes, her beautiful hazel eyes with their unusual mix of brown inner ring and blue outer, were dark. "Do you want to go to my room?"

"No." His thumb found her clit. "I want to fuck you up against this wall."

"I can't come like this."

"Why not?"

She shrugged.

"Then how long can you take this?" He shouldn't have grinned. But when her heavy eyes met his, he had no doubt about his ability to give her an orgasm. He lifted her leg and stroked her core with his rock-hard cock, then positioned himself just at her opening.

"Kiss me, Wynn."

She turned her face to his, nose to nose, mouth to mouth. He was kissing her when his thumb began a slow, easy pressure on her clit. He felt her body tense, could feel the way she held herself back.

"Relax. I got you. You aren't going to fall, not while I'm holding you."

"You can't hold me. I'm too heavy."

He grinned. "I am holding you. Let yourself go. I gotcha." He rocked slightly against her core, slipping just inside her then back out. She gasped. Her eyes became soft and unfocused. He did it again, timing his micro-thrust with the motion of his thumb on her clit.

She gripped his pecs, her nails digging through his black tee reflexively like cat paws. He changed the pressure his thumb was placing, changed the motion, went faster. Her hips jerked against his and she whimpered. He slammed into her, thrusting into her release. He lifted her other leg, leaning her body against the wall as his body pounded hers.

She was holding his shoulders now, groaning with the passion racking her body. When the first and second wave of it eased away, she wrapped her arms around his neck and kissed him as he made his final thrust. He moaned into her mouth.

It wasn't enough. He needed her again.

He eased her back to her feet. "Do you have some condoms here?"

"No."

"I do. In my bag." He removed the condom, then

put himself back together. He tossed it in the trash in the hall bath. "I'll be right back." Pausing at the front door, he looked back at her. "Don't even think about locking this. I will kick it in."

Wynn smiled just a little and pulled her bottom lip between her teeth. She looked rumpled and still warm from their sex. He came back and kissed her, pulling that lip from her teeth. She was warm and open to him. Standing there in that pink room—even with an étagère full of creepy little boy statues watching them—he felt more at home than he ever had anywhere.

When they broke apart, she gave him a little push. "Go, so you can come back."

Angel went out to his SUV and grabbed his go bag. He paused, remembering why he'd come down to see Wynn. He couldn't tell her now, before another round of sex. Nor before they went to sleep—it would give her nightmares. He thought of the man he'd seen her arguing with just before he pulled up to her house. They had a lot of things to go over. But not now. Not when she'd let him in to her house, and her body, and maybe her life.

Wynn was standing right where he'd left her when he went back inside.

He caught her hand, then nodded over to the glass case. "What are those things?"

"What things?"

"The boy statues."

Wynn laughed. "They're Hummels. Grams loved them."

He led her down the hall. "C'mon. Those creepers don't need to see what I'm about to do to you." At the end of the hallway, she paused, making him stop. He was uncertain which room they should take. "There a problem?"

She gave him a sheepish smile. "I just feel weird having sex in Grams' room...on her bed."

He looked at the twin bed in the guest room and made the decision for them by drawing her into the master bedroom. "I won't fit on that cot." He pulled her into his arms. "Besides, this is your house now. Your bed. Your room. Your life." He stopped himself from saying that Grams was gone, because she really was, and he had no fucking idea where.

"I know, but it still looks like she's here."

"You can overhaul it, later, when change quits raining down on you. It's probably best not to make those decisions right now."

She nodded. He kissed her nose, then leaned back to pull off his tee. Her gaze dipped to his chest, then moved from his shoulders to his pecs. Where her eyes went, her hands followed. Her palms were cool on his heated skin. She ran them over his tight nipples. He couldn't wait to do the same to her. The urgency he felt was as if their fast fuck in the living room hadn't just happened.

Her hands went to her waistband, pulling her shirt

from her skirt. He stopped them, then finished unbuttoning that for her and pushed it from her shoulders. She wore a white tank beneath it. Yet another layer to free her from. He kissed the soft skin of her shoulder. Undressing her was like slowly unwrapping a gift, anticipating what was inside. He ran his hands around the waist of her skirt, searching for the fastener.

She slipped her hands through his so she could unfasten her skirt, then pushed it down her legs...her long, smooth legs, revealing the pink panties she wore.

"Nice," he groaned.

WYNN FELT waves of heat followed by waves of cold. Hunger and fear. What if, when she was fully naked, he didn't like the looks of her? She wasn't a size four. Nor even a fourteen. She was a tall, curvy woman with breasts that barely fit in a tank top and hips that were wide. After that cold thought came a hot one as she remembered the way he'd taken her in the living room, the way he'd made her come despite her hesitance. It was as if he knew her body better than she did.

And now he was looking at her with those dark eyes and that hungry gaze of his.

"Angel...how long has it been for you?"

He met her eyes. "There's been no one since I met you. Before that, plenty. Doc Beck's given me a clean bill of health. How about you?"

"Longer than you. I don't do casual. I haven't before, anyway."

Something whispered across his expression, a fast-moving shadow. He didn't think what they were doing was casual. She was going to have to straighten that out. Afterward. This could only be a short-term thing between them. She was never going back into his world.

Still, she was grateful for this time with him. It was just what she needed. She didn't want to be alone right now. Not with Grams so recently buried and gone. Not with crazy men running around telling her that her parents were alive.

Angel was exactly what she needed right now.

He settled in one of the armchairs near the window to untie his boots. She sat opposite him, on the mattress.

"Open your legs."

"Angel—"

"Do it."

She bit her lip as she considered resisting, but then she spread her thighs apart and watched his heated gaze touch her core. She leaned back, bracing herself on the mattress. His hungry eyes moved up her body to her face, pausing on her lips, which parted on a shallow breath. It was almost as if he was actually touching her.

"Angel..." She saw he still had one boot to unlace. "Hurry up."

He straightened and looked at her. "Why?"

"Because I need to feel you again."

He finished and kicked off his boots then tore off his socks. He stalked over to her, then leaned over her, standing between her legs yet not quite touching her. "We could have been doing this at the team headquarters." He shook his head. "Think of all the time we lost."

"No." She could feel his heat arcing over her body. Gooseflesh rose on her skin.

"Yes, we could have. I could have been with you every night. Every morning."

"It wouldn't have been appropriate. I was there as an employee."

"So was I. You don't think teachers fuck?"

"Angel—"

"What?"

"Less talking..."

He laughed. He retrieved several condoms and set them on her nightstand. He gave her a frustrated glance. "It's all I got. I'll get more tomorrow."

She smiled. Four condoms. Four more encounters... in one night. It was more than she'd had in that many years.

He pushed his tan cargo pants down and kicked them off, revealing a tightfitting pair of black boxer briefs and a huge erection pressed sideways against his hip. She couldn't help herself. She reached out to touch him, stroking the long length of him, from his heavy balls to the broad tip. His penis jumped. She looked up at him.

"Take your tank off, Wynn."

She lowered her eyes, intentionally not looking at him as she revealed the pink lacy bra that matched her briefs. She looked down at her breasts and the mounds they made above the cups of her bra. Not for the first time, she wished she wasn't so well endowed. Why couldn't she just be normal like most women and have regular-sized breasts?

She looked at the fading bruises from the beating Jafaar had had his men give her.

Angel's hiss was audible. "Jesus. I forgot. I was so hungry for you."

"It's nothing. They don't even hurt anymore."

He wasn't fooled by her lie. "Lean back. Let me look."

She did, watching him. He straddled her leg and leaned over her, gently touching the fading marks. "Wynn, honey, it hurts me to see these."

She smiled. His hand was warm on her stomach. She put hers over his. His eyes showed he wasn't lying. "What about your ribs? They can take a long time to heal." He stroked the curve of her ribs on the side where she'd been kicked.

"It's okay. Really. They don't hurt."

He ran his hand over her stomach, from her ribs to the tender skin below her belly button. "You are unimaginably perfect. We don't have to do this tonight. Holding you will be enough until you're better."

"Yes, we do need to do this. I'm hurting, but not

48

from the bruises. I need you to finish what you started, Angel."

He looked into her eyes, then nodded. "I need that, too." He got off the bed and took off his briefs, freeing his heavy erection. It was so tight, it stood at a right angle from his body, pointing toward her from its dense nest of dark hair. She wrapped her hands around him, then kissed the wide crown of his head.

"Suck me, Wynn."

She let her tongue circle him. He tasted sweet and salty. His hips pushed himself closer to her mouth, but she controlled him. All she gave him was her tongue's wet caress. He reached down and pressed his thumbs against her teeth, forcing her jaw to widen. "Open," he ordered.

She did, and he moved inside her mouth. She pushed him back so she could lick at his crown, then took him into her mouth. Deep.

He uttered a long hiss, his teeth bared as he fucked her mouth. "Yeah. Like that." It wasn't long before he pulled free and ripped into a condom then covered himself. "Lie back."

She did, supporting herself on her elbows so she could watch him. He eased her panties off, then knelt between her legs and pressed his face against her core. His tongue was wicked, licking, pressing, stroking. Her first orgasm came fast, ripping through her body. She braced her heels against the bedframe's sideboard so she had more leverage to push against him.

He penetrated her with two, then three, wide fingers, stretching her, thrusting into her, preparing her for what was coming. She peaked again. He moved over her, drawing out her orgasm with his thumb instead of his mouth as he entered her, filling her. She bucked up against his thrusts. Never had she felt an orgasm as intense as she did then. No man had ever made her feel so complete or so connected.

It was shattering.

She cried out.

Her body wanted more. He pounded into her, moving her across the mattress. As her head started to dip off the other side of the bed, she felt him stiffen, felt his release pulse deep inside her. They were both breathing hard. Took a long minute to come back down. He moved her over slightly so that she was all the way on the bed once again. She looked up into his eyes. He brushed his thumb over her jaw. She had the crazy thought that he was as moved as she was by what just happened between them. She didn't want him to pull out. Not yet. Not when her body was still humming.

But he did withdraw. He kissed her forehead, then got off the bed to dispose of the condom. When he came back, he stood there frowning down at the bed.

"What's wrong?"

"You got more pillows? I sleep with a lot of them."

Wynn smiled. Never would she have thought a guy like Angel liked pillows. "I think so. I'll go look."

He caught her up against him. She shivered at the

feel of his body against hers. He grinned and reached behind her, unfastening her bra. "We forgot this." He tossed it on the ground and leaned back to look at her.

For the first time in her life, Wynn didn't feel heavy-set; she felt beautiful.

ANGEL FOLLOWED Wynn as she checked in the closet in the guest room for extra pillows. They found three more. He held them while she slipped pillowcases on them. They arranged all the pillows in two stacks, then he turned out the lights and held the covers up for her to get in. Grams' queen-sized bed was better than the twin in the guest room, but he was still going to have to sleep sideways or let his feet hang off the end. Thankfully, she had a headboard but no footboard.

He pulled Wynn against his side. The room was dark, but lights were still on in the living room, spilling ambient light into their shadowy space. He was holding Wynn. She was safe and relaxed. Now would be a good time to tell her about exhuming Grams.

He couldn't do it yet. Instead, he pressed his lips to her forehead and asked, "Why did you say no before, in the living room?" He felt her body tense.

"I wasn't saying no to sex. I was saying no to us."

"What do you mean?"

"I'm not going back to your world, Angel."

Yeah, that didn't hurt. He sighed. "I don't blame you." And now would be a good time to tell her about

Grams, since he was going to get the boot anyway. But he couldn't. Not when she was so soft in his arms. "But we're not done, Wynn."

"We have to be, Angel."

"Give us this weekend."

She nodded. "Okay."

"Can you sleep?"

She leaned up to glare at him. "With all these pillows? I'll be the princess and the pea."

He frowned. "The what?"

She turned on her side, her back to him though she was still in his arms, and pulled some of the pillows out from under her head, pushing them off the bed. "It's an old fairytale."

He rolled onto his side, spooning her. "I'd like to hear it sometime." Not that he was into fairytales, but he loved the sound of her voice. She took his hand and pushed it between her breasts. He tried not to react, but her breasts were heavy, warm, and soft. The way their bodies were aligned, she had to feel the instant erection she'd given him with that gesture.

She'd just nipped their future in the bud. But they had now. And whether "now" was hours, days, or weeks, he was going to make it memorable. He just wasn't sure he was going to be able to let her go when "now" became "then."

Yeah, that wasn't stalkerish. Much.

4

———

Wynn woke to the smell of bacon frying. She smiled. For a second, she thought she was having a sleepover with Grams, like the old days when she was in college...until she opened her eyes and saw the lone remaining condom on the nightstand. Everything came hurtling back to reality.

Angel. Grams. Angel's team and their hidden war. The man in the blue sedan stalking her.

She curled into a ball, feeling sore in places she hadn't felt in a long, long time. She felt other things, too. Replete. Content. And safe. That thought made her smile. Angel always had that effect on her.

She uncurled and stretched, realizing how sticky she was. Breakfast would probably take another few minutes. She had time for a fast shower.

She was just coming out of the bathroom a few minutes later when Angel came in with a loaded breakfast tray—bacon, scrambled eggs, a dish of fruit, a glass of orange juice, a cup of coffee, and all the fixings for it.

Her stomach growled as she tied the band around her kimono wrap. She was starving.

He nodded toward the bed. "Get back in. Gotta keep your strength up."

She was shocked at the heat spilling through her from the images his words conjured. She got back into the bed and pulled the covers over her lap. He set the tray there. One plate. Two cups of coffee. "Where's yours?"

"In the kitchen."

"You should take some of this. I can't eat it all. I didn't think I had bacon."

"You didn't. I went to the market."

"Already?"

He grinned. "Already? I went for a run, took a shower, went to the store, and cooked breakfast." He leaned over and picked up a big box of condoms. "I needed to replenish our supplies. Figured I'd leave them here for when I come back."

Cold fingers of panic slipped into Wynn's chest as she considered what that box meant. The longer he was here, the harder it would be to work on the problem of her parents. She couldn't put that off. If it was true that they were alive, then it was true they were in danger, from Angel and others.

Her eyes met his. "When you leave here, you can't come back."

He stared at her, then lowered his gaze to the tray. He nodded. "Yeah. No worries. I'll take them with me." He stood and shoved his hands in his pockets. He wasn't making eye contact with her. "I'm gonna go clean up the kitchen."

"Bring a plate and help me eat this."

"Not real hungry at the moment, Wynn." He left her room.

WHEN YOU LEAVE HERE, *you can't come back.* Those were the very words Angel had heard his mother say to his dad too many times to count—not that his dad ever listened to them. He knew his mom had loved his dad, but his dad was toxic to them. Trouble followed him and spilled over to Angel and his mom.

And now Angel was toxic to Wynn.

The fucking Omnis won again.

He was scrubbing the pan when Wynn brought her tray out to the dining room. She sat at the table to eat. He should leave after he cleaned up. No sense dragging it out. She didn't need to know that Grams' body wasn't where she thought it was. Just leave it alone. Get the fuck away from her so she could live her life and find some measure of happiness.

He looked at her as he dried the pan. "Who was

that guy yesterday? You were arguing with him just before I got here."

She shook her head and swallowed the bite she'd taken. "An ambulance chaser. He wanted me to list Grams' property with him. He keeps running into me."

Angel went cold as he stared at her. Her story didn't jibe with the info Greer sent back after Angel had sent him the guy's license plate. According to Greer, the guy was a middle manager for a local IT firm. Either she was lying to him, or the guy was lying to her.

He couldn't leave until he figured out which it was.

"Why did you come down yesterday?" she asked after the last bite of bacon.

"I wanted to see you." While that was only a partial truth, at least it wasn't a lie.

She brought her plate over. He moved aside so she could rinse it and put it in the dishwasher.

"How about giving me the tour?" he asked. The least he could do was make sure her house was buttoned up tight before he left.

"It's not a big house."

He shrugged.

"All right. Let me get dressed."

That wasn't an invitation to help, but his body sure responded as if it were. He folded his arms. "I'll be here."

She gave him an odd look, then caught his arm and leaned up to kiss his cheek. "Thank you for breakfast."

"Sure."

She turned around and took a couple backward steps when she was almost to the hallway. "You know, there's another reason we would never work out."

He lifted a brow.

"You're a morning person and I'm not."

He almost told her he could change, but he wasn't a man known for begging. When the door closed to the master bedroom, he wandered down the hall, beginning the tour himself in the two spare rooms. One was an office. It had wall-to-wall cabinets. Looked like Wynn had started going through things, for the tidy space had stacks of papers piled randomly, and there were trash bags on the floor.

The other bedroom was the one with the twin bed. Looked like a little girl's room. Flower wallpaper was on one wall; the other walls were a different shade of pink than the living room. The furniture was a yellowing white. There were sayings and quotes shoved into the edge of the mirror's frame on a little vanity. Angel leaned close to read one. *"Let your heart shine in your eyes"* and *"Do a kindness for someone else for no reason at all"* and *"Be kind. Be strong. Be yourself."*

This had to have been Wynn's room. The innocence and femininity of the space almost undid him. He'd been all fists, bats, balls, and colors of the local gang where he'd grown up in the projects, and she was sparkles and dolls and pretty things.

Just another way they were opposites.

Wynn's door slammed open and she hurried into the hall, coming to a full stop as she saw him. She sent a quick look over to the office, then turned her full attention on him. He smiled at her and nodded at the room. "It's a memorial to your childhood." A pink flush warmed her skin as if she were embarrassed.

"Yeah. Grams didn't want to change anything after I went to college. I bet your parents did the same thing."

"My parents are dead."

Her eyes went wide. "I'm sorry."

He shrugged. "Not your doing."

She cleared her throat, then stepped out into the hallway. He followed her. "So. The tour. There's the master. And my room. And the office."

He leaned against the doorjamb of the office, forcing her to stop with him. "What are you looking for in there?"

"Looking for?" She saw the stacks of papers he was looking at. "Oh, just anything that shouldn't be thrown away. Grams kept decades' worth of bills and receipts. I just want to make sure I'm not tossing something that I should keep."

"I can give you a hand with that."

She shook her head. "It's dreadfully boring."

He gave her a half-grin. "Dreadfully?" Her lips parted. Fucking hell, he could think of a dozen better ways to spend their time, but he'd help with her office if it let him see her secrets.

"Angel, don't you need to get back to Wolf Creek Bend?"

"Eventually. Show me the basement."

He followed her to the stairs, which were tucked away by the mudroom between the garage and kitchen. He had to duck as they turned halfway down to the lower level. It was finished with the veneer wood panels popular several decades ago. The ceiling was low. It was a dangerous place for a guy his height.

There were, he discovered, two more bedrooms, a bathroom, a rec room, and an unfinished storage and utility area. The rec room was filled with boxes and extra furniture—some of it blocking the door to the backyard.

Angel nodded to that pile-up. "That's a fire danger."

Wynn's face tightened. "I know. The lock's broken on that door. I haven't had a chance to mess with a locksmith."

"I can fix it for you. Or I can help clear out the office." He spread his arms wide. "Think of me as free labor today."

She shook her head. "You don't have to. I'll call a locksmith this week. And forget about the office." She gave him a little chuckle as she waved that off. "Not fun stuff. I'm not in a hurry to clear it out. Gives me something to do. And I'm kind of a control freak about seeing everything before it's tossed."

He took her hand. "Then let's spend today together. We could go downtown and walk around." He pulled her close, letting her soft curves ease his hard edges. "I'm leaving tomorrow morning." He brushed two fingers under a lock of her hair, smoothing it from her forehead. "And as it turns out, I won't be back. Give me today, Wynn."

Her face was serious as she studied his eyes. Just when he thought he was going to have to head out right then, she nodded. "Okay. We'll have today."

He tightened his hold on her. "Yeah?"

She nodded, then a shadow slipped across her features. "Will we be safe?"

Angel kept his expression neutral as he processed that question. What made her even question her safety? "Why wouldn't we be?"

She shrugged and stepped away from him. "I don't know. Just lingering paranoia from everything."

He tried to read her, but she'd turned at a slight angle. He slipped an arm around her, drawing her back against him. He reached down for her hand. "Yes. You will be safe today. And if you ever feel you aren't, I'm only a phone call away." He nuzzled her hair away from her neck and kissed her bare skin. He wanted to add that no one hurt his woman, but she wasn't his, was she? She didn't want to be in his world.

And he couldn't step out of it.

So they had today. One day. And hopefully, one more night.

Angel did a quick bit of research about things to do

in Cheyenne while Wynn got ready. Seemed the town had been slow to step into the modern world, but it was catching up with a vengeance. Local microbreweries, little boutique and antique shops, and restaurants serving new American and varieties of international cuisines were scattered down every block in the old part of town. It was a community finding its footing...as it had been since the days of the Wild West.

It was an entirely different culture than his inner-city East Coast roots. But this was Wynn's home, so everything about it interested him.

He looked up to see her step out of the hallway to the bedrooms. Her hair was soft around her shoulders, with a loose wave to it. Her face was just barely touched with makeup. She wore a taupe peasant top over a pair of jeans, which she filled out like a dream. A soft, flowery scarf was draped around her neck. He stood, blown away by the glow around her.

Her eyes widened as he stared at her. She looked down, checking herself over. "What? Is something wrong?"

He reminded himself that she wasn't his. She would never be his. *Don't say some dumb shit...like she's mine because my soul has already claimed hers.* "You're beautiful. And I'm in awe of you." He shrugged. "That's all."

Warm color flooded her cheeks. She smiled and dropped her gaze.

Way to fucking play it cool, schmuck. "You up for

walking around?" he asked. "You can give me a history lesson."

She stepped close and wrapped her arms around his waist. He loved the easy way she touched him. All of it...all of her...all of them. It was just so right. Except him. He was the monkey wrench in her bliss.

"Don't know about a history lesson, but I love walking around downtown."

He led her outside and waited while she locked the door. At his SUV, he opened her door. She smiled at him. Their eyes locked and held for just a breath too long. How the hell was he going to get through this day when every moment they spent together was one less they'd ever have?

It was a short jaunt to the old downtown portion of the capital city. They drove around, checking out the locations of all the places that were interesting to them before parking in a public lot. Angel took Wynn's hand and let her decide their direction. He had only one objective for their time together: make her happy.

They made their way through shop after shop, each with its own personality, but all of them strongly scented from soaps, spices, teas, potpourri, and candles. He kept his hands in his pockets and followed her through the dense arrangements of fragile whatnots, which made him itchy, but made her smile.

They went into a jewelry store that specialized in pieces made by Wyoming artisans. She found a pair of silver and amethyst earrings and held them up to herself in a counter mirror, but put them back when she saw the price. He loved them. They were beautiful with her blue-brown eyes.

On their way out of the shop, he noticed two of her little creeper statues in a display case. "Hey." He nodded toward them. "Do you have those two?"

She gasped when she saw them. "Grams doesn't have these." She looked up at him. "She would have been so excited to find them." The joy his find gave her was quickly followed by sorrow at not having Grams to share it with. He could have kicked himself for that. He shouldn't have pointed them out.

He led her outside, then turned to her. "Those earrings were beautiful. Will you let me get them for you? Something to remember today by."

She gave him a sad smile as she stepped close. "I don't need anything to remember today. I'll never forget this."

He stroked his thumb over her cheek, then kissed her brow. He made a mental note to come back and get those earrings for her. Maybe he could have the shop-keeper send them over to her.

"Hungry?" he asked. "Something about shopping until you drop makes me want to eat a full bull moose." He grinned. She laughed.

Jesus. He loved her.

He looked away, forcing his mind to the matter of

finding food for them. Didn't matter what he felt. Life was what it was. They could have no future together. And he was going to have to like that if he was ever going to live with it.

"I saw Thai, Chinese, French, and American. What's your poison?" he asked.

"French."

He nodded, then started toward that restaurant. "French it is."

The restaurant wasn't packed. It was between seasons, so not a lot of tourists were wandering around town. A few tables of locals were filled. The place had a lot of ambience. An antique bar filled an entire wall. The floor was covered with black and white tiles in a mosaic pattern. Crisp white tablecloths covered each table. Perfect setting for a French bistro.

They gave their orders. Angel had the seat facing the door, a logistical necessity, but it meant Wynn's face was shadowed by the bright light from the front window. "So what happens now?" he asked. "What are your plans?"

She set her napkin in her lap, then took a piece of baguette and put it on her bread plate. "I don't know. Grams had a modest life insurance policy. And of course the house was paid off long ago. I have time and options. I just don't know yet."

Angel leaned back in his seat and studied her. He closed his eyes briefly as he let her words swirl around his mind. That freedom to make her own life was exactly why he had to let her go. With him, there never would be any freedom.

"I envy you your freedom."

She met his eyes. "You can make changes, Angel. Choose to do something different."

He shook his head. "I guess envy's the wrong word. I made my choice a long time ago. And I wouldn't change it. But it's fun to be where you are and have your whole life open in any direction. That's exciting. I miss that."

She lowered her gaze to stare at her plate. As he watched, her breathing changed, became shallow. Man, he'd crossed a line again. Now he had her thinking about his world. It wasn't one of her options. It couldn't be. It would end her.

He had to distract her. "So the world's open to you, just waiting for you to take a step. What are your choices?"

"I could take my teaching certificate and start my teaching career. Here or anywhere. I could resume working on my master's in gifted ed. I could pursue a doctorate in education and become an administrator."

"But education's the ticket, huh? Why?"

As she considered his question, their meal was served. "I feel strongly about influencing the next generation of our country's citizens. I want to make a difference. I want them to know they matter. And I want them to understand that life is what they make it."

"The world's a better place because of you, Wynn."

She shook her head. "I haven't done anything to make a difference."

"Yet. You will." The waiter brought their meal over. They ate in silence for a few minutes. He had questions that he still needed her to answer. And there was the matter of Grams' remains. So much to fit into so little time before he left.

"What did your parents do?" he asked, though he knew the answer. Right on cue, the shadows slipped across her face, masking her from him. Why? Why was the topic of her parents so sensitive? Well, he had his own secrets, didn't he? Like the fact that Grams' body had been stolen. The thought made him sick. No fucking way could he tell her. Ever. Her life was too filled with chaos to chuck that in the mix. Let her have the peace of thinking her grandmother was where she thought her to be.

"They were scientists. My dad was a biochemical engineer. My mom was a molecular biologist."

"Those fields don't interest you?"

She shook her head. "I'm not smart enough."

Fuck that. "You have your own genius. Kids love you. Zavi is missing the hell outta you."

"I know. I miss him too."

"What happened to your parents?"

She met his gaze with her own hard stare. "You know what happened to them. You know everything about me."

"I know about you. I don't know about them."

She lifted a dark brow. "Is this an official inquiry?"

He stared back at her. "Forget it."

"They died in a fire in their lab. It was horrible."

He wondered what was worse—thinking your parents died a terrible death, or learning they never died at all but didn't bother to come back into your life? This was why he couldn't be in her life. The dead didn't stay dead. And the living all seemed to become victims.

Maybe she didn't know if her parents were still alive, but she sure was edgy about them. Still, he didn't think the answers he needed were going to come from her.

A man on the sidewalk went past the front window. He stopped and stood next to a sign. Angel frowned. "Isn't that the realtor who keeps pestering you?"

Wynn turned and looked. The color left her face. "Yeah."

Angel set his napkin on the table and stood. "How about I go set a few things straight with him?"

"No!" Wynn reached over and caught his forearm, halting him.

Angel sat back down, watching her curiously. "I don't like him bothering you."

"He's not bothering me now. The sidewalk is public space."

"But he just happens to pause where you can't help but see him? No. I'll take care of him."

"Angel." She shook her head. "Please don't make a scene."

"He's been following us all day," he said. Her eyes

widened and her lips parted. She really hadn't known he was tailing them. "So you want to tell me what's going on?"

"I told you. It's nothing. I guess I understand now why ambulance chasers have such a bad rep." She used her napkin, then set it on the table. "I think we should go. I think you should go."

Angel held her gaze. "Right." He dropped a few twenties on the table, then stood. He moved to the door ahead of her, wanting to be the first to leave the restaurant. The guy was gone. He stepped aside so she could come out.

The short autumn afternoon was quickly fading to dusk. They were silent as they made their way back to the SUV. Silent as they drove to her house. It was impossible to pack a lifetime of words into a few minutes, so he didn't try. He sent a look around when they got to her house, checking for that blue sedan. He didn't see it.

"I need to come in for my bag."

"Sure."

He held the screen door while she unlocked the front door. She stayed right there, waiting for him to come back. He paused by the door. Walking away felt wrong. She was looking at his chest, avoiding his eyes.

"Wynn, I wish Wolf Creek Bend wasn't so far away."

"I'll be fine, Angel."

He couldn't make himself tell her about Grams. It would only scare her more than she already was. And he didn't know yet if it meant she was still at risk. Maybe the Omnis got what they needed by taking Grams' remains. Maybe Wynn really was out of danger now.

"You know I'm only a call away."

"I know."

WYNN WATCHED Angel's broad back as he paused at the door. She crossed her arms, as much to give herself strength as to keep herself from reaching for him and begging him to stay.

When he turned to her, she had to fight to keep her expression calm.

"Wynn, I came here for a reason yesterday."

She studied his eyes. "Why?"

"We exhumed Grams."

"You did what?" Why would he do that? And without asking her.

Angel dropped his bag. "Grams was being held in a house leased by Syadne Tech. We think Syadne was behind the smallpox outbreak in a small community in Wyoming. They're why you had to get the vaccination. We've suspected for a while that Syadne is working on weaponizing another disease. The note the bikers left on Grams, marking her as a lab rat, just strengthens our fears. We had to know."

"You could have told me. You could have asked."

"Your approval wasn't needed. It was a matter of national security."

ELAINE LEVINE

That assertion briefly paralyzed her body while her mind went wild. Anything in the name of national security. Her parents didn't stand a chance with him. "I think you should leave."

"Grams' body wasn't in the casket, Wynn. That's what I came to tell you. Did you have her cremated?"

"No. She wanted to be buried, not cremated."

"There was a box of ashes in the casket. I don't know if they were human or animal or something else. We're having them analyzed. The cremation may have compromised the DNA in any bone fragments that remain. I don't know that we will ever be able to definitively say the ashes belong to Grams. My gut says they aren't hers."

Wynn felt lightheaded. She covered her mouth to keep from crying out. This felt every bit as if she were losing Grams all over again. Angel led her over to the sofa, then sat on the coffee table in front of her. "Breathe slowly."

"What happened to her? She was in the casket at the funeral home. I saw her. I made certain of it. I don't know why I did, I just did. She was there."

"Then sometime between when you saw her and when we exhumed her, someone switched out her coffin. The cemetery doesn't have security cameras set up where we could see Grams' grave. Their footage of vehicles coming in and out of the cemetery didn't show anything that stands out. None of their security logs noted anything unusual in the time after Grams' funeral.

The funeral home, however, had some glitch with their cameras the day of the funeral. I think that may have been when the switch happened. Greer's looking into it."

He leaned forward and took her hands. "I'm concerned you may not be out of danger."

"You think they're going to do tests on me?"

"I don't know. I don't know why or how or even *if* they used Grams—I just want to make damn sure you aren't next."

"I thought, by leaving you guys, that I would be safe. I thought I got away from what you were doing."

Angel brushed his thumb over the scar on her palm, the butterfly that Mr. Edwards carved into her skin. It was still healing, the skin rough in spots where he'd cut deeper. Angel lifted it to his mouth and kissed her palm.

She pulled free. "Don't. It's ugly."

"We all have scars, Wynn. They're what make us who we are."

"What are we going to do?"

"The way I see it, you've got two choices. You can let me stay and guard you. Or you can come back to Blade's. You don't have to teach Zavi if you don't want to. But if the Omnis want you, we can't let them have you. At Blade's, they'd have to come through all of us to get you."

She frowned. She'd kept herself so separate from the team when she was up at their headquarters that she knew nothing of what they were fighting or who their enemies were. "Who are the Omnis?"

Angel sighed. "There's a lot I need to bring you up to speed on."

Wynn stood and walked across the living room. "They can't just take my life away."

"Law-abiding citizens can't take your life away. These guys aren't law-abiding."

"Grams was just an ordinary person. You know that. Her death was just some horrible, useless, random event. No one was targeting her."

He shook his head. "Spies lead double—or triple —lives."

"She wasn't a spy. She was just a nice old lady."

Angel sent her a skeptical look. "Nice old ladies are of no interest to the Omnis."

Wynn sighed and looked out the window over the couch. "None of this makes sense to me."

"It doesn't to me and the team either. We need to keep you safe while we figure it out. You can help us with that."

Wynn blinked away the moisture filling her eyes. What did all of this mean for her parents? Were they working for these criminals? She nixed that. It was a lie that guy told her so he could get to her. But he'd said, that last time they argued, that her parents had done terrible things, criminal things.

"Angel, I can't do this. I don't want to be part of

this. I don't want to get any deeper into it. I can't. I really can't."

He came over to her. "I know. I don't blame you for wanting out. Help me keep you safe until you can get out. Yeah?"

His hands were warm on her arms, strong and reassuring. She bent her head as he pulled her closer. He was such a solid man. It felt nice to lean on him.

His phone rang. He fished it out of his pocket. "Go, Greer... Yeah... Shit... Copy." He sighed as he pocketed his phone. "Greer checked out that guy who's been bugging you."

"How?"

"I sent him the guy's license plate. He's no realtor."

Oh, no. He knew she'd lied. Wynn tensed.

"He's an Omni operative. I need to get you up to headquarters. How about you go pack what you're going to need. We should hit the road."

She nodded and started down the hall, but he stopped her.

"You'll be with us a while, Wynn. Don't pack light."

In Grams' room—her room—Wynn stood frozen. The world just couldn't stay calm for five minutes. It was like she was on the rails of a crazy ride she couldn't get off.

"Now, Wynnie."

She jumped at Angel's voice. She hadn't heard him follow her. He went over to the closet and pulled out her nested suitcases. He dropped them on the bed and unzipped them. Wynn shook herself from her daze.

"I got this. I'm good." She wiped at the tears on her face. Night was coming. The shadows were heavy in the room, but not dark enough to hide her fear from Angel. He didn't say anything. She couldn't read his expression. Was he angry with her?

She went to her dresser and grabbed things from the drawers to drop into the suitcase. She pulled things from the closet, folding them roughly. She was shaking. If he was in a hurry, she should be, too. She grabbed her shoes and shoved them on the pile. She made a few trips from the bathroom with the toiletries she'd need and put them into the smallest case. In bare minutes, the three suitcases were packed. She hooked them together and dragged them out to Angel.

While he took them out to his SUV, she packed up some things from the kitchen. Her apartment at the team's headquarters had its own kitchen. No sense leaving things here to go to waste when she could use them there.

She looked up when Angel came back inside. He locked the door behind him and shut off the lights. "Come with me, Wynn. Right now." He grabbed her hand and dragged her back to Grams' bedroom and then to the bathroom. "Lock this door, then hide in the tub. Keep your head down."

"Why? What's happening?"

He didn't answer that. "Don't unlock the door for

anyone but me. No matter what happens. Don't make a sound. Don't come out. If I don't come back, call Kit." He grabbed her phone from her dresser and shoved it into her hands. Her last sight of him was as he closed the door between them. She went to lock it, but saw that he'd already done that.

She jumped when he banged on the door. "Get in the tub, Wynn. Do it now."

5

—————

Wynn heard the back door in the dining room crash in. Her hands shook so much that it was hard to hold the phone. She didn't have Kit's number on her phone, did she? She scrolled through her contacts. Maybe Angel had put it there when he added his. She'd never looked for it. What was his last name? Kit what? Bolanger. There it was. She hit dial just as the first shot rang out, thundering through the house.

Dear God. Angel was alone out there.

"Bolanger here."

"Kit. It's Wynn. Angel said to call you if he didn't make it through. I don't know what to do. Help him. Please."

"Wynn. Be calm. What's happening?"

"I don't know. Some people are breaking into my house. Angel's fighting them."

"Got it. We're on our way. Where are you?"

"Hiding in the bathroom. They're fighting out there."

"As long as they're fighting, you know he's alive."

"Okay."

"Stay where you are, Wynn."

"I will. Should I call the police?"

It sounded like he was running. *"No. They can't help him. You understand?"*

"Yes." The line went dead. No, she didn't understand. He shouldn't have to be out there facing this alone. She had to help somehow. She sat up just a little. It sounded like a hurricane was trapped inside her living room. She doubted she'd even have walls left.

But that didn't matter as long as Angel survived.

She got out of the tub and faced the bathroom door as she tried to figure out how she could help him. She heard the bedroom door bang open. *Oh my God!* They got through Angel. *Oh, God.* She saw the doorknob turn slightly. Moving instinctively, she pulled the drawers of the vanity out so that they blocked the door.

In a panic, she looked around for something, anything she could use as a weapon. Her gaze touched on the lighter she used for the candles she sometimes lit while she bathed. A big bang sounded as whoever was on the other side of her door tried to kick it in. The drawers slowed them down, but not for long.

She cursed. A lighter was useless on its own... unless... She dug through the other side of the vanity

77

drawers for her can of hairspray. She didn't even know if this would work—she'd only seen it on TV. She didn't know how long the drawers were going to hold the door back. One kick. One more, then everything shattered—the door, the drawers. A man she didn't know stood in the yawning cavity. He stepped into the room, gun first.

Wynn clicked the lighter on just as she let loose a stream of hairspray. Flames burned the space between them, shooting over the man's arm and body, setting him on fire. He screamed and dropped his gun as he swatted at the flames. Wynn dropped her flamethrower stuff in the sink and scrambled to get his gun.

When she looked up, he was gone. The fire alarm went on, the wail screaming deafeningly. She cautiously stepped out of the bathroom and into the small anteroom between the his-and-hers closets.

The fighting had stopped in the main area of her house. She stepped to the doorway of her room and peeked around the corner. A tall man was coming toward her, shadowed by the light behind him. His height and width filled the narrow hall. Jesus, he was huge.

She looked back toward the bathroom and closet, but knew she wouldn't have time to make it to them before he came into her room. Too late, she tried to shove her door shut. His foot breached her doorjamb, blocking her attempt. She lifted the pistol, then realized she had no idea how to use the stupid thing.

"Easy, Wynn. You're safe," came a familiar voice.

Angel. She stepped back. "Angel."

"Yeah, me." He nodded at the gun she still held in her shaking hands. "How about you hand that to me?" He was bleeding from his nose and cheek.

He held his hand out. She put the gun in it. It was useless to her anyway. Just as she did, Angel was tackled hard. Some guy plowed into him from behind. Both of them rolled around on the floor. The other guy got the upper hand, arching his arm back then pounding Angel's face.

Wynn backed as far away as she could. The bathroom offered no refuge. She couldn't take her eyes off the horrible scene of Angel fighting. One of their blows would have killed her, and they were each taking several of them. Then she saw Angel do a maneuver where he locked his hands around the other man's elbow. He tightened his grip. She heard bones crunch.

His attacker screamed.

Wynn screamed.

Angel took advantage of the lull in the fight. He gripped the man's neck and tried to twist, but the man somehow freed himself. Angel reached for his throat, digging his fingers into the man's Adam's apple as he brought his knife up. All she had to do was shut her eyes, but she didn't. She watched the whole terrible thing, until the man dropped to the ground, sounds coming from the gaping hole in his neck instead of his mouth, where they should have been.

Wynn screamed again.

Angel started toward her. He wiped his knife on his pants and sheathed it. She panicked and tried to run from him, but he blocked her in the corner. Reaching over, he gently touched her face with his bloodied hands. "Be calm," he whispered. "I'm sorry, Wynnie. You shouldn't have had to see that."

Wynn flattened herself against the walls behind her. She was shaking so badly that her teeth rattled. Blood was pounding through her veins with such pressure that her ears started their own tinny scream. She was sucking air in great gasps and still couldn't get enough of it.

And all throughout her panic, she kept seeing him kill her parents in the same way he'd just ripped apart the man who'd fought him.

He stepped away, and she was vaguely aware that he went into the bathroom. She wanted to run, but where would she go? There might be more men outside—either from the team or their enemy, waiting to finish her. She slipped to the ground.

Angel came back into the room. He'd rinsed his hands and now knelt to hold a warm, damp cloth out to her. "Hold this to your mouth and breath through it. You're safe now. I gotcha."

She tried to resist, but he caught her head and held it still as he kept the cloth against her mouth. She took it from him, holding it with both hands. It did help. It was warm and soothing. Eventually, her breathing slowed.

When she pulled the cloth away, the smell of blood nearly suffocated her. It was on him, on her, in the air. The way Angel crouched in front of her blocked her line of sight to the man he'd slaughtered. Barehanded. She started to hyperventilate again, so Angel lifted her hand and put the cloth against her mouth again.

"Be calm, sweet Wynn. We need to leave."

She reached up to touch his cheek, and winced. He looked mangled. "You're bleeding."

"It's nothing." He wiped at blood that was spilling from his nose and the corner of his mouth, but he just smeared more over himself from his torn knuckles.

Wynn drew a ragged breath. There was no way they were getting out of this alive. Her gaze moved to the hallway. The fire alarm was still screaming. "Are they gone?"

"No. They're dead." He helped her to her feet. "We can't stay here." He walked over to the dead body lying next to her bed and went through his pockets. "By the way, that was fucking brilliant, what you did with the hairspray. How'd you know to do that?"

Wynn didn't answer. Her mind was still reeling from shock. If those guys had worked a man like Angel over so badly, imagine what they would have done to her if they'd been able to catch her. She looked toward the hallway door. "I don't understand any of this. Who were those men?"

"We'll talk about it on the road."

She followed him out of the bedroom, down the

hall, into the living room. The stink of fresh blood brought her up short. She saw three bodies lying where they fell. Blood was everywhere. On the walls, floor, furniture. Glass was littered across the room from the broken coffee table and étagère. One of the side chairs was flattened. The couch listed at an awkward angle, one of its arms broken and leaning wide, feathers everywhere from the cushions.

Angel dug through the pockets of the dead out there, too. Wynn looked away and noticed the brass frame of the étagère stood at an angle against the wall behind it. Shards of porcelain were everywhere. Only two of Grams' extensive Hummel collection remained intact. Wynn kneeled on the floor, unmindful of the blood-spattered debris digging into her as she sifted through the rubble to pick out the figurines. Her sight wavered through tears as she remembered the fun she and Grams had had hunting for them. She tried not to cry. She really did.

Glass crunched as Angel hunkered down next to her. Tears ran down her cheeks as she looked up at him, the Frankenstein monster she both feared and craved, his face battered by the men who'd wrecked her home. Her breath hitched. Still holding the Hummels, she pressed the back of her hand to her mouth.

"Baby, don't cry. I'm sorry, Wynn. I'm so damned sorry." He reached for her, but she pulled away. This war was becoming her life, as much as it was for him.

She blinked, spilling tears down her cheeks. "It's

okay. I'm just glad you were here and that you're all right. Pretty much." She cleared her throat, then started to stand. He helped her up. She walked over to the dining room and set the figurines on the counter that separated the kitchen from the dining room.

"Shouldn't we call the police?" she asked him. "Whoever it was that broke in here can't be allowed to do this to other people."

Angel shook his head. "This isn't a police matter. The more people we pull into this mess, the higher the body count's going to be. Those were Omni guys; they didn't pick you randomly. And they sure as hell aren't after your neighbors."

"I called Kit while I was in the bathroom. I think he's on his way down here."

"Good. I'll phone him from the road."

Something caught his attention outside the sliding glass door that opened to the backyard. She followed his gaze, but didn't see anything. He hurried outside, crossing the lawn to the gate in the back fence. That gate led to the alleyway where the trash service ran. A minute later, he came back into the yard and then the house.

"What did you see?" she asked.

He shook his head. "Nothing."

"Was it another of those men?"

Again, he shook his head, then looked outside. "I thought I saw a woman."

Wynn gasped. *A woman*. Could it be true? Was her

mom here? She bent and picked up some photos that had fallen in the fight. Pictures of her parents and Grams. She dusted the glass off one of them.

Angel frowned and picked it up, stared at it, then looked out the back door where he'd just been. "Who's this?"

"My mom." Wynn took the picture from him. Her hands were shaking. Had he seen her mom? "It's an old picture from when she and my dad were on their honeymoon." He was frowning at her. "Why?"

He shook his head, then ran his hand over his short hair. "Nothing." He looked at his watch. "We need to head out. Ready?"

"I just need to grab the kitchen stuff." She went into the kitchen, but saw another dead guy sprawled across the floor. The things she'd collected to bring with them were scattered everywhere. "Never mind." She backed out of the room. Angel caught her arm and led her outside.

The quiet outside was deafening after the wail of the smoke alarm. He held the passenger door open for her. She got in and buckled up. He was carrying a small plastic grocery bag, which he put in the back hatch before getting into the driver's seat.

She was silent while they made their way across town to the highway. Angel wasn't chatty either. In fact, he seemed pissed. He called Kit through the dashboard.

"You alive?"

"Yeah. Tell Lobo we need a cleanup at Wynn's."

"Already called it in. We're halfway there."

"I've got Wynn. We're heading up."

"Copy. You need to stop in at the clinic?"

"No."

"Yes, he does," Wynn interrupted.

"Which is it?"

"I'm fine. Still have all my teeth. Fucking miracle." Angel shook his head. "Those guys, I dunno, Kit. Something was off with them. Like they were on something. Super steroids."

"Copy. We'll have Lobo get them checked out."

The line went dead. Angel pounded the dash with his fist, making Wynn jump. "I almost left you there to face that alone."

"Did they want me alive or dead?"

He looked over at her then faced the road again. "I don't want to find out."

"Thank you, Angel. You saved my life."

"You did all right yourself, setting that guy on fire."

"I hated doing that."

"Only a sociopath loves that sort of thing. You protected yourself. I'm proud of you." He grinned. "And you called Kit. What did he say?"

"He told me that as long as there was active fighting, then you were still alive."

"Huh. That's one way to look at it, I guess."

Wynn stared at the road. The headlights caught the

white dashes they passed, like fast-moving dots. "I know you said we'd talk on the ride up, but can we wait until tomorrow? I don't know how much I can absorb tonight."

He sent her a quick look, then nodded. "Tomorrow sounds good. Or whenever. I'll answer all of your questions when you're ready to ask them. I thought keeping you out of this as much as possible was best, but that hasn't worked out as intended. There are things you need to know, Wynn. And there are things we need to know that only you can answer. Questions about your parents."

Wynn looked out the window, trying to keep her mind from looping the brutal way Angel killed the man in her room. The guy in the suit who told her that her parents were still alive had also said that Angel and his friends would kill them for what they'd done. But that guy had turned out to be one of their enemies, so was he lying about her parents? Were they alive? Had Angel really seen her mom tonight?

She folded her arms close around her middle, chilled now that the adrenaline was wearing off. Angel turned the heat up on her side. The only thing she knew as truth was that the closer they came to Wolf Creek Bend, the harder it was for her to breathe regularly. She didn't want to go back there—had never wanted to be there again. She'd had a taste of normal and now craved that life, the one she'd had before she ever took the job with the Silases.

They didn't talk about anything on the ride up. He looked angrier each time she glanced at him. And his mood did little to alleviate hers. Wynn felt tension twist in her stomach when they pulled off the highway into Wolf Creek Bend. It was like an invisible band of elastic was attached to her from this place. She'd tried to run, but it just let her go far enough to feel freedom before snapping her back.

He parked in front of Ty's big house. She got out and looked up at the sprawling mansion. The wind blew around her, smelling of a wood fire. She was so afraid. She knew without a doubt that she didn't want to go back inside that house and the maelstrom it represented.

But it didn't matter, did it? Like it or not, she was part of it.

She didn't look at Angel, couldn't take his lies that she was safe or things would be better soon. She had a crazy sense that she wouldn't be far behind following Grams to the other side...a disturbing thought that shouldn't have been so comforting. She needed time alone—to process what had just happened and what being back here meant. And she needed time to make a plan for what her next step should be.

How was she going to find her parents if she was stuck here?

Angel took the first step toward the house. She followed him. It was a relief that no one was in the living room. Wynn's feet felt frozen in place where she stood in the foyer. Her breathing was labored.

Angel nudged her. "Let's get you settled." He carried two of her suitcases up the stairs. She brought the smallest bag full of her toiletries.

6

Wynn was on edge as they turned down the hallway that led to her apartment over the garage. She was glad they didn't run into anyone. The key to her apartment was in her door. She unlocked it and pocketed the key. Angel brought her luggage in for her. She dropped her purse on the couch, then turned to face him and gasped. In the full light of her apartment, he looked twice as bad as he had at her house.

She grabbed his arm and gently touched his face, turning him so she could see both sides. "You should let me take you to the clinic."

He pulled free. "I'm fine. I'll go take a shower and wash the grime off."

Wynn still had trouble processing all they'd been through. Nothing in her life had prepared her for anything like it. She nodded. "Go. Shower. Put ice on your face." She looked at his chest. His injuries had to be as bad—or worse—than those she'd gotten when Jafaar's men worked her over. "How's the rest of you?"

His eyes were dark and intense. "Keep looking at me like that, you'll find out really quickly."

She shook her head. "Angel."

"There's nothing wrong with me that a night holding you wouldn't fix."

"Then come back after your shower."

"I will."

A knock sounded on Wynn's door. Angel went to open it. Greer was on the other side. "Need a word."

Angel looked back at her. "I'll be back in a bit."

Wynn nodded. She took her suitcases to her room. She was coming back into the living room when Angel walked back into her apartment. His eyes were full of demons. Had those monsters followed them here?

He walked right up to her and wrapped his arms around her, pulling her close to his body, his hold almost suffocating.

"Angel. What is it? I can't breathe—"

"Wynn. Wynn, honey, they burned your house."

She grabbed his arms and tried to push free, but his hold was unrelenting. "What?"

"The Omnis burned your house."

Her legs went weak. His arms were strong around her, holding her up. "No. That can't be."

"It's gone."

"My grandfather built that for Grams." When she

realized the last connection she had to Grams was gone, the floodgates opened. She leaned into him and wept for everything that was gone, everything that was broken...which was her whole life now.

When the first shock wore off, Angel led her back to her room. "We're both going to take a shower. If ever a day needed washing off, it's today."

Wynn was numb. She couldn't think, couldn't feel. Without Angel, she would have just curled up on her bed in a ball and waited for the night to pass. He stripped, then helped her off with her clothes. Normally, standing naked in the light in front of a guy like Angel, she would have felt a rush of insecurity, but not tonight. Tonight, she felt nothing.

He turned the water on, and while it heated up, he got a couple of towels out of the cabinet. Wynn took the things she needed in the shower from her toiletries bag that was on the counter. She stepped into the steaming shower and moved so that there was room for him. It wasn't a large booth, so they stood against each other.

"Lean against me," he said.

She couldn't. He was covered with bruises and scrapes from his fight. She ran her hands over them, then looked up at him. "Are you scared?"

He gave a slight shake of his head. "I am not afraid. I'm angry."

"I'm sorry you had to fight for me."

He touched her cheek. The water was pouring down

on their shoulders. "You don't get it, do you? I stand for *you*, Wynn. There is no end to how many battles I will fight for you. I will fight until there's no fear in your eyes, until there are no secrets you feel the need to keep from me, until you know only joy and hope and peace. There is no cost, no thing you have to do. Love me or hate me, I stand for you."

She couldn't understand the magnitude of his words. Such a creed would get him killed. "Why?"

"Because they don't have the right to take your life away. Because unless you're free to live the life you choose, none of us is."

She closed her eyes as the hot water poured over her. It helped that he pulled her close again and let the water run over both of them, rinsing the night away. The panic and dread she'd felt slowly eased away.

After a few minutes, they separated to wash. Wynn's gaze snagged on his heavy penis.

"Forget it. This isn't a night for sex. It just does that every time I see you. Or think of you. Or remember your eyes or your laugh or your scent. It has since I met you."

She studied his eyes, trying to see if that was true. She'd never affected a guy that way, as far as she knew. He smiled at her. "I'm not the most attractive woman."

"Bullshit."

"Look at me. I'm not slim."

He caught her hips and pulled her close. "You see what you're not. I see what you are. Hang around with me for a while, and maybe you'll start to see you from my eyes, because I see a beautiful woman, full of curves, soft skin, stunning eyes, gorgeous hair. I see a kind woman with a gentle nature. I see perfection."

She stared into his eyes, then couldn't help laughing. "Perfection. That's good. You almost had me believing you."

He wasn't laughing. He was serious. He caught her face in both of his hands. "I'm not lying. I won't lie to you."

Her humor slowly slipped away. "I don't know what to do with that."

"Accept it." He kissed her, slowly and leisurely. She started to cry again, wondering if this was love. Was this how Grams had felt about Gramps? Her mom about her dad?

That last thought was sobering. She couldn't risk falling for Angel, not with the possibility that her parents were alive and would become a target in Angel's war. She pulled free, trying to put some space between her and Angel, but there was no space to be had in the tiny stall.

He shut the water off, then got out and grabbed their towels. He handed her one. She wrapped it about her and went over to her bag of toiletries. Tomorrow, she'd unpack. Tonight, she just needed to brush her teeth, put some lotion on, and do her hair.

Angel dried off, then hung his towel up and walked out bare-assed to her room. She released a long sigh as she brushed her teeth. The man was gorgeous. She looked at herself critically in the mirror, wondering how she'd captured his attention. It was a mystery. She rinsed her teeth, then found her hair serum. She didn't feel like blow-drying it tonight, so she just let it air-dry.

Angel came back into the bathroom wearing a fresh pair of black boxer briefs. They hugged his thick thighs and emphasized his narrow waist. She was sitting on the closed toilet putting lotion on her arms. He looked at her, his warm brown eyes going black. She went still. He turned to the sink and started brushing his teeth. She met his heated glance in the mirror. She leaned forward and smoothed the lotion over her legs. His hand went still with his toothbrush in his mouth. She smiled and looked away. He was serious about finding her attractive. That realization sent liquid heat spilling through her.

She stood and tightened her towel around her. For some reason she couldn't explain, she felt suddenly shy around him. He watched her every move. She said nothing as she left the bathroom. He'd set her suitcases on the floor of her room. She dug through them for a nightgown. All of them were silky lingerie, which she usually loved. Tonight, she wanted something else. She found a pair of lacy boy briefs and put them on. Then she noticed Angel's go bag sitting near her suitcase. It was unzipped. She could see one of the tees he'd worn at her house. She pulled that out of his bag and pulled it on. As big as she was, his tee was still loose on her. And it smelled like him. She lifted the neck of the tee up to her nose and pulled a deep breath of his scent. Soap and man.

She heard him come into the room and turned to him. He smiled when he saw her. He led her over to the bed, then lifted the covers. "In." She scooted in. He turned off the light and followed her under the covers. As soon as he did, he pulled her over to him, holding her in his arms against his side.

"I'm sorry my hair's wet."

"I don't care. I just want you close. We have a lot to talk about, but I'm too tired tonight. Go to sleep, Wynn. You're safe. We'll start all over tomorrow. I'll bring you up to speed and answer all of your questions."

"All of them?"

"All that I can. You need to know the details of this world that you've been dragged into."

"I wish things were different, Angel."

He turned on his side and looked at her. There was enough ambient light in the room for her to see his worried expression. "I do too."

ANGEL LEFT WYNN SLEEPING SOUNDLY. A lock of her hair lay across her face. He wanted to sweep it back, but didn't want to chance waking her. He took his clothes and go bag and let himself out of her room. Dawn was still an hour away, so the household was quiet. He changed in his room and went for a run.

He came back inside through the kitchen. The lights were on. Two guys he hadn't seen in a long time were hard at work on the team's breakfast. One, wearing a chef's jacket, was cooking and snapping feverish orders to the other, who was nodding with each new command, his tan apron dotted with fresh stains.

"Sonofabitch. I guess they just let anyone in here now." Angel grinned at them. They looked up and laughed, then came over to greet him. The chef, Russell Scott, hooked thumbs with Angel, gave him a quick shoulder bump, then hurried back to the stove. His sous chef, Jim Reed, was in less of a hurry to return to his station.

"What are you guys doing here?" Angel asked.

"Owen hired us last week. We left the Army about a year ago," Jim said. "Russ has been wanting to open a restaurant, but he's such a perfectionist that he couldn't do it until he settled on a theme and had a core selection of recipes. Personally, I'd prefer we opened a bed and breakfast, so we've been arguing about it. Owen offered us some work while we get our shit together. The pay's excellent, and we can be backup for y'all when needed."

"So you're running the ranch now?" Angel couldn't help but be shocked by that news. They were two city boys, wicked in the field but without a ranching bone between them.

"No. Blade got his dad to take that over." Jim tugged at the bib of his apron and grinned. "I'm the house-keeper. Russ is the cook."

Angel smiled. "That's fucking awesome. We could use the extra hands—here in the house and when hell breaks loose, which it's doing ever more frequently."

Kit came into the kitchen. "Need to talk to you." He looked at his watch. "There's a little time before breakfast."

"Righto." Angel nodded to the guys. "Glad you're here. See you in bit."

"I see you've met our new household staff," Kit said as they walked to the den. "What do you think?"

"They're perfect. It's great to have a couple more guns. Frees us up."

"True that. Just so you know, they've been cleared, read in, and they're getting up to speed. Of course, their number one priority is maintaining the house and feeding us, but they'll also be our backup, when needed."

"They cool with that?"

"Oh, yeah. They got out last year, but have been drifting a bit. Russ wants to open a restaurant. Jim wants to open a B&B. This gives them the opportunity to test the waters for both of those things. And they get to keep a foot in the action. Who knows. Maybe they'll open a B&B for antiterrorist operatives." Kit grinned.

Angel had to laugh at that.

"Having them here lets us talk more freely, but I

don't want to cause our women more anxiety than they already have, so we'll be keeping our convos and work in here and in the bunker. Besides, we still need to be careful around the kids and Carla. She'll be here three days a week to do the bedrooms."

Carla was one of Kathy Jackson's friends who sometimes came in to help. "You trust her?"

"No. Not entirely. Her background check is clear. Greer ran it again and nothing's changed since the first check, but anyone can be bought, so we'll be doing sweeps after she's been here."

"Roger that."

Kit walked to the desk, then faced him. "What the fuck happened in Cheyenne?"

"I went to tell Wynn about Grams. Saw a guy following her, so I thought I'd stick around and find out what he was up to. Greer said his surface identity checked out, but he dug deeper and found he was connected to the Omnis. I got Wynn to pack to come back up here, but we were hit before we could bug out."

"And the bastards burned her house."

"Six guys hit us. Five died, one left on fire, thanks to Wynn. She made a blowtorch from her hairspray. As far as I know, he's the only one who got away. Did Lobo get the bodies?"

"Not before they were fried."

"Shit."

"You find out anything about Wynn's parents from her?"

"Still working on that."

"Make it a priority."

"Copy that. Any news from Owen?"

"Not yet. He's keeping his head down."

Greer came up from the bunker. "Hey. How's Wynn?"

"Wrecked. She's lost everything." As Angel said that, he remembered he'd grabbed a few things that she'd probably like to have.

"What's the Omnis' interest in her?" Kit asked.

"I'll let you know when I find out," Angel said.

7

Wynn was alone when she woke. The emptiness slammed into her, bringing with it the ugly reality of her situation. She sat up, sucking air as she fought a rush of panic. She realized she'd slept in one of Angel's tees. She pulled the neck up and drew in his smell, which seemed to be the one thing that calmed her. She settled down only by shoving everything back behind some heavy curtain in her heart. What was done was done. Nothing she could do to reverse it.

What worried her the most was that her parents, if indeed they were alive, were out in the world of those evil people. Her parents didn't deserve that. They weren't cruel. Selfish, maybe, if they left her and Grams for career reasons. Evil? Never.

She had to find a way to discover if they really were alive, but how?

She dressed, made the bed, then started to unpack. The best way to get on with life was just to get on with it. She was almost finished when a knock sounded on her apartment door. She doubted Angel would knock. She opened it to see Mandy standing there, a big smile on her face.

"You're back." She hugged Wynn. "Rocco told me what happened. Are you all right?"

Instantly, Wynn found herself fighting tears. She nodded, then shook her head.

Mandy stepped into her apartment and reached for her hand. "You will be. I promise. This will all be a memory you can choose to ignore one day."

Wynn hoped that was true. "I'm glad you're here. I wanted to give this back to you." She went to her purse and took out the check she'd written to reimburse them for the payment Rocco had given her at the cemetery. "I don't need it, and I have no right to it—I haven't earned it."

Mandy didn't reach for the check. "You know, when you're ready, you could resume teaching Zavi, if that fits with your plans."

"I don't know how long I'll be here."

"Where are you going?"

"Please don't take this the wrong way, but I don't want to be here. I don't want to be part of what's happening. I just want a normal life." Preferably one with Angel. Wasn't that like wanting the day and the night to happen at the same time?

"I'm not offended. Not in the least. I know just how you feel. When I was having problems with the construction of my riding center, it just seemed like bad luck at first. Then my brother came home with the team and I learned there was so much more going on. By then, I couldn't have gotten out because Rocco had my heart." She gave Wynn a long look. "I know you crave normal, but please don't do anything rash. You are much safer here with all of us than out on your own."

Wynn nodded. That was true. God, they'd burned her house. Where would she even go?

"Maybe you could wait things out here. You don't have to teach Zavi if you don't want to. Or you can take some time before starting up again. Just do what's right for you."

"If I'm going to be here, then I think I should earn my keep. I would like to work with Zavi again. Maybe I could start tomorrow? I'm still so emotional today."

"Tomorrow. Next week. Take the time you need. You tell me when you're ready." Mandy gave Wynn another big hug. "I'm not far away if you need to talk. They blew up my dream, my riding center. I know a little of what you're going through."

"I'm sorry. No one should have to go through this."

Mandy smiled as she paused at the door. "Come down for breakfast. Everyone will be relieved to see you."

Wynn nodded, not entirely sure she was ready for the whole group yet. Before the door fully closed behind Mandy, she heard her in the hallway talking to Angel.

"Oh my God. Look at you. Have you seen Doc Beck?"

"No. I'm fine, Em. This looks worse than it is. Is Wynn home?"

"She is. See if you can get her to come down for breakfast."

"Will do."

Her door opened. She'd been frozen in place, both excited and nervous to see him again. As soon as he walked through her door, everything seemed better. His cuts were taped in places, scabbed over in others, bruises blossoming everywhere. At least he wasn't actively bleeding.

He met her eyes cautiously. He was carrying a plastic grocery bag. "Hi."

"How are you?" she asked.

"Better. You?"

She shook her head, then blinked, refusing to cave to the emotions riding her so hard. "I think I'll be teaching Zavi again. At least while I'm here."

He nodded. She was glad he didn't try to argue against her leaving. "Do you know if my car was destroyed in the fire?"

"I don't know. I'll find out."

"Thank you." Strange how formal they were being with each other after all they'd been through. Really, she just wanted him to hold her and tell her that it was all a bad dream, that Grams was still alive, and her house was still intact, and the world was as it should be.

But he didn't. He just handed her the bag. "What's this?"

"I grabbed a few things yesterday."

Whatever was in the bag clinked. She looked inside and gasped, then carried it over to the table. Inside were the last two Hummels that had survived the fight, along with the pictures of her parents. She set them all on the table. They wavered before her. Her breath locked up in her chest until a pair of strong arms wrapped around her.

"I didn't mean to make you cry."

"I'm so glad you got these out." She looked up at him. "I would have had nothing."

He turned her in his arms. "I thought we could spend the morning together. There's a lot I promised to tell you to get you up to speed."

"I'd like that. I don't understand at all what's happening."

"How about breakfast first? I'll be with you the whole time."

Funny how that made facing everyone so much easier. Was she such a coward that she couldn't do this alone? "I am hungry."

"And wait until you meet our new caretakers, Russ and Jim. They're former Red Teamers, like the rest of us. They're another layer of security. Jim will do the housekeeping, Russ the cooking. I don't know if you ever met Carla, Kathy's occasional assistant, but she's starting to work a few days a week now that there are so many of us here. Russ is excited about the assignment because it lets him perfect some recipes he's planning on using when they open their bed and breakfast. I understand from house gossip that he and Ivy are best friends already. I think Kit would be insanely jealous if Russ and Jim weren't married."

"Oh. Are their wives here?"

His eyes twinkled. "No wives. They're married to each other."

"Ohhh." She laughed at that.

As they went downstairs, Wynn felt a strange blend of conflicting emotions. She'd missed everyone here, missed the familial relationship everyone shared. But she was angry still that she had to be in the middle of this conflict, one she didn't understand. When they came down the main stairs into the foyer, a little black-haired boy tossed himself at her. She knelt and hugged Zavi.

"Miss Wynn! You came back! Are you going to stay now?" Zavi eased his grip only enough to look into her eyes.

She was back, but for how long, she didn't know. Everything was so complicated that she couldn't even give the boy a straight answer, so she didn't attempt it. "I missed you."

He straightened, holding her shoulders as he looked into her eyes. "I missed you too. Are you going to teach me again?" He leaned his weight on one leg and gestured with his hand. "Because it's like this. Mom knows horses and helping people as good as I know languages, but she doesn't know teaching as good as you."

Wynn smiled, wondering where he learned to say such things. He picked up on everything he heard around him, absorbing it into his lexicon. "I'm sure Mom tried very hard."

"She did. I gave her a gold star." He leaned close and said, "But it made her cry."

"Well, no worries about that. I'll be back in the classroom with you tomorrow."

"Yes!" He threw his arms around her neck and squeezed.

Wynn laughed and hugged him again. She looked around for Casey, but remembered Ivy and Kit took her to school quite early. "Where are Mom and Papa?"

Zavi shrugged. "They had some things to talk about. They said Aunt Ivy would help me with breakfast."

"Well, I'll help you." When she stood up, Eden, Fiona, and Hope came up to greet her. It was overwhelming, all of it, everything her life had become. Angel took her hand as he stood next to her, silently offering her his strength. He also was a welcome diversion, for when the women noticed how banged up he was, he became the center of their attention.

As a group, they went into the dining room. She'd missed this. She really had. Being an only child raised by a grandparent had been a quiet and often lonely existence. She liked the chaos of a big family. She looked at Angel, wondering how he'd feel about having a half-dozen or so kids, then blushed furiously when she realized what she was thinking. He caught her expression and raised a brow as a very male grin curled his lips.

Breakfast passed without much drama, even after Kit joined the group. He looked at her and nodded, his eyes hard. She could tell he had all sorts of questions for her, and by the looks of his determined expression, she doubted she'd be comfortable with any of them.

AFTER BREAKFAST, Angel took her outside. It was a sunny autumn morning, crisp but not cold. They were walking in the lower terrace. The grass had turned brown already from a string of hard frosts.

"You asked about your car...I'm sorry to tell you it was destroyed in the fire. When the investigation's finished, Owen's company will send a crew to clear out the debris, but that won't be for a couple of weeks, I expect."

"I should call my insurance company today, I guess."

"Just tell them the fire is under investigation and that you don't know the details yet. If it turns out not to be covered because you have an act of terrorism exemption, Owen will make it right."

That surprised Wynn, but it also eased some of her

worry, though not her sorrow. The house that Gramps built for Grams was gone, and nothing was going to bring it back.

He stared at the grass for a while, lost in thought. "I don't know where to begin. There's so much to tell you."

She reached for his hand, such a comfortable gesture. Odd that it was, when so much was at risk. "Then I'll start by asking questions. Who are the Omnis and why are they after me?"

"It'll sound crazy. Hell, it is crazy. They're a secret organization that's existed for centuries. Seven or so, to be exact. They were created to protect scientists at a time when the world was driven by religious dogma, not science or logic."

That triggered a thought. "They're an organization of scientists? Still?"

"They were originally. Still? Can't say for sure. Why?"

Oh, hell. She'd opened herself to that. She sent him a questioning look, not liking the coincidence. She didn't want to tell him about what she found in Grams' papers, but she had to accept that she couldn't do this alone. She'd been in this spot before, and look how that had ended for her...and for Grams. And yet, how could she risk involving the team? If her parents were alive and had indeed done bad things, Angel and the guys wouldn't hesitate to end them. Their moral compass was very neatly defined by clear black and white sides.

She stopped walking. He turned to face her. "Grams kept some of my parents' things, especially anything that had to do with their careers, their published papers, stuff like that. In those papers, I found a certificate of membership in a scientific organization that had the word 'Omni' in its name. I can't remember the exact name. I didn't think it was connected until what you just said."

"Shit." He looked up and away. "Okay." He sighed, then met her eyes. "I need you to trust me. I know that's a big ask. You may know things that will help us help you. I need there to be no secrets between us right now."

Wynn's eyes watered. It was a big ask. "I want to trust you."

He nodded. "We'll start with that. Let's keep on. There may be other things that pop out at you. If they do, I need you to tell me." They resumed walking. "When the Omni organization was formed, science and research weren't well understood and often ran counter to religious doctrine. Because scientists were being persecuted, the group built a sophisticated organization to hide and protect both researchers and their work. Jump forward to the twentieth century, and things changed. It wasn't necessary for scientists to hide. And the corporations who funded the scientific advancements owned the rights to that work, so it couldn't be easily shared. The original reason the group was formed was no longer relevant. However, its sophisticated secret structure did have relevance. The group suffered some sort of schism, which we don't yet fully understand. The faction favoring the secret society grew stronger, while the half composed of dedicated scientists grew complacent."

Wynn frowned. "This is the group you and your team have been fighting?"

Angel nodded. "We didn't know it at first. We thought we were dealing with international terrorists here inside the country, but that was just an Omni smoke screen. They've become a violent and destructive group. They've infiltrated governments internationally. They own lawmakers, gangs, wealthy and elite citizens, banks, corporations, you name it."

"Why are you fighting them?"

He thought of the hell the Omnis had made his parents suffer. "They're terrorists who've partnered with other domestic and foreign factions to do evil things. They're the ones who released the smallpox into the Friendship Community. We believe it was a test of bigger threats they're working on."

Wynn gave that some thought. "My parents were scientists. You aren't against all scientists, are you?"

"I'm not against any group of law-abiding people, Wynn. But I've vowed to fight anyone who thinks to bring down this country or harm innocent civilians—to the death, if needed." They sat on the terrace wall separating the upper and lower levels. "Tell me about your parents."

"I'm sure you know all about their history."

"We know a lot about them, but they're just flat facts on a screen. Nothing we know shows them as they were, parents, spouses, members of society. Tell me about the people you knew them to be."

"They died in a massive explosion in their lab." She shrugged. "Honestly, I didn't know them that well. I was young when they passed. What time we had together they spent being very busy working on important things. Grams pretty much raised me, even before the explosion."

Angel grunted. "I know that feeling of being an afterthought to your parents. I didn't know my dad very well. I always thought he was a drug dealer or in some crime org. He didn't come around much."

"I'm sorry." She glanced at him. "Is that why you took up this line of work?"

"Maybe. It would have been reason enough, I guess, if the Red Team hadn't come for me."

"What do you mean?"

"It wasn't until recently that I understood why my dad never was around. The Omnis owned my mom. She was promised to them, but she broke that commitment by falling for my dad and having me."

"What do you mean they owned her?"

Angel stared at his hands, which were folded between his legs. She could tell he was trying to find the right way to say what he had to tell her. "The Omnis have become something of a cult. Maybe they are a full-on cult. I don't know. A faction of them in the early part of the last century was into eugenics big time. After the Second World War, they used their secret world to continue their breeding program."

"Why? That's disgusting."

"It is. But it's what they did. They believed there was a perfect human race, and I guess they wanted to corner the market on it. Anyway, we've learned, from Ace—who grew up in their world—that they have a caste system that divides their populace into nobles, aristocracy, and commoners. My mother's family was a member of the Omni aristocracy. She was supposed to marry another member and have a batch of perfect children. Instead, she fell in love with my dad, son of a Puerto Rican dockworker. Because of that, the Omnis punished them. My mom lost everything to keep my father and me. The Omnis dogged their every step, made it hard for them to keep jobs or get a mortgage or build any kind of life. They couldn't even live together. I didn't understand any of this until recently." He looked at her. "It's why I get your need to keep space between us. You're either all in or all out. I respect your choice."

She folded her arms about her middle and rocked herself a couple of times, then nodded. "How have these Omni people been allowed to exist?"

"They kept a low profile. The group, which now calls itself the Omni World Order, has spent a century infiltrating world governments and the upper echelons of society. It owns powerful people and is, in itself, powerful. It supports them in times of financial or criminal need." He stood and shoved his hands in his front jeans pockets. "We've recently learned that it's not uncommon for people to fake their deaths when they enter the Omni world. They just slip away. I know it sounds crazy, but there's a chance that your parents are still alive. They may have done that."

Wynn looked up at him. Trusting him with the whole truth was her only option, but why did it feel like jumping off a cliff? "That man who was following me in Cheyenne said they were alive."

"You said he was realtor."

"What he was telling me made no sense. I thought he was bonkers. I didn't want to give credence to it." She winced. "And I was afraid what he said might be true."

He nodded. "Okay. What did he say?"

"He told me my parents were alive but in danger and that he would take me to them. He said they'd done terrible things and that you and your team would kill them."

Angel sighed. He leaned his head back and looked up at the clear blue sky.

"If it's true, if they are alive, are you going to hurt them?" Wynn asked.

He met her hard gaze. "If they try to harm you or my team or anyone living here or any civilians, I will not hesitate to end them. If it's true that they are alive, I suspect we're going to need them alive. If they've committed crimes, they'll have to face the penalty, but I'm not a judge or jury. Let's not get ahead of ourselves, Wynn. We need to find them before we can know if they're with the Omnis, and if so, why."

"Why would they have faked their deaths? They were doing important work and gaining accolades for it."

He shook his head. "Great questions. I wish I had answers for you. Perhaps your parents were working on a project the Omnis wanted. Perhaps you and your grandmother were threatened if they didn't comply with the Omnis' wishes. We need to find out what they were working on when they 'died.'"

They fell silent. Wynn played that alternate version of reality through her mind. "My parents wouldn't have left me, left Grams, for their work."

Angel nodded. "Okay."

Wynn blinked and looked away. "They wanted me."

God. The hell of that statement. Wynn wished she could unsay it.

Angel looked angry. "How could they not? You're perfect in every way. Kind, smart, brave, beautiful."

A choppy breath broke from her. She wiped her eyes. "Grams said she saw them when she was sedated at Jafaar's. We both thought she was just having a dream about them."

"What if it wasn't a dream?"

Wynn nodded. "What if?"

"The Omnis are involved with a company called

Syadne Tech. They're the ones who rented the house where Jafaar kept Grams. We're afraid Syadne is working on a new infectious disease, which I've mentioned before."

Wynn's mouth opened in shock. "That note that the bikers left on Grams. It claimed she was a lab rat." She put both hands on her cheeks. "Did my parents cause her stroke?"

Angel shook his head. "We don't have any evidence of that—or that they're even alive. We're playing catch-up right now. It didn't help that someone stole Grams' body."

Wynn got up to pace. Maybe the man she'd run into in Cheyenne had been right about her parents. Maybe they had done terrible things. If they were involved in the work Syadne was doing, Angel would kill them. And maybe they deserved what they'd brought on themselves. But surely she didn't deserve to lose them twice.

"Grams had a ton of info on my parents at the house. It's all gone now."

"Maybe that's why they torched your house."

They were silent for a few minutes. She was trying to pick out any memory she could reach that put her parents in a suspicious light. They'd always been busy, missing her school events. Half the time it was Grams who went to her parent-teacher meetings or checked over her homework.

She thought about the days before the lab explosion. It was so long ago that she couldn't remember much about the specifics of how they'd behaved, if they'd acted differently.

She looked over at Angel, who was watching her intently. "Do you think my parents really could be alive?"

He nodded. "Several people we thought dead have been discovered alive, living inside the Omni World Order. Blade's dad. Owen's girlfriend. Ace. Maybe Owen's dad. We haven't yet sorted out who belongs to which side of the OWO. These people are ruthless. They have hundreds or thousands of foot soldiers who are completely expendable and willing to follow any order, like mindless automatons."

"Were they trying to kill me? Those men you fought in Cheyenne?"

"Don't know. Maybe your parents are alive, and the Omnis wanted you for leverage against them...now that they don't have Grams. But, if that was the case, why would they have ordered the hit on Grams?" He shook his head. "Your guess is as good as mine. All I know is that your life is in danger. You might be in the crosshairs between the two Omni factions."

"And there's no end in sight?"

"Oh, there's an end. And it's coming fast. But what'll still be standing when it's all over...I don't know. I told you that the team and I recently discovered we'd been involved with the Omnis for a long time, a lot longer than we ever knew. For some of us, that involvement predated our births. I wonder if that might also be the case for you."

She shook her head. "No. It isn't."

"Maybe you were and didn't know."

"Then how would I know now?"

"Let's look at your life differently. It's what we had to do with ours to find the connections. Your parents were scientists. The Omnis were originally formed to protect and propagate scientific knowledge. How old were you when they died?"

"Eleven."

"Do you remember much of your parents?"

She considered his question, then nodded as she frowned.

"Do you remember what they were working on?"

"They were researchers for a pharmaceutical company. They were working on something that had to do with nanotechnology. It was the early days in that field when they disappeared." She sifted through her memories of that time, more than a decade ago. "I remember how distraught their peers were. One of them even said to me at their funeral that their deaths set the field of nano-research back decades."

"Do you know what happened to their research, their papers, the work they left behind?"

She shrugged. "The building they worked in was destroyed in the fire. Everything was lost. The company declared bankruptcy shortly afterward. The only documentation I know of, their white papers and such, were lost when Grams' house burned. Why are you asking these things?"

"I'm just wondering if the Omnis are singling you out, or if any of us would do as a hostage. It makes a difference in how we approach this." He sighed. "That's as good a place as any to leave it for now. If you think of anything, come get me. You've got my numbers. I'll be in the bunker."

She nodded. He came and stood before her. His eyes looked sad as he touched her cheek. "I'm sorry that you had to come back, but I'm happy as hell you're here."

She smiled and stepped into his arms, wrapping hers around him. He held her in a gentle grip, one he seemed in no hurry to end. "Thank you. For everything." She looked up at him. "Grams was right—you are an angel."

8

L ion sent a glance around him at the weary boys he'd been putting through their paces. They'd almost finished the five-mile trek back to the campsite where they were now living.

They'd been relocated twice since leaving their original home on the White Kingdom Brotherhood compound. He had a gut feeling another move was imminent. He and Hawk had been uncertain whether their current circumstances were an improvement or a setback. They were away from the acid vats in the silo under the WKB compound, but he didn't like being out of contact with his sister or Mad Dog and his team of fighters.

For that reason alone, he'd decided this change had been intended to isolate his pride, break with tradition and everything they held familiar. And worse, with winter coming, they wouldn't be able to rely on supplies from the Friends. Nor did they have close access to the food stores the bikers maintained. They were truly on their own if King decided to stop supplying them—or if weather made their remote location impassible for a supply dump.

That was why he and his second in charge, Hawk, had kept up with the cubs' training. He'd let their education slide a little bit in favor of teaching them to become self-reliant in the wild. They did drills covering everything Lion knew to teach: how to stay alive if you're lost in the woods at night; what to do if a sudden snow squall dumps feet of snow, keeping you from returning to the camp; how to set snares for small game; how to hunt large game; how to field-dress whatever game you take; how to start a fire and put it out; how to cover your trail while leaving signs for other cubs to follow.

They'd run specific exercises sending the boys out into the woods, showing them how to evade capture, how to hide until it was safe to return to camp. These were drills he'd run through with the boys at the WKB compound. Nothing new, just in a new location. They'd walked the five miles to the highway and back a dozen times in the weeks they'd been there.

Today's drill had to do with emergency bug-outs. He and Hawk had set out caches of blankets, medical supplies, and food stores. These were all camouflaged as squirrel nests above trees marked with what looked like bear scratches. They'd visited every single one of the caches on their way out to the highway, and hit them all again on their way back. The cubs looked ready to drop.

Lion was confident the boys knew what to do in almost any circumstance that he might deem an emergency. Most of all, he'd had them sew into their jackets and backpacks Mad Dog's address in Wolf Creek Bend. If any of them got lost and needed to be rescued, they'd know a destination that was safe.

The boys were as ready as ever to make a run for it. He decided that tomorrow morning would be the time for them to head for Mad Dog's house. They could travel between fifteen and twenty miles a day. It would take each group of three boys about three to five days—if they had to travel on foot. By hitting the highway, it was possible they could do it much faster. Taking a ride from a stranger was a dangerous proposition for the cubs. That was why he assigned an older boy to lead each group of cubs. There'd be less danger to each boy if they traveled in packs.

The boys reached camp in a jubilant mood. Lion hadn't told them they were going to be leaving in the morning. He meant to save that news for after breakfast, otherwise they'd be too excited to sleep.

As he came out of the woods near the mess hall, Lion came to a full stop. Two black SUVs were parked out front. No one was in sight, but that didn't mean whoever was visiting couldn't see them quite clearly.

He turned to the boys. "Stay alert. We aren't going with them this time. If I tell you to run, you know what to do. Group up with your travel buddies now. Follow my lead."

Though they'd run the drills, slipping out into the woods was a risky proposition for the boys—especially for the younger ones if he and Hawk weren't with them. He'd taught them to stay in groups of three or four. But would they remember everything he'd taught them when danger was all around?

Lion led the boys into the mess hall. He recognized Mr. Edwards. There were five other men with him, whom Lion didn't know.

Edwards didn't look happy. "We've been waiting for you for hours."

Lion didn't answer.

"Where've you been?"

"On a hike." Lion shot a look over to Hawk, whose face was tense. Six men to fight and thirteen boys to protect.

And one of the men was Edwards, King's chief enforcer. Lion felt the hairs on the back of his neck lift as he met the bastard's blue eyes. He was the one who'd told Holbrook to drop cubs into the acid vats until the remaining boys learned to obey him. One of his men carried a tray of small plastic cups and a big thermos.

Edwards smiled at him. Lion didn't respond in kind. Edwards moved past him, walking around the group. He stopped in front of Beetle. The boy fearlessly met the old man's cold stare and skeletal smile.

"What brings you here today, Mr. Edwards?" Lion asked, redirecting the man's attention.

Edwards smiled again and slowly made his way back to Lion's end of the room. "You've been here almost two months, yes?"

Lion didn't respond. Obviously, Edwards knew the answer.

Edwards grunted and nodded as he cast a look around the camp. "It's time for a change."

"What kind of change?" Lion asked.

"I think you and your boys should come in closer to the fold. Be among us."

"I thought we were one of you."

Edwards gave him a fast, closed-mouth smile. "You were. Until you weren't."

Lion frowned. "Meaning?"

"You had charge of King's gold. You were his favorite sons. Until you took up company with his enemies."

Lion and Hawk exchanged looks. "No one took his gold."

"No. No, they didn't. It's the only reason you're still alive." Edwards glared at Lion, then slowly smiled. "I'm here to bring you back to us, now, before irreparable harm's done." He shot a glance around the room. "I see you have your things collected already. Uncanny how you do that, but all the more reason why we want you with us."

He waved to one of his men, who began pouring out

a purple drink into the small, clear plastic cups. "We've brought you boys a treat. Cookies and juice." He pointed toward the table. "Why don't we sit down?"

"No."

"Then we'll have our treats standing." Picking up one of the cups, Edwards moved around the group of boys, returning to Beetle. Why single him out?

"You see, it's just a sweet grape drink." He waved Beetle forward and handed the cup to him.

Beetle looked at Lion, who gave a short shake of his head.

"Pass them around," Edwards said, waving the man with the tray on.

Lion took up one of the cups. He held it up, catching the attention of the cubs. The milky purple drink didn't look like any juice he'd ever seen.

"Everyone, take one," Edwards said.

"Wait," Lion ordered. He stared into the eyes of the man with the tray until his fear showed. "You first."

"No. I have only fifteen cups."

"Then you and I will share." Lion didn't break eye contact. "You first."

The man looked at Edwards, who waved his hand. "So be it. You can refill his cup."

The man's hand shook as it hovered over the tray. He looked at Lion, then downed the cup's liquid. Lion stood unmoving, watching him. If the cups contained poison, who knew how long it would take to strike its victim?

"Now, you," Edwards ordered Lion, nodding toward the tray. "You see, there is nothing to fear." He turned and looked at the boys in the room. "All of you. Now. Come take your cups."

Lion stared into the other man's eyes. The whites were turning red—burning from holding his stare or from the beginning effects of a poison?

Lion reached for a cup, but shoved the tray aside before any of the boys could take one. He grabbed the steel thermos and shoved it into the soon-to-be-dead man's forehead, shouting, "Run!" to the boys. He spilled the thermos contents on the ground.

Hawk tackled the guy nearest him. The boys were running every which way, around, under, and over Edwards' men, slipping into the woods...all except Beetle. Edwards had him by the scruff of his neck. He swung him up off the ground and slammed him down on a picnic table. The boy's mouth fought for the air that was forced from his lungs. Edwards pulled a flask from his breast pocket. He held the boy down with his elbow as he unscrewed the silver lid.

Lion ran toward them. He managed to kick the flask from Edwards, but was grabbed by two of his men before he could free Beetle.

Lion wasn't in the same weight class as Edwards' henchmen, but he was well schooled in hand-to-hand combat and fought with the viciousness of a cage fighter. When the knives came out, Lion ordered Hawk into the woods. One of them had to survive for the cubs.

He was vaguely aware of Edwards dragging Beetle to one of the SUVs. Lion tried to reach him, but the two men he was fighting wouldn't let him get free. He executed a hand lock on the man closest to him, immobilizing the hand holding the switchblade, then tightening his grip until he broke the man's arm at the elbow.

Pain made the man go limp, letting Lion pull him in front of him to block the forward thrust of Edwards' other man. Lion pulled the knife from the grip of the dead man. Tangling his feet with those of the second man, he followed him to the ground and stabbed his neck with the knife.

All was silent as he looked around the campground, expecting more of Edwards' men to come at him, but they were gone—as were both SUVs...and Beetle.

Why hit the campground, try to kill everyone, then make off with one of the cubs? Was it just random that Edwards took Beetle? Or had he come for Beetle?

Lion walked around the mess hall. He found the man who'd tried to serve them the grape juice in the dirt where he'd fallen. Frothy saliva was oozing from his mouth. His eyes were open, bulging slightly from their sockets. Anger speared Lion. What had his cubs ever done to deserve such a terrible death?

He remembered the boys Holbrook had dropped into the acid vats on Edwards' order—one that doubtless had come from King. What lesson was King trying to teach now?

Lion went to the picnic table. He searched through the scattered debris for Edwards' flask. He found it several feet away. He sniffed the contents. It was sweet smelling, but not like the grape juice that Edwards had tried to get them to drink. It was some other liquid, but still might have contained a poison. He found the cap and closed the flask. He would give it to Mad Dog and have it tested when he reached the team's headquarters.

9

G reer sent Val a text. *Gym hallway. Now. Alone.* He needed privacy, 'cause he was about to lose his shit. He shut off the hall's cameras.

Didn't take Val more than a few minutes to join him. "This has to be epic. I don't usually get to see Drama Greer."

Greer tossed his tablet on a hall table, then paced away from it and Val, his hands on his hips. He was sucking air in long, slow breaths. When he turned back toward Val, he couldn't hide the tears in his eyes.

"Shit." Val's humor left him. "What's going on, G?"

"I've been looking into Santo. He was good at avoiding the camera when Ace recorded him. But we have technology he didn't anticipate. I was able to make a composite of him." He picked up his tablet and showed an image of Santo to Val.

"Yeah, that's him."

"I cleaned him up. Made him younger." Greer swiped over to another image. "Look at these side by side." He swiped again, showing the composite image he'd made alongside another pic of a middle-aged man.

Val went still. "Who is this?"

"Henry Myers. Santo is my fucking grandfather." Rage boiled to the surface. He tossed the tablet onto the hall table then fisted the wall. Val looped an arm under his, spinning him around before he could throw another punch and break his hand. Greer punched both hands against Val's chest, shoving him back a few feet. "He knew. All this time. He knew Ace was his granddaughter. He let her live in hell. He left her there, my baby sister who bled out all over her nursery." Greer pressed his fists against his temples and paced away. Ten feet from Val, he dropped his hands. "He taught me honor. He taught me family before all else." A hollow laugh broke free. He looked back at Val. "It meant nothing to him."

Val clicked his comm unit on. "Kit. Need you out here."

"Copy. Where?"

"Gym."

"You know, I feel nothing when I kill," Greer said. "I became a monster for him."

Val nodded. "He trained Ace, too."

Greer caught Val's tortured eyes. They were both thinking of all Ace had been through. "I can't put the pieces back together," Greer said. "I can't give her back her life—the life her own grandfather took from her."

He and Val had the next thought almost simultaneously.

"Did he take her from your house that night?" Val hissed.

Greer's lips trembled as he answered. "Probably. Remember, there was no evidence of forced entry."

The door from the house opened and slammed shut. "S'up?" Kit asked as he joined them.

Greer had no words. He gave a shake of his head. Val picked up the tablet and showed Kit. "Santo is Henry Myers."

Kit looked at the pictures. "Motherfucker." He glared at Greer. "Jesus, bro. I'm sorry. Go get him."

Greer shook his head. "No. I'm going to kill him. I'm going to rip his lying tongue out of his mouth, cut out his eyes, and tear his goddamned heart from his chest. He's done. He's so fucking done. I'm going to end his life with all the years of pain he gave Ace packed into fifteen minutes. I'm going to watch him bleed and suffer."

Greer was vaguely aware of the rest of the guys coming into the hallway.

Kit shook his head. "That ain't the way it's gonna go. We need to know what he knows. Why are so many we thought dead coming back to life? Why would he do what he did? He helped found the Red Team. Why would he do that, then give his granddaughter to the enemy?"

The guys were handing the tablet around. Greer shook his head and started to plough through them. Kit stopped him, which earned him a fist in the jaw. Kit slammed him face first against the wall. They grappled until Max stepped in, pulling Greer away.

"*We'll* go get him." He caught Greer's head in his hands. When he leaned close, forcing Greer's attention on him, tears streamed down Greer's cheeks. Max caught him in a bear hug. "Fuck him all to hell, G. We gotta know why he did what he did."

Greer shoved free and started down the hall.

"Max. Go with him," Kit ordered. "I want Myers alive, feel me?"

"Loud and clear."

THE HALL WAS silent after they left. Ace came in seconds after Greer and Max left. She looked around at the team, standing frozen in place. Val had an awful feeling in the pit of his stomach. He was going to have to break the unthinkable news to the woman he loved beyond life itself.

He sent Kit a desperate look, seeking wisdom or strength or some fucking thing he couldn't name.

"What happened?" Ace asked as she made her way through the group to him. She walked up to him and set her hands on his chest. He loved the easy way she touched him. He caught her shoulders, but his gaze stuck at her chin. Goddammit. He couldn't bear to look in her eyes as he told her what he had to, but look he did.

"It's Santo."

She frowned. "Is he okay?"

"SweeTart." Val shook his head. He wanted to vomit. He wasn't man enough to tell her. "Greer did some research on him. He's Henry Myers. He's your granddad."

Her beautiful green eyes widened. Her lips, in their shiny purple gloss, parted on the word "no" but no sound came from them. She frowned. "Henry's dead."

Val shook his head.

Ace sent a glance around the room, looking shattered. She started sucking air like her brother had. Val caught her up in his arms, afraid she was going to hyperventilate. She didn't fight him. He kicked the door to the walkway open and went out into the night. His only thought was to get her up to their room before she had a public meltdown.

Privacy was the only kindness he could give her.

It was late when Greer and Max made it to the Friends' village. No children ran to greet them, but the dogs still started a ruckus. A light went on in Mrs. Haskel's cabin. Greer knocked on her door.

"Who's there?" she asked through the heavy portal.

"It's Greer, Mrs. Haskel."

She cracked the door, holding a lantern before her. "It's late, Mr. Dawson."

"I know, ma'am. Can you tell me which cabin is Santo's?"

She frowned and looked from Greer to Max. "Yes. One minute, please. I need to get a wrap." She shut the door, then joined them a moment later. "What is the need to rouse us all at night? Why couldn't this wait until the morning?"

"Because it couldn't." Greer didn't offer any excuses.

She went down the walkway by the public square, then pointed down a short street. "His cabin is two blocks down that road, then the first cabin on the left."

"Thank you, ma'am," Greer said, presenting a far calmer front than he felt.

They moved silently through the dark street. No streetlights lit their way. Only the faint glow of a sliver of a moon. They paused on Santo's doorstep. Greer knew how dangerous his grandfather had once been. And judging from the training he'd given Ace, he might still be.

He nodded to Max, then they moved in sync through the door, flashlights and guns sweeping the room...the empty room. The cabin was a simple one-room space, so it took little time to clear. The bed was made. A piece of paper lay on top. Greer holstered his weapon, then picked the paper up. It contained only one sentence: *I never wanted to be in the game.*

Greer handed it to Max, then started checking the cabin for anything else San—Henry—might have left behind. There was nothing. Greer stormed back to Mrs. Haskel's cottage. He pounded on the door. She opened it while his fist was still raised.

"Where is he?"

She frowned. "I showed you his cabin."

"He's gone. When did you last see him?"

"He was here this evening. He was talking with us at supper. He didn't say he was going anywhere."

Greer gave her his card. There were no phones in the village, but it was still under quarantine for the smallpox outbreak. Several CDC doctors were still on site. "If you see him again, go get one of the doctors to call me. Immediately."

"All right. Is there a problem? Is he in trouble?"

"Yes."

She waited a second for him to elaborate, but he didn't. "Are we safe, Mr. Dawson?"

"Not if Santo is here."

She nodded. "He seemed so peaceful. I'll get the word out in the morning."

"Thank you."

Max looked at the buildings and little houses around them. "Want to wake the fucking village and toss each cabin? Your call."

"No point. He's gone." They started back for the SUV.

"How did he know we were coming?"

Greer shook his head. "He always did that sort of thing. He has a heightened sense." He looked at Max. "What did that note mean? What game is he talking about?"

Max didn't answer immediately. "He obviously isn't working with a full deck, so who knows."

Greer wasn't convinced. "You don't know my grandfather. He never did anything without clear intent. Never. He drummed that into me as well. Think something all the way through. Do it fast. Make your move. Let every action have a purpose."

Max shook his head. "Pisses me off how our puppeteers are fucking sociopaths. And we never see it until we're in the middle of the dance they make us do." They reached their SUV. "Hope Ace is okay. This can't have been an easy discovery for her. Are you going to tell your parents?"

Greer thought about that. "No. He's already dead to them. I'm just going to kill him. For real, in a painfully slow way. Send him back to the fucking devil." He smiled at Max. "I'm going to do what he trained me to do."

"You can have him, but not until we get the info we need."

10

Something lingered around the edges of Wynn's mind as she tried to sleep. It danced at the corners of her awareness like something she should know, something she should have thought about.

Unable to identify what it was, she went through all that Angel had told her that morning. It was hard to grasp the fact that enough people had faked their deaths that it was a known pattern. She wondered if it was really possible her parents were still alive. The idea filled her with hope...and anger.

If it was true, then it was a terrible indictment against them as parents: they'd rejected their own child in order to fully pursue their own careers...their own glory. No wonder she'd always felt like an afterthought around them; she was the albatross around their necks.

Well, her life was her own now, to do with what she wanted. And the past was done. How many times had

Grams said that very thing to her? She had to find a way she could leave her own footprint in the world. The small way she could make a difference. Maybe things happened for a reason; maybe her relationship with her parents had put her on that path. They were why she'd chosen to work with children.

Again, she tried to go to sleep, but still that niggling feeling haunted her. It wasn't until she'd almost fallen asleep that she realized what it was. She sat up. It changed everything. *Everything*.

She reached over to the nightstand for her phone and called Angel. One ring and he picked up.

"S'up, babe?"

Babe. In that deep voice that felt like home to her. "I need to talk to you. Which room is yours?"

"Last across the bridge, just before the hallway to the southern bedroom wing. But stay put. I'll come to you."

Wynn threw the covers off and slipped into her kimono robe. She paced in the living room, but didn't have long to wait. She'd propped her door open so Angel wouldn't have to knock. He pushed the door open, then closed it behind him. He was wearing only a pair of jeans. His hair was too short to be mussed from sleep, but the rest of him still looked bed-warmed.

She reached for him. He caught her upper arms as she flattened her hands against his chest. "I can't believe I didn't see this earlier when we talked."

"What?"

"I told myself I didn't want to get pulled deeper into this mess."

"I know. I don't want you to either."

"But if my parents left the real world to go work for the Omni World Order, then I've already been pulled into it."

He frowned.

"You see, I blamed you and the team for what happened with Grams, for putting me in this spot."

"It is our fault."

She shook her head. "But if my parents are working for your enemies, then I was already neck deep—because of them. It isn't your fault."

Angel straightened. He moved away from her and ran a hand over his short hair. "Wynn, when you got involved doesn't matter. Once you're in, you're owned by the Omnis. It's like quicksand. The more you struggle to get out, the faster it consumes you. We don't know yet if your parents were or are involved in any way. But whether you came in through Grams, through your parents, or through us, you're still in. And you're still in danger." He came back to her. "There's nothing more that I want for you than your freedom."

"I'm sorry I ran away. I just needed to hide for a while."

"Don't worry about it. Every wild animal I know holes up while it heals."

Wynn laughed. "But I'm not a wild animal."

His smile seemed sad. "That's what the Omnis do to

us." He touched her face. "Get some rest. I'll see you in the morning."

"Night, Angel."

"Night, Wynn."

ANGEL QUIETLY CLOSED Wynn's door. He walked a few steps down the hall then stopped. He couldn't fully understand her new attitude. No matter who brought her in, she was still in Omni quicksand. And he was just going to watch her slowly sink deeper and deeper if he couldn't bring an end to the Omni World Order —and fast.

He could hear muted laughter from the billiards room down below as he went back to his room. He wasn't in the mood for company. He shut his door and sat on the end of his bed without the lights on. Just because Wynn was here again didn't mean he got to steal her life from her. He had to get his shit locked down before he spent much more time in her orbit.

The longer he sat alone in the dark, the more intense his hunger for her became. He tried to fight it, but images of her in the shower with him, of holding her luscious body through the night, of how soft her eyes were when she looked at him...all those things ate at him. He had a hard-on that he couldn't ignore. The pain was brutal. He ran his hand over himself. That contact only made things worse. He could ease himself, but his hunger for Wynn would come back as soon as he finished.

He shoved a few packs of condoms in his back pocket, then went back through the house to Wynn's room. He pounded his fist on her door. It probably wasn't locked. He could just walk in, but he wanted her to invite him in.

"Wynn. Wake up." A flush was heating up his chest. How could she sleep when he was on fire? He lifted his fist to pound at her door again, but it opened, framing Wynn with her loose hair and her big eyes and soft lips.

"What is it?"

"I don't know how long we have, but I want to spend the time we have together." He stepped into her space and slipped his hand into her hair, catching her by the neck. He pulled her close, feeling her body line up with his, his hard dick like a pole between them. He kissed her, crushing her mouth beneath his. She leaned into him, surrendering without hesitation.

His hands couldn't touch her enough. Her face, her hair, her body. He moved her backward as he stepped into her apartment. Her hands slipped over him as feverishly. He leaned her against the wall next to the door and fucked her mouth with his tongue, egged on by the sharp sting of her nails kneading his back. When he broke the kiss, her worried eyes swept his face. He stroked her cheek. "I don't want to lose you, but I know I can't keep you. I know that, Wynn."

He took her hand and led her back to her room. It

was darker in there. The shades were drawn. Took his eyes a minute to acclimate. He helped her remove her silky, long nightgown. The calluses on his hands caught in the soft fabric. He tossed it aside and filled his hands with her breasts. A shiver passed through him as he buried his face in the curve of her neck. Her hands were on his shoulders, soft and cool, stroking him. Fanning the fire already licking at him.

He pressed her against the bed, then held her as he lowered her to it. She still wore a pair of white bikini panties, and he still had his jeans on. He couldn't pause long enough to remove the rest of their clothes. He had to feel her body against his. Now. Right now. She scooted across the mattress. He settled between her legs, rocking himself against her core as he covered her body with his.

He kissed her mouth, her neck, her chest, then buried his face between her breasts, luxuriating in their fullness. He'd be damned if he had ever fucked another woman with tits like hers. Hell, he couldn't even remember any other woman. Wynn filled his heart and his mind, pushing the others out.

She cried out when he held one breast and sucked her nipple. "Angel." She dug her fingers into his hair. "Take me."

"Soon." He stroked her over her panties. She pushed herself up into his touch. Her lips parted. She was an amazing lover. He brought her to an orgasm just to watch the passion rack her body. He wished it was even lighter in the room. He wanted to see her eyes as he entered her. He moved farther down her body, easing her panties down her hips so he could taste the pleasure he'd just given her.

She sucked in a sharp breath, then sat up to pull him back up. He smiled as he looked at her from between her legs. He caught a breast in his palm and pushed her back down. She needed to come about a half dozen times before he took her. His tongue set her over the edge as she surrendered to him. Twice more, then he straightened, kicking off his jeans and shorts to cover himself.

"Wait." Wynn crawled over to the edge of bed. "Not yet," she said, looking up at him. Bracing herself on one hand, she wrapped her fingers around his cock and took him into her mouth. He pushed her hair back, but he was blocking what little ambient light filtered in from the hall. He eased himself from her hot, sweet mouth.

"Hold on." He switched on the light from her night-stand. She was kneeling at the edge of the bed. Her skin was flushed. Her silky brown hair, with its slight curl, swirled around her shoulders. He grinned at her. "Okay, now."

She smiled at him as she reached for him again. She licked her lips. His cock jumped, a fresh rush of blood hardening it. He got on the bed and knelt before her, making it easier to reach him. She leaned over and took him. Her lips were soft, her tongue hot. Christ, he almost came right then. He was too close to take much more.

"Wynn, Wynn—no more." He hissed a long breath. "I want to come in you."

She looked up at him as her tongue made a last pass over the wide crown of his head.

He groaned. "That was cruel."

She smiled, biting her bottom lip. He bent over and kissed her. She was everything to him. All his life he'd searched for her, yearned for her, hoped he'd find her. And he was going to have to set her free.

It was going to fucking kill him.

He pulled back, shoving those thoughts away as he ripped into a condom pack. He covered himself, then pushed her back on the mattress. He slowly entered her, savoring their connection and the way her eyes darkened as she watched him move over her. Contrary to the painful tightness in his groin, he wasn't in a hurry to finish this. It was heaven looking into her eyes as he made love to her.

He changed his thrusts, grinding himself against her mound. Her lips parted. Her eyes went unfocused. He reached between their bodies and massaged her clit. Her response was instant and volatile. She cried out as she pushed up against him, her hands hooked under his shoulders. Her release brought his. He slammed into her.

When they finished, he was sweating and she was glowing. "Wynn." He caught her face in his hands.

"When we end the Omnis, you have to leave. Promise me."

The passion in her rosy cheeks faded as her eyes focused on him. She frowned. "You want me to leave?"

"When it's safe. You have to go."

"Why?"

"Because you deserve peace, and you'll never have that with me. There will always be another fight, another enemy, another war. It's all I know. It's what I do. You deserve better."

"Angel...I don't have anywhere to go."

"You could rebuild on Grams' lot."

"I don't know that I want to do that."

"You mentioned graduate school. You could do that."

"Sure, but finding a school and getting admitted is a lengthy process."

"You have options, Wynn. You could buy a house somewhere. Someplace you want to be."

She pushed him off her. He got up to dump the condom, then faced her from the bathroom.

She sat up. "Anywhere, as long as it's not with you. That right?"

Holy fuck, this hurt. "Yeah. That's right."

She nodded. "Got it." She grabbed his clothes and threw them at him. "Get out. Don't worry about me. We're done. I can take care of myself."

"You can take care of yourself when the Omnis are finished."

"You don't get a say in my life, Angel." She grabbed her kimono and slipped it on. Instead of tying it, she crossed her arms in front of her and glared at him.

"I repeat, until the Omnis are put down, you aren't to leave here."

She pivoted on her heel and left the room. He yanked his jeans on and shoved his underwear in a pocket. When he walked down the hall toward her living room, he found her standing beside her open door. He paused, hating that he'd hurt her. "Wynn—"

"Don't come back here. Don't talk to me. I don't much like being a conquest, Angel."

"You're not a conquest." He shook his head. "No. You're much more like a wild horse that's been run into a paddock before a storm breaks. When it's safe again, Wynn, I'll open that gate. I swear it."

Her nostrils flared and her eyes were on fire. It was all he could do to not take her back to the bedroom. "When it's safe, I will run that gate down myself."

He stepped into the hall. She slammed the door behind him. He sighed, then leaned against the wall. He realized his assessment of her may have been off by a sizable amount. She wasn't a fragile woman made of flesh and bone. No, she was a fierce woman made of forged steel and pure grit.

Of all this war with the Omnis had cost him, losing Wynn was by far the worst.

11

A ngel was in the conference room with the rest of the team as they worked on discovering Omni real estate holdings. Once they had something to work with, they might be able to zero in on where King was and where Owen might be headed.

Kit's phone rang. "Bolanger here." There was silence on Kit's end, then he sent a sharp look around the table. He got to his feet. "Send me the coordinates. We'll meet you up there." The call ended. "That was Lobo. Sheriff Tate received an anonymous tip about a possible homicide at a hunting camp in the Medicine Bows. When the sheriff got there, he called Lobo. Three men were dead—two from a fight, one apparently poisoned."

"Poisoned?" Max said. "What about the cubs? Did he see them? Were they hurt?"

Kit shook his head. "Lobo said the sheriff also found

cups of a purple juice spilled in the room. Said there were fifteen cups, but no sign of the boys." Kit's phone beeped. He looked at the coordinates. "He's on his way up there. Max, Angel, gear up. You're with me. The rest of you, find every property between the WKB and the tunnels in Colorado that was ever owned by anyone whom we know to have been in the OWO. I have a feeling they keep those in the organization, even if it's been sold. And remember, Ivy, Mandy, and Eden need to be accompanied if they leave the house. Even just to go to the stable or kennels." He looked at Greer. "If Remi has to go to the university, you drive her. I don't want them to get to us through our women. If I'm not back before Casey gets out of school—"

"We got it covered," Blade told him. "Get outta here."

THE CAMP WAS deep in the backwoods of an uninhabited mountain ridge. The way in was a barely passable forest service road rough cut through the terrain. Judging from the road, the campsite had to have been abandoned long ago. They parked next to the sheriff's vehicle. Lobo was there already. Kit nodded to Deputy Jerry then followed him into what looked like a hunting camp, with several smaller cabins surrounding a larger one.

"We found the bodies in the mess hall over here,"

Jerry said. "If this is some of your doing, well, it ain't gonna make the sheriff too happy, but you might as well fess up and spare us all wasted time investigating it."

"It wasn't us," Kit said.

They stepped inside the long building. There was an open kitchen at one end, a long table in the middle, and doors on one side and at either end. Kit shook hands with the sheriff and Lobo.

"How'd you know to call Lobo?" Kit asked.

"You kidding?" the sheriff asked. "Three dead guys and what looks like a bunch of spilled poison? That's weird. And weird shit belongs to you. Didn't have any of it until you came back to town, boy. I've just about hit my limit with it."

"True that. Me too," Kit said, nodding.

"We don't know that it's poison, Sheriff," Lobo said.

Kit looked at Lobo, who didn't appear any happier than the sheriff. "You think this is where they kept the boys?"

"What boys?" the sheriff asked.

"There's a group of kids that belong to the Friendship Community," Kit said. The boys came from a wider group than the Friends, but no need to open that can of worms with Tate. "They've gone missing."

The sheriff stepped closer to him. "You didn't think to fill me in on that?"

"I did think about it, but the less you're involved, the better. In fact, now that you've handed this over to the FBI, you guys should take off."

"I think we'll stick around."

"Kit's right," Lobo said. "I've got a crew coming in. We'll process the scene. There's nothing more for you to do here."

Tate gave Lobo a hard glare. "We'll secure the site until your crew gets here."

Kit took out a pair of black nitrile gloves. "Max, Angel, check out the cabins, then the woods. We need to find the boys...or figure out what happened to them."

The mess hall was a shambles. Chairs were upended, some broken. One of the shelves that had housed dishes was turned over, the dishes scattered in broken fragments. The dead men were big guys. Two had bruises on their faces, necks, and knuckles. Probably elsewhere, too. Both had been stabbed.

The other guy, in the kitchen area, had dried froth around his mouth. His eyes were open, bulging slightly from their sockets. Next to him was a tray and more than a dozen little Dixie Cups in puddles of purple liquid.

Kit knelt next to the dead guy, then looked back at the room, trying to picture what had happened. "Doesn't appear the boys took the poison."

"No. Looks as if they fought their way out."

"How long ago, you think?"

Lobo caught the corner of his lip in his teeth and shook his head. "A day, maybe."

Kit stood, then walked out one of the open doors to look at the other cabins and the woods surrounding them. He stood there, looking, listening. Lion and his pride had been gone almost two months now. Had they been here the whole time? Were the boys still nearby?

Wide tire tracks marred the dirt. Looked like a couple of big vehicles had been parked outside the kitchen. He moved around them and followed Max into one of the cabins.

"Find anything?"

"Someone's been living here," Max said. "The cabins are as squared away as their dorm had been back at the WKB compound. A few of them left their packs behind. I found this in each of them." He handed an empty backpack to Kit, showing him a label that had been sewn into it.

Kit read it, then looked at Max. "It's Blade's address."

"Yeah."

"There's sixty miles between us and Blade's, thirty of it rough going. No way those boys could make that trek safely."

Max folded his lips into his teeth, then shook his head. He stepped outside and did a three-sixty turn, looking at the woods. "I've seen these boys in action. It's a mistake to underestimate them. Have some more of the team come up. We need to go through the woods. If they're still hiding nearby, they might come forward."

~

WHEN MAX and the team got back from Lion's camp, he had to tamp down his anger. They'd found nothing that indicated anything conclusively about Lion and his cubs' situation. The dead bodies had had no IDs on them. Without a complete roster of Omni members, there was no way to know for sure if King had sent the three henchmen. Maybe Jafaar had done it. If the team could connect the dead men to an Omni family, they might have their answer. Lobo had taken the men's remains into custody. Greer had started a facial-recognition search, but that could take a while. Max was anxious to ID the dead.

The only thing they knew for sure was that two vehicles had recently been to the cabins, and both had left. None of Lion's watchers knew how to drive, so they hadn't escaped that way. And if they had taken control of the vehicles and somehow managed to get to the highway, they would have been here by now. So they'd either been moved, or they'd run into the woods.

He hoped like hell that none of the boys drank the poison. The fact that their search hadn't discovered any dead boys or recent graves gave him hope.

The team went around him and into the house. Hope was in the garage, standing on a stool, bent over the engine of one of the team's SUVs. Max leaned against a nearby workbench. Folding his arms, he waited for her to finish what she was doing. He was in no hurry to give her more bad news.

Didn't take her long to lift her head and shoot a look

his way. He shook his head. She bit her bottom lip, then returned to her work. A minute later, he heard sniffling from under the hood of the SUV. He pushed off the workbench and went over to put a hand on her back.

"Hey. I have some news. It's not all bad."

Hope turned to him as she stepped off the stool. She had grease marks on her cheek and chin. He brushed a bit of hair that was too short to reach her ponytail behind her ear. She had a wrench in her hand. He hoped she didn't hit him with it when he was finished updating her.

"We found a camp where Lion and his cubs had been, as recently as yesterday."

Her mouth fell open. "Where?"

"Not more than an hour from here, but in a different spot in the mountains. There was a fight. The boys cleared out." He opted not to tell her about the poison. No need to panic her unnecessarily. "We found a couple of backpacks with Blade's address on a label that was sewn into them. I think they're headed here."

"All of them? Lion, too?"

Max shook his head. "We don't know. We searched the woods thoroughly. We found a couple of caches of food and clothes, and several that looked as if they'd already—and recently—been emptied. I came back to get the drone. I'll go back after dinner. Kelan's coming with me. We'll crash at the campsite. We might be able to spot a camp more easily by its campfire tonight. If not, we'll keep searching until we find them."

"Okay." She nodded. "Okay." She leaned into him, tentatively at first, as if she feared smearing him with engine grease.

He pulled her tightly against him and held her. "This is good news. Really good news."

"I want to go with you tonight."

"No. Too dangerous. I don't know what might be out there."

"Lion and his boys know me."

"They do. But they're not what I'm worried about lurking in those woods. Come up with the team in the morning. I'll tell them to grab you."

She nodded, but didn't look happy.

WYNN WAS WATCHING Zavi and Casey playing soccer. Casey was faster and more agile, but she was careful to play to Zavi's capabilities. It was a great way for the two of them to burn off energy after a day spent cooped up in classrooms. Homeschooling Zavi let Wynn have more flexibility to structure his days around his energy and mood—and hers. Today, with it being her first day back in almost a week, she went light on academics. They'd gone to the stables and helped with the chores, then they got to watch Mandy work with a client. They spent a lot of time outside, which was nice, because they both needed the sunshine with the days growing ever shorter.

Everything would almost feel like just another regular day if it weren't for Ace and Selena bracketing the field, watching the woods, armed to the teeth...a reminder that normal had left the station a long time ago.

Wynn looked over at the house and saw Mandy coming out to join them. "How did it go today? You feel all right working again?"

"Actually, it was great. I needed the distraction. Zavi and I had a lot of fun catching up with each other and watching you work. Thanks for letting us do that."

"Absolutely. Some of my clients aren't ready for an audience, but some love the encouragement observers give. Anytime you want to come out, just ask." Mandy's face got serious. "Angel told me that he's been working on updating you with what's happening. He doesn't want you kept in the dark."

Wynn looked away. "I had no choice before. I didn't want to know because it endangered everyone here."

Mandy hooked her arm through Wynn's. The friendly gesture put her at ease. "Something happened today that you need to know about."

Wynn's stomach went cold. "What?" Had Angel been hurt?

"Let's take a little walk." Mandy waved to Selena, alerting her that they were going to make a circuit around the lawn. "I don't know if Angel mentioned any of this to you, so if he did, you can stop me. A few months ago, Hope met Max when she was looking for her brother. She'd been separated from him at his birth and had been searching for him for a while. Someone gave her info that her brother was living on the White Kingdom Brotherhood's compound."

Wynn gasped. Those were the men who'd beaten her at Jafaar's. The story Mandy told her of a band of orphaned boys who were watching King's gold that was stashed in a missile silo under the biker compound was beyond fantastical—it was crazy. What kind of people were these Omnis?

One word came to her mind: evil.

"The guys got word today that the FBI found where Lion and his pride had been hidden. The boys were gone, but three of King's men had been killed. And it looks as if an attempt had been made to poison the boys. The team didn't find any bodies of the boys—or any survivors. Hope is beside herself." Mandy looked at Wynn. "Just thought you should know what was happening if you saw Hope and Max upset when you come down for dinner."

Wynn nodded. "Thank you. It does help to know what's going on." She wondered if Angel had sent Mandy to update her since Wynn had shut the door on his talking to her. At least he was honoring her request for distance.

She and Mandy had arrived back at their starting point near the kids. "Dinner's at six tonight." Mandy looked at her watch. "I hope you'll join us."

Oh yeah, Angel had definitely sent Mandy to talk to

her. He didn't want her left alone in the group. It was bad enough that she was here and he was here and they couldn't be together. But even with the door slammed shut on their dead-end relationship, Angel was still looking out for her, and that made her doubt resolve about keeping him at bay.

She reminded herself that he'd made it clear their fling wasn't going anywhere. It would have to end sooner or later. Better sooner than later, when her heart was set even deeper on what couldn't be.

"Thanks, Mandy, but not tonight. Zavi wore me out. I think I'll just have a quiet night in my room." Plus, she really didn't want to run into Angel yet. Not when everything she felt for him was still so raw and near the surface.

"No worries. Want me to bring a plate up to you?"

"No, I have some supplies left in my kitchen here. I have plenty to eat." That thought slammed her back into the reality that Grams' house was gone. She'd better start making plans for what would happen next, after the team finished with the Omnis. Angel wasn't her employer, so he couldn't fire her, but he had sway with Rocco. It was just best to have a plan B. And probably a plan C as well.

ANGEL and the others came upstairs from the bunker. They'd been reviewing the results of their searches in the woods by Lion's camp. Greer had showed a map pinpointing all the caches—intact and emptied—that the team had found.

Dinner was ready. The women were gathering in the living room. Angel sent a quick look around the room, searching for Wynn. Mandy came over to speak to him. He had a bad feeling she knew Wynn wasn't going to show.

She kept her voice low. "Wynn said she wasn't hungry. I think she just needs some time alone. I'll check in with her tomorrow. She did good today with Zavi."

Angel ground his teeth, then nodded. He lowered his gaze so his friends couldn't read his disappointment.

Dinner was an unusually somber affair that night. He appreciated the silence, actually. He cut into his steak with a vengeance. The sooner he finished his meal, the sooner he could leave. The vacant seat beside him was making him itchy. He should have taken his and Wynn's dinner plates up to her apartment. Angry with him or not, she should eat something. It would help her get back to normal. She'd probably just throw the plate at him and order him gone. The fuck of it was that he couldn't blame her.

Val's boot hit his shin, interrupting his mooning over Wynn. "What?" Angel snapped at Val.

"What what?" Val widened his blue eyes in a confused look.

"You kicked me."

"I didn't kick you. I was just stretching."

"Well, stretch against someone else's shin, would you?"

"Sure, if you quit glowering at everyone."

Angel pushed to his feet—fast enough that his chair slammed to the floor. "Since when are you the team attitude adjuster?"

Val got to his feet as well, but without tumbling his chair. He grinned—then he didn't. "You got some kinks to work out, it seems. Let's go."

"*Jay...sus*, you two," Kit growled from his end of the table. "Sit the fuck down or I'll adjust both of your attitudes. You'd think you'd had enough fun for one day. Don't bring your shit to the dinner table, feel me?"

Ace yanked on Val's arm. He took a seat without further prompting. Angel looked down at his plate. Russ' gourmet dinner suddenly had no flavor. He didn't look at the empty seat next to him, didn't need the reminder there was no one to hold him to the standard of his higher nature, like Val had.

Fuck. It. All. He and Wynn were done—because of him. He had to let her go.

But he'd had a taste of heaven, and he wanted more.

He flashed a dark look Kit's way; he didn't want to be here, sitting with everyone, pretending this was just another regular day. He sent a look around the table at his friends and their loved ones. Russ and Tim had joined the group for the meal. The team's family had grown. Angel noticed no one sat in Owen's empty seat.

Its emptiness was louder than Owen's quiet presence ever was.

Everything was not fine.

Their boss was still gone—somewhere. The Omni trackers were stalking Wynn. Lion and his cubs were fuck knows where. And the Omnis were secretly furthering their agenda—one that may or may not include Wynn's parents. Rage was simmering inside Angel. One more quiet trigger, and he knew he was going to lose his cool...and when he did, it would be goddamned epic and not something he'd be proud of.

His gaze snagged on Rocco's. The two glared at each other. Seemed ever since he and Rocco had faced off during Rocco's crisis, they were strangely tuned in to each other. Rocco gave a slight nod toward Angel's plate. Angel stared at his unfinished meal. He'd lost his appetite. He straightened the chair he'd knocked over, dropped his napkin on his plate, and left.

Val was right. He wasn't fit company for anyone. Angel cut through the living room and down the southern hall, heading toward the gym wing. A few hard rounds with a boxing bag might burn off his rage.

Then again, it might not.

≈

ANGEL LOST track of time in the gym. His body hurt, not just from the bruising he'd received at Wynn's a few days ago, but from the long circuit he was close to wrapping up. Val strolled in, his hands in his pockets. Angel put the barbell back in its cradle and sat up. He grabbed a towel and wiped the sweat from his face.

"Yo. Sorry about dinner," Val said, a hint of humor in his eyes.

"No big deal. I'm a little on edge."

Val feigned shock. "No. Really?"

Angel flipped him off, then went over to a line of hooks where he'd left his shirt. He picked it up, but it just hung limply from his hand. "Wynn and I are done."

"No, you aren't."

"Yeah, we are." He met Val's gaze. "I cut her loose. She doesn't deserve the life I can give her."

"You don't think that's her choice to make?"

"No."

"You're a fucking idiot. You two are made for each other. You know it."

"I didn't say I didn't love her, but I'll be goddamned if I'm gonna drag her deeper into this Omni hell we're fighting. I saw what happened to my parents. I don't want that for us."

"Yeah. First off, you guys aren't your parents. They did the best they could with the knowledge they had. But you're a whole hell of a lot better informed. And trained. And for all you know, she's in this way deeper than anyone suspects. Besides, she does have a choice, and you're man enough to give it to her."

Angel shook his head.

Val gave him a half-smile. "If she doesn't want you

the way you want her, she'll have your jewels in a French twist in seconds flat. Go for what you want, Angel. The rest will sort itself out." They glared at each other for a long second. "Look at it this way. Life is short. No day, no minute's guaranteed. If she's your heart, and you're hers, why fight it?"

Angel sighed. He looked at the ground. He'd burned that bridge but good. That sucker was ashes in the wind. There was no going back to what might have been.

LION HEARD A DRONE. Sound bounced around the bowl of the valley, making it impossible to tell where it was coming from or where it was headed. He hurried down a steep incline, rushing toward a rocky ledge near a creek where periodic floods over millennia had carved out a pocket in the cliff deep enough to hide a man. It wasn't easy terrain to navigate in the dark, but he made it in one piece. He slid to the ground, then rolled inside the covering. Depending on which way the drone was headed, it might or might not see him. He hoped the latter.

Whose drone was it? Did it belong to Max and his team or to Mr. Edwards? He couldn't risk hoping it was friendly. Max had told him guns could be fitted to a drone so that people could be killed while the shooters remain safe, miles away from the fight.

He was glad he'd learned about such a weapon—he and Hawk had folded that new knowledge into their training with the boys. He just hoped that the others who hadn't yet made it to Mad Dog's house heard the drone and did what they needed to avoid it. They'd never had one to include in their training, so the sound would be unfamiliar to them—that would be the very thing that clued them in to the need to hide.

12

ax came out to greet the team as they pulled into the camp. He wished Hope had stayed back at the house, just in case today was the day they found bodies of cubs who'd been poisoned, but he knew some activity, any action toward finding the boys was better than sitting at home.

Everyone on the team except Kit, Greer, and Rocco had come out for the search. Even Ace had come. They'd brought three vehicles so they'd have room to bring back any the boys they found. Wishful thinking at its best. Hope came over to hug him.

"It's okay," she said. "Whatever it is, we'll deal with it. Better to know than this terrible wondering and worrying."

Max sighed. "I hope you're right." He called the group together. They'd already been briefed about the scene at the camp. They'd gone over the search grid at

Blade's, but Max spread a map over the hood of one of the SUVs.

Val looked from it to Ace, who was too short to see much of the map. "Want me to put you on my shoulders?" He grinned. She punched him, then stepped on one of the tires and hoisted herself up to stand precariously above the map. Val put a hand on her ass to steady her.

"The caches of supplies that we found were here... here...and here," Max said, pointing to different areas on the map. All were between the highway and the camp. "Because of the patches sewn into the backpacks we found, it's my guess the boys would be heading down to the highway. If you find more caches, make a GPS note of them." Max assigned the sections of the search grid to each pair of searchers. "Cover your quadrant, then meet back here. Unless you find something. I don't think they would have set out booby traps, simply because Lion would have known it would be hard for the younger boys to remember all the places to avoid in an emergency evac situation. Doesn't mean we should be complacent. Remember the cubs are damn good at blending in with their environment. They've had years to perfect that behavior. I don't even know the names of the boys we're looking for, but if you want to do a shout-out, call for Lion. Or Hawk, who's his second-in-command."

"And Beetle," Ace said.

Max frowned at her. "You know for a fact that Beetle's one of the cubs?"

"Yeah, I do. My handler said that's the name the pride gave to Owen's son."

"Shit," Max said. "All right. We got two names."

"There's one called Mouse." Selena touched a thin scar on her face. "He carries a riata."

"Copy that. Call for Lion, Hawk, Mouse, and Beetle, then. Lobo's team has processed the main campground. I'm going to take another look around, then Hope and I will take our search section." Max drew a circle around the camp that showed where the team had searched yesterday. "We've already covered this area, so let's move through it quickly and focus on the outer areas of our quadrants. Greer's going to man the drone I'll be sending up. Questions?"

No one had any. Each group of two searchers headed off into the woods.

Max launched the drone. It had an infrared sensor that would help detect a human who might be hiding. It could cover the entire search area in less time than the group together. What it couldn't detect, though, was a dead body. For that, they needed the team.

Max didn't reach for Hope's hand as he led her into the campsite itself; she was keeping her shit together, but only by sheer will. Any show of sympathy or concern on his part might break her resolve. He even tried not to keep a worried eye on her, but it wasn't easy.

Lobo had cleared out the dead bodies and every-thing else that had anything to do with the attempted poisoning or the fight that had taken place. Max followed Hope as she went through each little cabin and the mess hall.

He wished like hell he had some good news to give her. When she walked up to him, the pain in her eyes was like road rash on his heart. He pulled her into his arms and just held her for a long moment.

"Usually, no news is just no news, but in this case, I think it's good news. It's clear that Lion had prepared the kids for the worst. Yesterday, we found all those caches of food, clothes, and supplies that had been emptied out. They were ready to bug out. King's men would not have found or used the cached goods. So whatever happened here, we know at least some of them survived."

She looked up at him. "Do you think Lion was one of the survivors?"

Max fingered a wisp of her long blond hair, pushing it behind her ear. "I'll tell you what I do know. Your brother puts his cubs first. He made sure they'd have what they needed for an evacuation. I admire the hell out of him." He stopped. His words were just making her tear up. He kissed her forehead. "Come on; we have a wide area to search."

It took Angel and Blade almost three hours to get to the highway. They'd passed two more supply caches, which they photographed and marked the GPS coordinates for. None of the supplies had been disturbed. They left the caches as they'd found them, in case any of the boys might still need them.

Angel crossed the two-lane highway and went into the woods on the opposite side. Maybe some of the boys had come over to this side for some reason. He found nothing.

Blade was leaning against a pine massaging his thigh when Angel came back. "You hurting?"

"No." He quit rubbing it. He'd kept pace with Angel the whole way down. He was as worried as the rest of them about the fate of the boys.

"If you want, you can wait here for a pick-up. We'll get you on our way out."

Blade straightened. "I'm good. Ready to head back?"

"Yeah. Didn't see anything on the other side, either."

They started back up the slope. The forest was filled with evergreens—fir, spruce, and pine—with the occasional grove of aspens. Deer had trimmed away the lower branches of the evergreens. Other than rough outcroppings of granite, there was little cover to be had in the understory of the woods; there was almost no place for a boy to hide without climbing high into the trees.

For that reason, Angel made vertical as well as horizontal visual sweeps with each step he took. Blade was doing the same. Greer's drone hadn't alerted them to any hotspots in its passes over their search area. Where the hell had the boys gone? They couldn't have simply disappeared. They were either holed up in spots outside the search grid or...someone had them. If they hadn't been able to execute their planned evacuation, then God alone knew where they were.

"How's Wynn?" Blade called over from a few yards away. Angel was glad for the distraction.

"Confused. Scared. Determined. She's a lot of things I wish she never had to be."

"Yeah. We all feel that way. At least she has you now."

Angel didn't respond. *Don't come back here. Don't talk to me.* Her words floated up to haunt him. She didn't have him at all, and that was for the best. He was everything that was bad for her.

WYNN OPENED her apartment's back door and stepped out into the still air of the night. She'd gone down for supper, but only because she'd learned that Angel was still with the search group and wouldn't be back in time for the meal. It wasn't easy avoiding him, not when she craved every stolen glance she could sneak in.

She sighed, leaning back against the wall of the house. The landing was small, only room for a single chair. Sometimes, when she'd first come to work here, she'd sit there and watch the colors of the summer sunset or wait for the moonrise.

Tonight, she wore her slippers, nightgown, and kimono, but was still chilled. She went inside to grab the throw from the couch and pull it around her shoulders. This tiny spot was one of her favorite places here at the team's headquarters. It was quiet and private. The stairs led down to the parking lot behind the garage. Her apartment was probably originally planned for staff housing.

An owl was exchanging hunting calls with its mate. She crossed her arms as she leaned against the wall behind her, listening to the two raptors.

Mandy told her about the set-to Angel and Val had had at supper last night. It was petty of her, but she hoped Angel was hurting as much as she was. Losing him left her feeling raw and orphaned all over again. She hated that feeling. She knew he was a heartbreak waiting to happen—had known it from the first time their eyes met.

Her small deck overlooked the lawn behind the house. The moon was already up, spilling light over the tiered grounds. Lights from the long patio that spanned the length of the house cast shadows over the lawn and illuminated the distant edge of woods.

As she looked that way, a white figure seemed to move just inside the woods. It was small. Maybe a coyote. Surely not a wolf? Were there wolves in this corner of Wyoming? No, couldn't be. It was just the night and the shadows making the thing appear pale.

Still, whatever it was lifted the hairs on the back of her neck. She watched the shape change; it became taller as it stood up. Wynn leaned forward to get a better look at what she was seeing. The thing took a step out of the woods. Finally, she could see it clearly... and knew she was looking at a boy! Not Zavi—this one had blond hair.

"Hey!" she called to him, waving at him. He waved back. She gestured for him to come over, but he just stood there. She remembered what Mandy had said about the watchers. Was this boy one of them? If so, it explained his odd behavior, showing up at night, being afraid to come closer. She couldn't let him get away. If she went in her apartment to call someone, he'd disappear. She couldn't lose sight of him.

She hurried down the stairs then ran across the lawn. This was no place for a boy to be wandering around. She jogged across the grass, down the short set of stairs to the lower level, and across to the edge of the woods. The boy didn't run away. He looked behind him, then at her again. He shook his head, then waved his arms as if to warn her off. Why? Was she afraid of her? He took a sideways step, watching her as he slipped back into the woods.

"Wait!" The shadows swallowed him. "Wait! I won't hurt you." She followed him into the woods, going in deep enough that the light from the house behind her was blocked from the thick evergreens. It was colder out here than by the house, where she'd been sheltered from the breeze.

Breathing hard, she stopped to get her bearings. She could only hear the whine of pine needles in the wind. She tightened her blanket around her. "Where did you go? Please, I won't hurt you," she called into the darkness. No answer. She should go back to the house and get the guys. Was this boy one of the watchers they were looking for? "I'm going to get help. Stay put. Please. No one here will harm you."

There was a sound off to her right. She turned, trying to see if the boy was there. "Come with us," a man said in a soft whisper that sounded deceptively near her. Fear slammed into Wynn. Oh. God. She'd come out here at night. Alone. No one in the house even knew she was out there.

She backed away, then spun around, landing against a man. He grabbed her arms, but she slipped out of the blanket and ran from the woods. It was like a nightmare she'd had often as a kid. She'd wake herself up running from some amorphous threat that chased her. Many were the nights she'd slept with Grams after one of those nightmares.

She heard the man behind her, heard the branches break under his heavy boots. She stumbled up the steps to the upper terrace, shooting a look back to the woods. There were two men running toward her. She knew she'd never get up her stairs to her apartment before they caught up with her, so she ran to the main portion of the house. She reached the dining room's French doors first. They were locked. She banged on them to get someone's attention, then ran to the doors from the living room. Again they were locked.

She was crying now. She hurried down the patio to the next set of doors, where light was spilling onto the patio. The billiards room. The men had to be almost upon her now. She looked over her shoulder toward the woods. Her hair blocked her sight. Someone grabbed her. She screamed—and screamed again as her face was pulled against a heavily muscled chest.

Strong arms encircled her. "I got you. Wynnie. I got you." Angel's voice slipped into her mind between the pounding beats of her heart. She threw her arms around him and held on as tightly as she could. "What are you doing out here?" he asked.

She looked up at him. Some of his friends spilled out onto the patio. She looked from him to them, then over her shoulder to the woods before answering. "I was sitting on my deck. I saw a boy in the woods and went after him."

"Why didn't you get us first?" Angel asked.

"I thought he would run. I thought I'd lose him. But when I got to the woods, I couldn't find him. There were men in there. Two of them. They tried to catch me."

Kit barked some orders: "Max, check surveillance. Greer, get the drone up. Blade, get Eden and Tank, then do a sweep with Val and Rocco. Selena and Kelan—gear up and keep an eye on things here. I'll alert Jim and Russ." He nodded toward her and Angel. "Get her inside and stay with the women."

"Want them to go to the bunker?" Angel asked.

"Not yet. Let's see what we find."

Angel led her into the billiards room. Mandy and Ivy hurried toward her. Angel pulled the drapes closed after he locked the French doors. "Let's head down to the den. It'll be faster to get you to the bunker if needed."

"Should we go get the kids?" Ivy asked.

"No need to bother them yet," Angel said. "We'll be closer to them in the den. Let's see what the team finds first."

"What happened?" Mandy asked.

Wynn told them what happened as they walked down the hall. She felt the shiver that went through Mandy. In the den, Angel again pulled the drapes and checked the outside doors.

Hope sat next to her on the sofa. Facing Wynn, she took her hands. "You said you saw a boy."

"I did," Wynn said. "I thought I did. He was just at the edge of the woods. Yes, I'm sure it was a boy." As Wynn thought about it, she replayed it in her mind. What if it hadn't been a boy? What if it'd been one of the men squatting or kneeling down? She'd jumped to the decision it was a boy when that made absolutely no sense at all. Maybe boys were on her mind after her conversation with Mandy.

"My brother runs a group that he calls his pride," Hope said.

"Mandy told me about them."

"They were taken from their camp about an hour west of here a couple of months ago—and from their latest camp sometime in the last few days. They ran these woods and the mountains like wild things. I wouldn't at all be surprised if one or more or several of them showed up here. They know about us. They would come here if they could."

"I hope that's what I saw." Wynn looked around at the group. "But why would men be with them?"

"Their leader, Lion, is my brother. He's twenty-one. His voice is deep. There's another kid in the group who's about that age, too. Maybe that's who you heard?"

"Maybe. There were two of them, but I didn't get a good look at them."

"What did they say to you?" Mandy asked.

Wynn shook her head. The male voice had been a silky whisper. "He said 'come with us.'" She looked over to where Angel stood near the hall door to the den. She wished he was sitting next to her, but she understood his need to be ready. He caught her looking at him.

She glanced away, frustrated with herself for finding comfort in him after all that had happened.

Someone was running up the bunker stairs. Greer burst into the room. "Remi's coming down." He turned down the hall toward the living room. A minute later, they both walked back into the den.

"What's happening?" Remi asked. "Another attack?"

Greer shook his head. "Not an attack, exactly, but maybe only because Wynn ran away fast enough." He pulled out his phone and showed Remi a video. "I sent the security footage to you, too," he told Angel. "Remi, stay here with the group. I need to get back downstairs."

"Go. We'll be fine."

Wynn saw Angel's brows lift as he watched the video. He reset it and played it again. Wynn walked over to him. "Can you see anything?" He lowered the phone so she could see. The video was grainy, just at the far edge of what the house cameras could pick up. In the footage, there was a small, whitish shape next to a tree. Impossible to tell if it was a child or a man crouching down. The video showed Wynn going into the woods, then nothing, then it showed her running out, stumbling on the stairs. The terror on her face was unmistakable.

Mandy came over to see the video. Wynn handed the phone to her, then covered her face as she remembered that horrible feeling of a near-death experience. Angel put his arm around her and turned her against his body.

When her shivering stopped, he leaned close and said, "Wynn, honey, you can't go off investigating stuff on your own. Not now. Not with our enemies so close all around us."

She nodded. "I thought we were safe here."

"We're safer here than anywhere, but our enemies have penetrated our home before. You were here for one of those times."

"I know. I wasn't thinking. I just saw a boy. Alone. In the dark."

"Next time you see something odd, get me. Get Selena. Get someone on the team—and wait for us."

"I will. Next time, but I hope there isn't a next time." She leaned her head against his broad chest. He wasn't wearing Kevlar, so she could hear the steady thud of his heart. She told herself that she would feel as comforted if any of the team held her, but she knew the truth was that only Angel made her feel safe.

ALMOST AN HOUR PASSED before the team joined them in the den. The room wasn't a large space. With the girl-friends and wives taking up the sofa and side chairs, the rest of the team only had standing room. Jim and Russ came in with the others.

Kit leaned on the big mahogany desk. The room got quiet. "I've seen the surveillance footage." He looked at Wynn. "There definitely was someone in the woods with you tonight. I think you did see a boy—we found footprints that were considerably smaller than the adult sets with him. Tank tracked a scent out the far side of the woods where Blade has a dirt road that leads from the main road in to his pastures."

He straightened and set his hands on his hips. Spreading his legs, he gritted his teeth then sent a look at the women in the room. "I can feel this coming to a head. Things are going to get worse before they get better. I hate to think of you caged in here, but for the next few weeks, I think it's best if you stay inside the wire. If you have to leave, make sure you take a couple of the team members with you."

"What about Casey?" Ivy asked. "The school year's only just begun, really. I want to keep things as normal for her as possible, but I don't want to compromise her safety or that of her school because she's there."

Kit nodded. "We can talk about homeschooling her if you like."

"She can join Zavi and me in the classroom," Wynn offered. "I can set her up online with a national K-12 program."

Again, Kit nodded. "I like that option. But for now, let's leave things as they are. I'll take her to school and pick her up. We've already spoken to the office to let them know no one other than Ivy, myself, or one of the team here are allowed to pick her up."

"Think that through, Kit," Ty said. "I don't know if the guys tonight were here specifically for Wynn or if they would have taken anyone they could have. If any of us will do, then Casey is definitely at risk at school, especially if they came in at gunpoint."

Kit exchanged looks with Ivy, then looked at Wynn.

"How long would it take to get her set up in an online class?"

"We can do it over the weekend. She can be ready to go Monday."

Kit nodded. "Make it happen. Mandy, Eddie—we'll need to make some changes for when you're at the stables or the kennels. We can't be casual about that anymore. Ivy, for the time being, do as much as you can from home for the diner. One of us will escort you when you have to be on site. Remi, I know you've received a grant to continue your work with the Friendship Community, but the same restrictions go for you as well. One of us will drive you to the university or to the Friends when you have to leave the house. Hopefully, this won't last long."

"We'll make it work," Remi said.

"The Omnis are tightening their noose. We have to make sure it's around their necks not ours until we can wrap this up." Kit's lips thinned as he looked around at the group. "Val, Kelan, help Max and Greer with a sweep of the house. For the rest of you, stay aware. Stay vigilant. This lockdown won't run the rest of our lives. This thing's coming to a head...and fast."

Wynn stood up with the rest of the group. She tightened her kimono, scared suddenly to return to her room. What if these Omni people broke in to her apartment while everyone was sleeping? They'd broken into her house in Cheyenne. They could do it here too.

If they hit fast, they could have her through the woods and off Ty's property in no time at all.

Everyone was filing out of the den, but Wynn dreaded returning to her apartment.

"Hey," Angel said, drawing her to his side as the room emptied. "I could stay on your couch tonight, if it would make you feel safer."

She nodded. "It would."

They walked up the backstairs and down her hall. He opened her door and flipped the lights on in the living room. Before he stepped inside her apartment, he drew her against the wall in the hallway. "Wait here. If I scare up anyone, you can trip them on their way out." He gave her a sideways grin.

"Angel!"

He flashed his full grin at her, then went into her apartment. She could hear him moving around, checking inside each nook and hiding spot. He locked the door to the backstairs before he came back for her.

"All clear." He smiled at her. Heat slipped down her spine, warming all the cold spots inside her. "I'll just go get a couple pillows and blanket."

Wynn lowered her gaze to the center of his chest. "If you'd rather sleep in your room, I'll understand. I know I'm a coward. They aren't going to unlock the back door and get me."

"No, they aren't, but I'm happy to stay with you. And most important of all, you aren't a coward." He caught her scarred hand in his and rubbed his thumb

over its ridges. "You're a long, long way from a coward."
He ducked his head toward her in a way that made her
look up and meet his eyes. "Yeah?"

She didn't answer.

"Don't lock the door. I'll be right back."

ANGEL CAME BACK into Wynn's apartment and dumped
his blanket and pillow on the couch. Wynn wasn't in the
living room or kitchen. A chair had been wedged under
the outside door in the kitchen.

"Wynn?" No answer. "Wynn?" Angel called from the
living room side of the hallway leading to her bedroom.
Still no answer. He went down the hallway, but stopped
outside her bedroom. "Wynn?"

Silence was his only answer. Fear filled his gut. He
pushed his way into her room. She was standing in the
middle of it, statue-still.

"Hey. What's goin' on?" He wanted to reach out to
her, but was still trying to respect the boundaries she'd
set. He moved around in front of her. Dim light from
the master bath shared enough light in the dark room
that he could see all the shadows in her haunted eyes
when they lifted to him.

"There's no place to hide."

Fuck. He could feel her slipping back into her shell.
"Yes, there is."

"Where?"

He reached for her. "In my arms. Hide in me. I'll shelter you." But he hadn't, had he? Even keeping a close watch on her, she'd still almost been taken tonight.

"I can't, Angel." She shifted her gaze away from him. "This is my life. I have to be able to deal with it. You said I have to leave when this is done."

Angel drew her close, if only to block him from seeing her empty eyes. "Yes, you do. Doesn't mean you have to be alone through all of this."

She leaned back and looked up at him. "I saw a child out there tonight."

He nodded. "You did."

"Mandy said the boys that are part of a group that Hope's brother leads might be headed this way?"

Angel stared at her for a minute, trying to decide if she had the strength to know. He realized that hearing the truth was better than filling a void of knowledge with supposition. "I'll tell you everything I know."

He took her hand and led her from the room. In the kitchen, he set a kettle on the stove. There was a ceramic container on the counter labeled "Tea." He opened it, then winced at the smell of herbs that floated into the air. "Earl Grey for you?"

A fleeting smile eased the persistent strain on Wynn's face. "Yes. I'm guessing it's cocoa for you?" She got two mugs down from the cabinet.

"Yup. I've got to remember to bring some beer up for me."

"You can go get some. I won't go anywhere. No matter what."

Angel glanced at her. "I'm not leaving you tonight."

"So what's this about boys? Mandy told me some of it, but it's hard to believe."

"More Omni World crap. Centuries ago, the Omnis had a robust network of people who supported the work the scientists were doing. They included packs of boys who were out in the world and could watch the goings and comings of anyone who was friends or enemies of the Omnis. These boys were called watchers. As far as we can tell, in recent times—the early part of the last century, anyway—there were no watchers in play. It looks as if when the recent divide in the Omnis took place, they began to employ watchers again.

"These boys are taken from Omni members or from other distantly connected groups. King, the head of the Omnis, uses cults and isolationist groups for various purposes, which we also still don't fully understand. Remember when you had to get a smallpox vaccination?"

She nodded. The teakettle was whistling, so she poured hot water into their two mugs. She stirred his and handed it to him, then prepared hers with honey and lemon.

"Well, we believe the Omnis were testing an outbreak of smallpox on a nearby isolationist group called the Friendship Community. It was a nasty outbreak, but one we quickly contained. There was a watcher group assigned to protect the Friends. They were also in charge of guarding a horde of King's gold that he kept underground beneath the WKB compound."

"Mandy mentioned that."

"Those boys went missing in the mayhem of the smallpox outbreak. Literally minutes before Max went to pick them up, they were secreted away. We've been looking for them ever since."

"Does the government know these boys are raising themselves? In, what, a cult of some sort?"

"The FBI knows. There were several of these groups. Ace has recovered a few of them. As far as I know, they've been taken out of service, but what became of them, I'm not sure. It's a big deal that we find these boys and get them away from King. We believe that Owen's son is among the boys. And we recently learned that King tried to have Lion's pride poisoned."

"A pride is the group of watchers?"

Angel nodded.

"God. I can't even imagine. Were they hurt?"

"We don't know. We've been searching where they were being held. There was clearly a fight. Three of King's men died there, but we couldn't find any of the boys—alive or dead. It's significant that you saw a boy in the woods tonight."

"What kind of people are these Omnis, using children to do their evil work?"

"They are evil. I told you Ace said they have a caste system. People who fall below a certain mark are just used in their programs, whatever those may be. They used your grandmother. They would use you if we let them. They destroyed my parents. They killed Hope and Lion's mom, Fiona's mom, Val's mom. And Blade's. We have to end them before they can unleash whatever it is they're working on."

Wynn looked disbelieving. "How can you, a small band of fighters, end a distributed and integrated force of secret cult members?"

Angel smiled, but not in a nice way. "That is the very thing we trained to do in the Army. We're closer than we've ever been. We'll end this soon."

"You're an optimist."

He caught the look she gave him and laughed. "Not really. I'm just pissed that those goddamned bastards couldn't leave you alone. You weren't doing anyone any harm." A muscle bunched in the corner of his jaw. "All you wanted to do was live in your pink house with your little boy statues. They had to fuck it up."

Pink? Oh. Yeah. The light mauve had kind of looked pink. "Hummels."

"What?"

She smiled. "The little boy statues. They're Hummels."

"Right."

"Grams collected them for years."

"And I took them out in a few short minutes. I'll replace them, Wynn."

She shook her head. "Most of the ones Grams had were antiques. Irreplaceable. I never liked them, really. It was just one of the things Grams and I would do on weekends, go looking for them at estate sales. They can't take that, can they? My memories of Grams and me?"

He caught a lock of her hair between his fingers. "No. They can't take your memories. As far as I know."

She met his eyes. A wave of warmth washed through her body. How easy—and wonderful—it would be to take him to bed. Right now. But if they had no future, then they sure as heck had no present.

She wasn't interested in a short game.

13

Kit stood up as Ivy brought Casey into the den. Both of his girls looked nervous. He couldn't blame them. What he had to say wasn't news his daughter would like. Ivy and Casey sat on the leather sofa. Kit paced over to the French doors and stared outside for a minute, preparing himself for the fight to come.

He faced his daughter. "Casey, things here are taking a dangerous turn for the worse."

She nodded. "I heard about Miss Wynn. I can't believe I slept through all of that. Is she all right?"

"She's fine," Ivy said. "She was just a little shaken."

"The people we're fighting are circling close," Kit said. "Our weaknesses put all of us here in this house and in the community in danger. There are some changes that we need to make. They may be short-term, but they may be longer-term as well."

Casey frowned at him, trying to understand what he was saying.

"Your attending school is one of those weaknesses. You're an easy target for our enemies, as is your entire school." Kit pulled a deep breath. "We need to home-school you for a little while."

Casey looked from him to Ivy. "Do I have a vote in this decision?"

Ivy looked at him. Kit nodded. "You do. But be warned, your mother and I do as well."

Ivy took hold of Casey's hands. "Honey, you don't live a regular life. You never have. From living in a car, to staying in friends' living rooms, to living in a shelter, to finally putting some roots down here, nothing has been the kind of normal that your friends know. And that hasn't changed. To keep you—and them—safe, we need you to be here until your dad can make things safe again for everyone."

Her angry eyes went from Ivy back to him. "You said I get a vote." Her voice was quiet. Kit mistrusted the calm.

"You do."

"How did you two vote?"

"We voted to keep you and your school safe by homeschooling you here," Ivy said.

Casey nodded. "That's my vote as well. At least until it's safe enough for me to go back."

Kit nodded. "Then it's unanimous."

"Will I at least be able to bring my friends here?"

"Not for a while. Not while we're so actively under scrutiny. You don't want them to be used to get to us."

Casey nodded, but she looked as if she was fighting tears. She went over to hug Kit. "I love you, Dad."

Kit held her cheek. "You, your mom, and your new brother or sister are my entire world. As soon as I can reverse this, I will."

"I know, but this whole thing scares me. I don't want to lose you again."

He hugged her. "Not gonna happen, baby."

"Miss Wynn will be getting you set up with an online classroom," Ivy said. "Things will be a little frustrating and confusing while we make this transition, but we'll have to work through it."

Casey hugged her, too. Ivy looked at him over her head, surprised at her easy acceptance of their edict.

"Can I go to school tomorrow to say goodbye and get my things?"

"You can go with Dad tomorrow. It'll be your last day."

"Okay." She glanced at both of them, then nodded and left the room.

Ivy went over to slip into Kit's arms. "She's tough, like you."

Kit smiled down as he looked at Ivy's dark blue eyes. "I think you're tougher than me. I'm glad she took it so well."

"I'm not worried about the impact this will have on her academics, but I am worried about how this will affect her social development. Middle school is a critical time for a teen. How long do you think this situation will last?"

"The way things are intensifying, it won't be more than a few months, max. She should be able to rejoin her school after the holidays."

"I hope so."

Kit kissed Ivy, a gentle touch of their lips, and then he deepened the kiss. "I do, too."

"Kit, got some heat coming to the front door," Max said via their comms.

Kit straightened and touched his ear, letting Ivy know he was receiving a communication. "Who is it?"

"Your friends, Sheriff Tate and Barney Fife."

"Barney's not my friend."

"Uh-huh."

The doorbell rang. Kit left the den to answer it. "Sheriff. Deputy. How can I help you?"

"Can we come in?" the sheriff asked.

"Sure." Kit held the door open and stepped back. "Want some coffee or something?"

Tate shook his head. "No. This isn't a social call."

"Ah."

The sheriff stared at him. Kit lifted his brows, waiting. "You got something you want to share with us?" Tate asked.

"About?"

"Anything unusual happen around here lately?"

"You mean like our tutor's grandmother getting shot

in town? Or the dead guys at that camp a little way down the highway? Unusual like that?"

The sheriff sighed, then opened a photo on his phone. "This look familiar to you?" The picture in question was of a rectangular piece of leather with the team's headquarters address written on it in black permanent marker...along with the name Mad Dog. The label was hand-sewn on an area of sheep fleece, like the winter clothes Lion and his boys wore. It was the same label they'd found on the backpacks at the camp.

The hairs lifted on the back of Kit's neck. After what happened at the watchers' camp, and then last night with Wynn, he knew exactly what this was, but this sample had come from a piece of clothing belonging to one of the cubs. Someone had seen them. "Where did you get this?"

"That's what we'd like to know," Deputy Jerry said.

"Don't fuck around with me." Kit glared at him. "Where did that come from?"

The sheriff sighed again. "It was inside a jacket worn by a boy who said this was his home, said he'd broken free from some human traffickers. You know anything about that?"

"No. I told you the kids belong to the Friendship Community—and possibly others like it in the region. They aren't traffickers, as far as I know." Kit frowned, waiting for more info. "Where's the boy?"

"Again, that's what we'd like to know," the deputy said.

The sheriff looked disgruntled. "A very distraught couple stopped at the police station to make the report. Said they picked up the little boy hitchhiking down the highway in the Medicine Bow Mountains, about forty-five minutes from here. The boy said he'd gotten free and was trying to get back to his family. Showed them the address sewn into his jacket and asked them to bring him here. They got all the way to your driveway then stopped. While they debated leaving the boy or coming to us first, he jumped out of their car and ran away. You happen to see him?"

"No. We haven't, although our tutor said she saw a boy in the woods behind the house last night. We looked for him but didn't find him. What time did this happen with the boy and the couple who picked him up?"

The sheriff looked at his watch. "About a half-hour ago."

What the hell? Didn't sound like it was the same boy as the one Wynn saw last night, unless he'd ditched his captors and come back this way.

"Mind if we look around?" Jerry asked.

"Yeah, I mind."

"If you're trafficking children..." the deputy sneered.

"Fuck that," Kit said. "The only kids here are Rocco's son and my daughter. If others show up, I'll let you know. Send me that pic, Sheriff."

"You expecting others, son? You say these boys are

connected to that camp?" the sheriff asked, studying him as he waited for an answer.

If it had just been Tate here asking the questions, Kit would likely have told him about Lion and his boys. He didn't like Jerry Whitcomb. Didn't trust him for some reason, maybe because of the shit that had happened to Mandy before Rocco came to town that the deputy just let happen or brushed off as inconsequential when she'd asked for help.

"I'm not expecting anything." Kit glared at the sheriff until a thought occurred to him. "You get the couple's info?"

"We did." He sent the label pic to Kit.

"Think they're on the up and up?"

"Looks like it. But we'd like to find the boy and have a word with him."

Kit nodded. "We'll do a search for him. If we find him, we'll let you know."

Max was in the den when Kit returned, looking as edgy as a bottled hurricane. He pointed to the sheriff's picture of the label on the tablet he held. "That's the cubs' winter-issue wardrobe."

"Figured that. Lion's a smart kid, sending the cubs this way. We still don't know where they're being held, but it may not be as far away as we feared. Get a few of the team and go search the property."

"Copy that." Max pivoted and headed to the hidden bunker stairs. "Afterwards, I'm taking a drive back up the mountain. Want to see if there are any more strays making it out of the woods and down to the highway."

"Good. Take Selena with you."

~

W YNN WAS in the kitchen of her apartment, cleaning up after making a batch of brownies when she heard a knock on her door. Her heart jumped at the thought that it might be Angel. He'd been gone when she woke this morning, and he'd spent the day with the team, continuing their search for Hope's brother and his boys.

She dried her hands on a tea towel then hurried to the door, forcing herself to be composed as she opened it. Angel was there, filling her field of vision. He didn't look happy—until he got a whiff of what she had baking.

"That smells like brownies," he said with a moan.

She nodded. He'd been kind to her last night, as he always was. He was such a solid guy. Too bad he didn't want the future she saw for both of them. "I cook when I'm nervous."

"Can I come in?"

She opened the door wider. "Sure." Angel followed her into the kitchen. "Do you have news of the watchers you were looking for?" she asked. "Or the boy and the men I saw last night?"

"No." He picked up a towel and started drying

dishes as she washed them. "It's been awful for Max and Hope. They're both shredded."

Wynn looked up at him. "I don't understand how the Omnis could take boys from their families and force them into a *Lord of the Flies* existence, and no one reports them."

"It's an easy thing to do when you've raised them outside societal norms. Lion is a helluva leader, fierce in caring for his boys. He'll get them here safely."

"How can all of this be going on so near us, near mainstream society, and we not know anything about it?"

Angel shrugged. "My guess is that the real world doesn't want to know about it. They've heard of the polygamist communities in the area and turn a blind eye. They've heard of the White Kingdom Brotherhood prison gang and don't want to know more about them. They haven't heard of the Omnis, so the drivers of this secret world are completely under the radar, but they use the gang and the isolationist groups as entry points like a magician's slight of hand; people know about those groups but ignore them, so they see only what they expect to see. One secret begets another until there's an entire hidden world, and no one puts the pieces together."

He folded his arms and gave her a look that put her nerves on edge. "A thought occurred to me about your parents. Can we talk about them some more?"

She looked down at the sudsy water. "I've told you what I know."

"I had a revelation of sorts. Bear with me—before we get to your parents, there are things you need to know about me."

Angel was leaning against a big section of cabinets where she needed to put some dishes away. Just having him in the room shrank the size of her little galley kitchen by half. When he didn't move, she looked up at him. His dark eyes were frightening, like a city alley at night, teasing her curiosity with shadows and mysteries. She froze in place, her knees inches from his. "Like what?"

"Like who I am. Who my people are."

She pulled her gaze from his, letting it span his wide shoulders. Odd. She'd never thought of him as a child, an infant who'd had loving parents. He was so perfect, so fearless, that he seemed like an ancient warrior God had spawned fully formed.

"Does it matter?"

"It does."

She nodded and bit her upper lip. "Who are you, then?"

"My parents came from the same city, but entirely different worlds. My dad was the son of a second-generation Puerto Rican dockworker. My mom was the princess daughter of a real estate magnate. He was dark and she was light and they were everything together."

"You don't have much of an accent."

He gave her one of his slanted smiles. "My mom raised me. I was never allowed to talk Nuyorican like my father and his people. She thought it would hold me back."

Wynn frowned. "Was she right?"

"Dunno. Maybe. She did what she thought was right. She felt her people had greater power than my dad's, so she wanted me to fit in with them." He held his arms wide. "But look at me. I could never pass for a WASP. Mostly, I think, it was just her own insecurities. Whatever it was, it set me up for a lot of fights before we got out of the projects."

She frowned. "I don't think you look like a bug."

He grinned and shook his head. "Not that kind of wasp. A White Anglo-Saxon Protestant."

"Oh. Yeah, no." She smiled. "But how did your parents meet if they were from such different worlds?"

"A school event. Mom was pregnant with me before the end of her senior year. When her parents found out, they kicked her out of the family."

"Just like that?" Wynn touched his forearm. "How terrible."

"Maybe not. Forced my folks to figure out what was important to them. They chose each other. They got married. Moved in with Dad's parents for a little while. It wasn't like they were adrift without anyone to guide them."

"Sounds like they were strong. I don't know that I could have done without Grams at that age."

"I doubt she would have forced you to make that choice."

"She adored you."

He grinned. "I asked her to put in a good word for me with you." His gaze moved across her face. "Life was a struggle for my folks. My dad was a hard worker but couldn't keep a job. They had one setback after another. My mom wasn't raised to fend for herself—she didn't always understand how life worked. My dad had to leave us to find employment in a different town. Every day was a fight for survival for them. I even began to suspect that my dad was in some kind of gang, that that was why he'd left town."

Wynn's eyes widened. "Was he?"

"It wasn't until a few weeks ago that I learned the truth. The Omnis targeted my parents for the crime of loving each other; they dogged them their whole lives. My dad had to fake his death to break contact with them. He didn't warn my mom. He was depending on her reaction to the news to be so legit that it fooled the Omnis into believing he really was dead. But he didn't anticipate the effect it would have on her."

The pain in his eyes was as raw as if this was a recent event. "When she heard he'd been shot in a street fight, she killed herself. He only lived a few months after her death before he shot himself. They'd made plans to start fresh in a new town, with new jobs. They were within hours of living their dream." He blinked away tears. "The goddamned Omnis stole everything from them."

She looked into his stormy eyes. "Why would they do that?"

He sighed. "This is the point I wanted to make. My mother's family were aristocrats in the Omni World Order. My mom was the result of careful breeding meant to select the genes with the most intelligent, athletic, and beautiful features."

"The eugenics program you mentioned."

"Yeah."

"But that was a short-lived madness that never, thankfully, took root in our society."

"Not in the light of day, but it did in a secret world —the world of the Omnis. My mother had a sacred mission in the Omni organization to marry and procreate to carry on their genetic engineering. She bucked them by marrying my dad and having me."

Wynn blinked. "How could they have rejected you? You're as perfect a human specimen as possible. Look at you. You're smart, loyal, strong, fearless. Gorgeous."

Angel grinned at her. "That's how you see me?"

"Yeah."

The humor left his eyes. "Well, that's not how the Omnis see me. I'm not white. I'm a descendant of Caribbean peoples, a cocktail of American Indian, African, European, and Asian ancestors."

Wynn smiled. "You're a perfect mix of all humanity."

He nodded. "But to the white supremacist Omnis, my blood has been tainted with the colors of humanity, see? Because of that, my mother had to be punished. The Omnis stalked my mom her whole life."

"I wish I could have met your parents. I know I would have liked them."

"They would have loved you." He gave her a sad smile. "What occurred to me today is this. Your parents were geneticists working in the field of nanotechnology."

"I know."

"Put it together...the Omnis had a eugenics program. Selective breeding is a slow, slow process. Results can't be fully measured for decades. What if the Omnis wanted to speed things up by altering existing humans? Or editing genes in utero? What if they moved from eugenics to epigenetics?"

Wynn gasped. "What if they *did* alter Grams? Oh my God, Angel." She pressed her hands to her face. "What if...what if the Omnis needed her body to see if the modifications worked? Those weren't her ashes in the casket; I just know it. They took her body because she was a lab rat, like the note that the bikers left with her said. You didn't see her right after her stroke, the long weeks where she couldn't even communicate. She was barely alive. But you did see her when she was here. She was so vivacious, so ready to tackle the next thing." Wynn gave Angel a sheepish look. "Which, I'm afraid, was matchmaking us."

The look he gave her was full of regret. The oven began beeping. She grabbed some potholders, then took out the long dish of brownies. The rich scent of warm chocolate filled the little kitchen. She set the hot dish on the stove and turned off the oven.

"You gonna cut those brownies?"

"Yes, but they have to cool before we eat them." Wynn slowly cut the bars. She set the knife down, but couldn't meet Angel's eyes. "What if my parents are behind all of this?"

He took her hand, turning her to face him. "We don't know that they are, although it's looking ever more likely. But we also don't know how complicit they are with the Omnis. Maybe they were forced to work for them. The Omnis have ways of doing that. Let's give them the benefit of the doubt until we know the facts."

Wynn blew out a long breath, relieved that he wanted to take that tact. "Grams said she saw them while she was at Jafaar's. Do you think they somehow escaped the Omnis?"

"It's possible. It would explain why the Omnis are after you—they need you now that they don't have Grams. What it doesn't explain is why they killed off Grams to begin with." He straightened and held up a finger as he tapped his earpiece. "Go, Greer." Pause. "You did? What did you find?" Pause. "Great, we're coming down."

She handed Angel a piece of hot brownie on a plate. He took up one of the forks and dug in. "What did Greer say?" she asked.

"He found something on a video from a business

next to the funeral home. Wants us to take a look." He frowned down at his plate then looked at her in awe. "This is incredible!"

"Grams' recipe. All from scratch. She was a stickler for real food, not processed junk full of preservatives."

Angel polished off the brownie, then set his plate in the sink. He sent the brownies a regretful glance. Wynn grinned at him. "We can take one for Greer."

"Yeah...or we could take the whole thing and eat them down there."

"That works too."

Angel took up the pads and carried the glass dish. They left her apartment and passed Rocco and Mandy's wing. The TV was on. They'd just stepped into the main hallway when Rocco caught up with them.

"Hang on. Where you going with that?" Rocco asked. "I could smell that from your apartment. I was hoping you were bringing them for us." He smiled at Wynn like a child begging for a treat.

Angel didn't look inclined to share. "We're heading down to see Greer," he said. "He got new footage of the funeral home. And we have an interesting theory on Wynn's parents."

Rocco looked at the brownies. "Huh. Guess I'll go with you."

"Wait!" Mandy called after them. She punched Rocco's arm, then smiled sweetly at Wynn. "You can't seriously think you can walk those past a pregnant woman without sharing, do you?"

Wynn laughed. "Help yourself. There's more than we can eat."

Mandy took a square and moaned as she walked back to the sitting room outside their bedrooms. "I may need a whole batch just for myself," she called after them. "Don't tell Ivy about these or you won't have enough to share with Greer!"

Angel grinned. "Good point. We'll take the stairs at the end of the hallway."

Val and Ace were in the sitting room of their wing. They hurried over to get a brownie. When they heard where Wynn and Angel were headed, they followed them down. The five of them were a tight squeeze in the elevator.

Max was downstairs. He helped himself to a brownie. "Wait till you see what Greer's got." He reached for another brownie, but Angel blocked him.

"No. One for Rocco, one for Greer, and the last is Wynn's," Angel said.

Wynn smiled as they moved into the ops room where Greer was. He stood up. "Let's take this in the conference room...there's more space."

"Sure, but Wynn brought you a surprise," Angel said, holding out the pan.

"Thanks, Wynn," Greer said. He took a bite, then closed his eyes and savored the treat.

"Last one's yours," Angel said to Wynn.

"That's okay. I don't really want it. You can have it," she said.

"That's not fair. You had two," Val said.

"How do you know?" Angel asked.

"Like you didn't eat one hot out of the oven." Val shook his head. "Not like you to delay gratification."

Wynn blushed, feeling somehow they were talking about her. And Angel. Being intimate.

Angel set the dish on the conference table and took the last brownie. "You're right. I don't...unless the outcome is very, very important to me." He finished off the brownie in one bite and stared at Val through narrowed eyes while he chewed it.

Val laughed. Angel almost choked. Wynn wished they could get on with whatever it was Greer wanted to show them.

"You think we should call the others down?" Rocco asked.

"Already did. They should be here shortly." As soon as Greer said that, the door on the opposite side of the conference room opened. Kit, Kelan, Ty, and Selena joined them.

Selena sniffed the air. "I smell brownies."

"They're gone. Sorry," Wynn said. "I made some for Angel, but they didn't make it very far."

Angel's brows shot up. "You made them for me?"

Wynn felt her cheeks heat up again. "Well, yeah."

"Whatcha got, Greer?" Kit asked, refocusing the team.

"This." Greer clicked footage from the business next to the funeral home. It filled the big smart screen. He sent Wynn an apologetic look, then explained what they were seeing. "This is Grams' casket being loaded in to the hearse. This was happening in the rear of the funeral home while we were waiting in the front. Notice the other hearse parking here." He pointed to a black vehicle that pulled into the back area, then blocked the way while it reversed into a parking space.

Wynn saw the driver get out and go over to Grams' driver. He wore the same black suit, white shirt, and gray tie as the driver of Grams' hearse—or maybe it was just the monochromatic nature of the footage. They spoke for a minute, then the driver handed Grams' driver some money and they switched hearses.

Wynn gasped. She looked up at Angel. "I told you. I told you they stole Grams' body. They didn't cremate it."

He reached for her hand. "Can you get that license plate any clearer?" he asked Greer.

"No. The driver knew where the camera was and was careful to keep his face and his license plate off screen."

"But why? Why switch out Grams?" Ty asked.

Angel looked at her and nodded. "Tell them our theory."

"Grams said she saw my parents while she was at Jafaar's house," Wynn said. "She was heavily medicated. She and I thought she'd just been dreaming about them. But then that note left on Grams after she was murdered called her a lab rat. These Omni people that you're fighting, they come from an organization made up of scientists. My parents were scientists. The Omnis have a eugenics-like breeding program. My parents were geneticists." Her breath hitched. "It's possible they aren't dead. Maybe they're working for your Omni people. Maybe they were involved with Grams' stroke... or with her rapid recovery. They could be helping the Omnis move from a slow eugenics program to a fast one based on epigenetics."

Angel finished for her: "We think the Omnis may have taken Grams' body to examine the effects of whatever they did to her."

Kit whistled low. He set his hands on his hips and ducked his head as he weighed their words. "Wynn, have your parents tried to contact you? Has anything unusual happened?"

"Beyond being attacked at Grams' house or almost grabbed here?" Beyond every waking minute of this whole experience? "No." She looked at Angel. "Although you said you saw a woman outside my home the night we were attacked there."

He nodded. "Could have just been shadows. But there was that guy who was bugging you in Cheyenne about going with him to help your parents." Angel looked at Kit. "I think he was trying to nab her for leverage. It could be that her parents broke free when they were helping Grams at Jafaar's house...the house that Syadne rented for him."

Angel watched Kit for a second, then looked around

at the rest of the group. "Syadne had three silos of labs in the tunnels in Colorado. It's possible the genetic developments were being worked on there."

"Or in the restricted levels of the silo under the WKB compound," Max said.

"If her parents are still alive and still plugged in to what's happening with Wynn, maybe their loyalties shifted after Grams was killed," Ty suggested, "if they were ever loyal to the Omnis."

Wynn crossed her arms. The mere thought of her parents having faked their deaths so that they could be rid of her and Grams—and their familial obligations to them—shook her to the core. Like a giant billboard shouting to the world her ugly secret of being unwanted. So much so, they ditched her, ditched the life they'd built, ditched their peers and career to join a secret organization working on a project that might harm all of humanity.

"Oh fuck." Ty shoved his hands into his hair and paced a few steps.

"Spill, Blade," Kit said.

"It's Lion's Armageddon."

"How so?" Kelan asked.

"Wynn just said it." Ty pointed at her as he faced Kit. "The Omnis have been slowly engineering perfect humans through painstakingly careful breeding." He shot a glance over at Angel. "It's why your mom was so severely punished when she bred you. You're a deviant to Omnis. They've been doing this for a long time. The initiations—forced breedings witnessed by senior OWO leadership. They figured out a way to speed things up by altering our genes. It's the Armageddon."

Angel nodded. "That's exactly what we were thinking."

Val chuckled. "You make it sound like shapeshifters and creatures from a Frankenstein lab."

"May not be far off," Ty said. "We don't know what alterations they made to Grams. And now we don't have a body to even investigate. Beck said he didn't have her blood samples, right?" he asked Angel.

Angel nodded. "She was DOA with a clear cause of death, so no samples were taken." He looked at Max. "I thought Lion and his boys were studying engineering and infrastructure for the advent of the Armageddon."

"They were," Max said. "Lion mentioned some dams and bridges he and his boys were supposed to hit when Armageddon came. If the end days he was talking about have to do with altering humans, why have the boys focus on infrastructure?"

"My mom's papers said the Omnis wanted to drop the world population down to half a billion people," Ty said. "Maybe they're working on a way to do that. They could tag everyone who's an Omni so the Armageddon passes over them. Or they could give all Omnis an anti-dote. Or they could just infect certain genetic strains of humans. Who the hell knows?"

"Maybe Lion's plan to hit infrastructure is merely a distraction for the bigger fight," Angel said.

"We're guessing now. Our job isn't to write a fucking sci-fi novel. We have to find King." Kit looked around the room. "It's late. Let's hit this again in the morning."

Angel picked up the empty brownie dish. He caught Wynn's arm and turned her toward the hallway leading to the ops room. Kit followed them into the elevator. Her head was spinning. It couldn't really be possible that these evil people had a way of wreaking so much devastation, could it?

No wonder Angel was putting this war before their relationship.

The elevator opened. Kit and Angel followed her out, but he stopped them before they reached the hallway. "Too bad about the brownies."

She looked at him.

"Next time, make a double batch. I hear they're hall-of-famers."

She smiled. No matter how you looked at it, these guys were overwhelming—in a group, one on one, angry or smiling. But even more surprising than that, she liked them.

Angel caught her hand and led her down the long hallway. Halfway to the stairs in the north wing, he grumbled, "Fuck that. I'm not sharing the next batch."

"Heard that, Angel!" Kit called down the hallway.

Wynn wrapped her arm around Angel's and leaned close to whisper. "I'll do a secret batch just for you."

"Heard that, too, Wynn!" Kit shouted.

Angel laughed. Wynn frowned at him, wondering

how Kit could hear them when he was almost out of sight. Angel pointed to the comm unit in his ear as he tapped it off. Wynn opened her apartment door. Angel followed her inside. She remembered his answer to Val about not rushing when something was important to him. Did that mean there was a chance for them, somewhere in the future?

He went into her kitchen and set the dish down on the counter. She followed him. Their eyes met when he turned. He came toward her. She backed up until she hit the wall in the hallway.

He didn't stop. Bracing his arms on the wall behind her, he stared into her eyes. "Tell me something, Wynn. Are you ready for what's coming between us?"

She studied his face. "You said we had no future."

His nostrils flared. "I have this dream for you. A wish, really. I want you to live free. In peace. Living the life that you want."

"You don't even know what I want."

He shook his head. "It's true. I'm only thinking of what I want for you."

"I want you, Angel."

"I'm a bad choice, Wynn. I'm a warrior. I will always find another enemy to fight. You will always be in danger because of me and what I do."

Her gaze lowered from his eyes to his chest as she struggled to find the right words to ease his fears. "Fair enough. You've warned me. You said you want me to live the life I want."

He nodded.

"I want a life with you."

His face hardened. He straightened, then shoved his hands in his pockets as he glared at her. "I didn't say you could make bad choices."

"I don't think you get to judge my choices. Not when they're the right ones for me. Not when they give me the only future I want."

He huffed a breath. "Some of the guys think I only have one speed: fast. It isn't true. We'll take this slow so you'll have time to get off the ride if you change your mind."

"I'm not going to change my mind. I rarely do once I've made a decision, because I don't make them lightly." She put her hands on his chest. His body was warm and solid through his black tee. "Besides, I understand it isn't like you to delay your gratification," she teased, remembering what Val had said.

"It isn't. But I want to savor this, the start of us. I want to remember every minute. I love the way your eyes darken, the way your breathing goes shallow. You're like a runner's high to me. You take me to a place where there's no pain, no fear, only a curious sense of ease and elation. I've never felt that before with anyone. It's damned addictive. I want more of it. More of you. More of us."

She smiled, struck by his words. "When I was at Grams' house, I felt guilty to realize I missed you more than I missed her."

He cupped her neck. "I spent those days we were apart coming up with lame excuses to pop in on you. I am sorry the Omnis forced you to come back. But I'm not sorry you're back." He kissed her forehead, then stepped away. "I'm gonna make sure your apartment is locked up tight."

He checked the deadbolt on the back door in the kitchen, then disappeared down the hall. Wynn didn't move. Her body was still zinging with the possibility they were going to continue exploring their relationship. *"...unless the outcome is very, very important to me,"* he'd told Val. Was she important to him?

"All secure," he said as he came back into the kitchen. Seeing her, he frowned. "You okay?"

She nodded.

He took her hand and led her into the living room toward her apartment door. "If you want, I can stay another night."

Wynn shook her head. "I'll be fine. Get a good night's sleep, Angel."

"All right. You have my number in your cell phone. And it's on the list of speed dials on the house phone. If you need me, if you get scared, call me."

14

_____

Max sent a quick look over at Hope. They'd left Blade's well before sunrise so that they could hit the highway corridor where the boys might be if they were traveling toward Blade's. "We'll go slow. Watch the woods. The boys, in their beige wool and lambskin clothes, will blend in with the brown ground cover. Best thing to do is to watch for movement. They're going to be as alert as deer, but even more secretive."

"You're sure they're heading this way?" Hope asked without taking her eyes off her search.

"I'm not sure of anything when it comes to the watchers. But we do have evidence that they were each told about Blade's house. And they had my name."

Hope sent him a glance, her eyes filled with worry. "I know the boys are self-reliant. I know they're capable of navigating these woods...but what kind of life is that for a kid? I hate King for doing that to them. That and so much more."

"I know. I'm looking forward to gutting the bastard. But as for the boys, I'm not sure it's a terrible life. They get to live a Peter Pan existence, running free and wild outdoors, constrained only by the rules of their pride. I would have loved to have grown up that way. Lion makes sure they're fed and cared for. Your brother has all the makings of a phenomenal leader."

Hope sniffled as she nodded, returning her focus to the hills slipping past her window.

WYNN WENT to Zavi's classroom after breakfast. Rocco and Mandy were just leaving. She stopped them on their way out to see if it would be all right for her to take Zavi on a picnic lunch.

Mandy smiled. "I think that would be a wonderful thing to do. The day's supposed to be the warmest one this week."

Rocco nodded. "Just don't go farther than Eddie's kennels. And take Selena with you. I'll let her know you'll call her when you need her. If she's busy with Eden or Mandy, I'll take you."

Wynn had no intention of going near the woods without some protection. But she wanted to insulate Zavi from what was happening. The boy needed time outside. Lots of it—combining that time with a class lesson was always a bonus for an energetic kid like him.

"Perfect. We're going to have a picnic after we collect some leaves for an autumn project. Then I think we'll go see Aunt Eddie and her dogs. I hear one of her rescues might be expecting puppies."

"Puppies?" Zavi's eyes got big. He looked at Rocco, but was shut down before he could ask the question.

"No puppies for us. We already have Yeller and Blue. And Eddie has Tank. And Uncle Ty has Sebastian. Four animals in the house are enough."

Mandy winked at Zavi. She linked her arm through Rocco's as they walked away. "But it is a very big house, Papa..."

Zavi gave Wynn a big smile. "I want a puppy so bad."

Wynn smiled and ran her hand over his dark hair. "Well, even if you can't have one of your own, maybe Aunt Eddie will let you help her with the pups in the kennel. It's a lot of work, though."

"I'm a good worker. I make my bed. And I help you clean the classroom."

"Very good points. Still, taking on the care of an animal isn't something that can be done impetuously."

Zavi frowned. "What does that word mean?"

"Impetuously? It means doing something without careful thought."

"Oh." He nodded. "I'll give it careful thinking, then."

Wynn smiled. "Let's go make our lunch. After that, I'll call Selena. We'll have fun collecting our leaves."

∾

ZAVI GOT off the chair at the kitchen table where Miss Wynn was cutting some carrots for their picnic lunch. "Is it ready yet?" he asked.

"Almost."

Mr. Russ was humming to a song on the radio while he did something at the big counter. Zavi was restless. He wandered over to the French doors that opened out to the patio and the lawn and looked out over the big grassy area. They were going out there later to collect leaves for a project Miss Wynn had in mind.

"Can I go outside?"

"Yes, but don't leave the patio," Miss Wynn said. "We'll be ready to go in just a minute."

"I won't leave it." He pulled his jacket on as he stepped outside. While he stood at the edge of the patio, he saw something move at the edge of the woods. He frowned as he tried to make sense of what it was. Maybe a deer.

No, it was a boy. He straightened. There was a boy out in the woods. Zavi waved to him. He waved back. Zavi looked over his shoulder toward the doors. It was so bright outside that he couldn't see into the dark interior of the kitchen. He could run to the woods and be back before Miss Wynn missed him. There was a boy out there! Maybe he could make a friend.

Zavi rushed across the lawn, jumped off the retaining wall, and headed straight for the spot at the edge of the woods where he'd seen the boy. He stepped into the woods, looking around. The day was sunny, but the pine woods were dark. Inside the woods were other big trees, their branches bare. Those let in more light, so he moved in that direction.

"Over here," a boy said.

Zavi turned in that direction. Twenty feet away was the boy he'd seen from the patio. He wore leather pants, handmade boots, a thick wool sweater, and a vest of animal skin with the fur on the inside. A memory flickered at the edge of Zavi's mind about the winter clothes he'd worn back in Afghanistan. But this boy was blond, not dark-haired, and his skin was super pale, not warm like his and Papa's. He was taller and older than Zavi, but still too young to be in the woods by himself. Zavi looked around to see if he really was alone. "Who are you?"

"I'm Fox. Who are you?"

"Zavi. I live here."

"Do you have food, Zavi? I'm hungry."

Zavi nodded. "There's lots of food inside."

"Bring me some."

Zavi shrugged. "Sure. But why don't you come inside?"

The boy shook his head. "I can't. I shouldn't even be talking to you."

"Why?"

"Because I'm a watcher. We're not supposed to be seen."

Zavi rumpled his face up. "What do you watch?"

"Everything. Hurry. Go get me some food."

"Zavi?" Miss Wynn was calling him. Oh no. He'd been gone too long. "Zavi! Where are you?" Her voice was sharp. He was going to get in trouble.

He looked back at his new friend, but the boy was gone. "Fox, come with me. Miss Wynn is nice. She won't hurt you." His words fell into the silence of the woods. "Fox! Come out. You don't have to hide."

"Zavi! There you are," Miss Wynn said as she rushed to his side. She gripped his arm in an almost painful hold. "Why did you come out here? You know you should have gotten me first."

"I made a friend."

Miss Wynn knelt and frowned as she looked at him. She sent a quick glance around them, but he knew she wouldn't see Fox. He was already hiding. Miss Wynn's lips moved, but she took a second to ask him her question. "You made a friend? I don't see anyone around here."

"His name was Fox."

"You made friends with a fox?"

"No. He's a boy. He was here. He said he was hungry. We have to bring him some food."

Miss Wynn got to her feet. Zavi could see the fear in her eyes as she searched the woods around them. "Okay." She grabbed his hand and hurried out of the woods. He had to run to keep up with her. She kept looking behind them with fearful eyes. Mr. Russ was hurrying toward them. Miss Wynn picked Zavi up and ran the rest of the way into the house.

Zavi could feel her shaking. He caught her face in his hands and forced her to focus on him. "Fox isn't a bad guy. You don't have to be afraid." His words didn't ease the fear in her eyes.

He heard the heavy footsteps of men running. Papa was the first into the kitchen. One look at his face, and Zavi knew he was in big trouble. He wrapped his arms around Miss Wynn's neck and buried his face in her shoulder, but his papa was stronger and pulled him from her.

THE ADRENALINE POUNDING through Wynn's veins began to fade. She put a hand over her mouth as she tried to calm her breathing. Zavi was safe. They were all safe. That was all that mattered. Angel had come into the kitchen with Rocco and Kit. He came over and wrapped his arm around her, drawing her close.

Zavi started to cry. Wynn did, too.

"I'm sorry, Papa. Miss Wynn told me to stay on the patio."

"Then why didn't you?" Rocco asked.

"Because there was a boy in the woods. He waved to me."

Wynn saw the fear that washed over Rocco's face. "What happened?" he asked her, his dark eyes intense as he focused on her.

She shook her head, wiping at her tears. "I was making our lunch. Zavi asked to go out to the patio. I asked him to stay there, but he saw something in the woods. A boy, again. I didn't see him, but Zavi did."

Zavi caught his father's face in his little hands, capturing his attention as he'd done to Wynn earlier. "You aren't supposed to know about him."

"Why not?"

"Because he said so. He's hungry. Can we feed him?"

"Max reinforced the perimeter after what happened to Wynn," Angel said. "How could a boy—or anyone—breach it without us knowing?" He looked at Kit.

Kit tapped his earpiece. "Max, I need you to do a sweep of the estate. Someone may be in the woods. Alert Blade and Kelan—they're with Eden and Mandy."

Rocco set Zavi on his feet, then knelt in front of him. He held his son's shoulders. "No one's in trouble, son, although when Miss Wynn gives you an order, you follow it as if it came from me. Understand?"

"Yes, Papa."

"Just tell me everything. We aren't angry with the boy in the woods. What did he look like?"

"He had hair like Casey's, but not as long. He had a fur vest. He said his name was Fox. He said we aren't supposed to see him or talk to him because he's a watcher. What's a watcher, Papa?"

Kit cursed under his breath.

Rocco stood. "Watchers can be dangerous. Stay in the house for now." He looked at his boy then at Wynn. "Both of you."

"Yes, Papa," Zavi said. "But someone needs to feed Fox."

Rocco set his big hand on Zavi's head. "We will. We'll get him some food." He looked at Wynn. "Go on back to the classroom. I'll give you an update when I can. And Zavi, you're not to go anywhere without letting Miss Wynn know first."

She reached for Zavi's hand. "We made a big picnic lunch. Maybe you could give that to the boy?"

"Good idea," Rocco said.

Angel went upstairs with them, walking them to the classroom. Wynn tried to tamp down the lingering effects of the fear she'd felt. She wondered if that was the same boy she'd seen in the woods.

Angel was watching her. He gave her a fortifying smile as he squeezed her arm. "You're okay. Just breathe."

She tried to return his smile. His gaze went to Zavi, and he frowned. "Zavi, I need you to promise you won't go outside alone. Papa wasn't lying when he said watchers can be dangerous. Do you remember when Selena's face was cut up?"

Zavi nodded. His eyes were huge.

"A watcher did that."

"I promise, Uncle Angel. But Fox wouldn't do that."

Zavi went into the classroom. Wynn stayed in the sitting room to talk to Angel. "Surely a little boy like the one he saw wouldn't be much of a danger," she said.

"Watchers were organized to serve at the interest of the Omnis. They're taught guerrilla warfare from an early age. It's hard to know exactly what they might do, especially if they're acting on orders. They tried to kidnap Casey once. That's when Selena was hurt. They are mostly a bunch of feral boys."

Wynn folded her arms and rubbed her hands over them, feeling chilled suddenly.

Angel caught her shoulders. "I'm sorry you were scared. It was brave of you to go after Zavi like you did."

"I couldn't leave him to face whatever was in the woods. And I'm worried for that little boy out there. The adults in his life have abandoned him. I can't imagine what he's been through."

Angel nodded. "We'll find him."

"When you put food out for him, put some warm blankets or a sleeping bag out there, too, just in case he evades you again. The nights are so cold now."

"Good idea." He studied her a little longer. "You'll stay inside, yeah?"

"We will. I'll watch for Casey to come home. She can stay with us too."

Wynn went into the classroom. Zavi was standing next to one of the bookshelves. His shoulders were slumped as he absently fingered the spines of the stories. "Would it be okay if I watched Papa and my uncles search for my friend?"

Wynn smiled. "He's your friend already?"

Zavi nodded. "He needs one."

"How do you know that?"

"Because I need one."

Wynn was careful not to show a reaction to that admission, but it hit her hard. She held out her hand to him, then led him into her apartment. She drew a chair over to the door that led to the backstairs down to the lower parking lot behind the garage. Zavi stood on it and watched the back yard.

A couple of the guys fanned out from the steps to the lower terrace and went into the woods. They were fully armored and carried rifles of some sort. Wynn looked at Zavi to see if that bothered him. It didn't seem to be anything unusual for him. They waited five minutes, then five more.

"Hey, let your papa do what he can for the boy." She nodded toward the kitchen table. "We have shapes to study."

Zavi's dark eyes looked like she'd told him to kill a puppy. "He's hungry, Miss Wynn."

She tried to smile. "Papa will take the picnic lunch we made out to him."

Zavi blinked. "My friend will like that."

15

It was late that afternoon when Wynn next saw Angel. She was in the kitchen, visiting with Mandy, Ivy, and the kids. Both moms had the afternoon off, so Wynn was technically off the clock.

Angel looked tired and frustrated. His gaze went around the group, then settled on her. "Wynn, can I see you for a minute?"

"Sure." She got up from the table.

"Uncle Angel, did you find my friend?" Zavi asked.

"Not yet. But I think we will soon." He stepped out into the hallway.

"What's up?" Wynn asked. "Have you found Fox?"

"We have him cornered in the stables. I just came to get some treats to entice him out."

Wynn sighed. "He's a little boy, Angel. Go in there and talk to him."

"He's not a boy, he's a watcher, wily like his namesake. He's escaped every time we've gotten close to him."

"Then let me talk to him. I'll get him to come out."

He thought about that for a moment. "No. Too dangerous."

"You'll be nearby."

"No."

She gave him her irritated teacher look. "You do want to catch him today, don't you?" He didn't shoot that down. "I'll bring him an apple. When I have his trust, we'll come to the house."

"Okay. We'll try it. But don't get too close to him. The guys and I will be only feet away, watching over you."

Wynn went into the kitchen to grab a couple of apples from a bowl on the counter. "I'm going to take a walk with Angel. I'll be back in just a little while."

Mandy and Ivy gave her curious looks, but kept things light for the kids. "Have fun!"

Wynn looked up at Angel as they went down the back patio. He'd shucked his rifle and Kevlar vest. Now he just wore a tan tee and a black fleece pullover that matched his cargo pants and boots. The pullover hugged his bulky arms and showed off his narrow waist.

"What?" he snapped.

She shrugged and smiled. "I was just thinking how hot you are."

"Now? You're thinking that now?"

"Well, yeah."

He grunted an answer that she couldn't quite make out.

"I guess I can't compartmentalize as well as you can," she said.

"Thanks. Now I can't either." He stopped and drew her to a halt as well. Glaring down at her, he seemed to struggle for words. "Hold that thought."

"I do. All the time. When I should be sleeping, but I'm not, I think of you. And when I'm watching Zavi do his lessons, I think of you. And when we're having a meal at the big dining room table and you're glaring at me—like you are now—I think about you."

His brows lowered. "What is it that you think about me?"

Her mouth suddenly felt dry. "What you look like with your shirt off."

His eyes went wide open, as did his mouth. A wave of tension moved through him. "Shit." He looked away from her, then back at her. "Shit." He started walking again. "I'm not thinking about that right now."

Wynn fell into step beside him. "That's fine. But I am."

"You don't know what you're getting into."

"With you or with the watcher?"

"Me. We've got the watcher covered."

"I think I do," she said without looking at him.

He stopped again. So did she. She'd never seen a look on a man's face like the one he had just then. "Wynn. Wynn." He frowned. "I tried to let you go."

"I know."

"I should still let you go."

He started walking again. They were nearing the stables now. Wynn saw some of the guys standing outside. None of them wore their full gear. Maybe they thought it frightened the boy.

Wynn walked past them right into the shadows of the stables. There was a bench just inside the entrance. Sitting on it was the cooler she and Zavi had used earlier. Wynn felt a huge sense of relief. She opened it. Empty plastic bags were all that remained. The boy had to be starving to have eaten all they'd packed. At least he'd had a chance to eat before spending the day hiding from the men.

She looked around the long alley of the stables. There were so many hiding places—in the stalls, in the storerooms—and he could be anywhere. "Hey. I don't know if you can hear me, but thank you for bringing the cooler back."

No answer.

"I can put something warm in it for you to eat tonight. And if you don't come up to the big house, I'll be sure to bring you some blankets."

"Thank you," came a muffled voice. She looked over toward the stalls, but couldn't quite place him. Each of the stalls had an outside run, so sound bounced off several walls.

"What's your name?"

"Fox."

"Fox." Zavi had been right about his odd name. "I think little boys shouldn't have to live out here, fending for themselves."

"I'm not a boy. I'm a watcher."

That was just what Angel had said. Wynn figured out which stall he was hiding in. She walked over to lean against the wall next to its gate. She had to keep the boy's attention so that he wouldn't see the guys moving in from the run.

"Do watchers like apples?"

"Yes."

"I do too. I have one for you."

"Roll it under the gate."

"No. It's dirty in there. I'll hand it to you under the gate."

"You'll grab me."

"No, I won't. It's too awkward. I can't reach that far."

"You're trying to make me get caught."

"No, I'm just talking to you. The men outside would like to catch you. But me, I would just like you to trust me."

"Did you poison the apple?"

"Poison? No. See?" She took a bite of hers.

"Take a bite of the other one."

She took a bite of it. "They are both good. What made you think I would have poisoned the apple?"

"Mr. Edwards tried to give us poisoned juice. Lion saved us."

Mr. Edwards. The bastard. To think that fiend had been near these boys. "I don't like Mr. Edwards. He's an evil man. He hurt me. See?" She flattened her hand and held it so he could see it, even though she wasn't entirely certain where he was inside the stall. "It still hurts."

The boy stepped out of the shadows. He looked to be maybe eight or nine years old. His hair was blond and shaggy. He wore odd clothes, roughly sewn like something from a medieval village. Wynn's heart started to beat hard. Despite the boy's unusual appearance, she forced herself to remember he was like any other kid his age.

She was still holding her hand against the open bars of the stall gate. Tentatively, wary of any sudden movements, he walked over to her. Keeping his body a little ways from the gate, he reached out to touch her scarred hand through the bars. "He took Beetle. Lion told us to run."

The sight of the boy wavered through the tears in Wynn's eyes. To think even one of the boys was in the grasp of that bastard was a nightmare. "I'm glad you came here. Truly, the men outside are only worried for you."

"Did they make you come here to talk to me?"

"No. They don't make us do anything. I came because I was worried about you."

"Lion worries about us."

"I'm sure he does. He must be sick not knowing where you are."

"He told us to come here."

She handed him the apple. "So why are you hiding? Why not come inside the house?"

The boy took a bite. "I'm waiting for the rest of the watchers. I need to tell them how things work here."

"Well, I'll tell you how things work. One of the women who lives in the big house keeps the horses here. She uses them to teach people different things. Another of the women trains dogs at the kennel. Did you see it?"

"Yes."

"One of her dogs may be having puppies soon. Zavi desperately wants a puppy."

"I like puppies. Sometimes I would sneak away and go play with the ones the Friends have. Sometimes I would help the dogs the bikers were mean to."

Wynn took another bite of her apple. "That's where you came from, isn't it?"

"No. We were moved to another camp."

"Who moved you?"

"Mr. Edwards."

Wynn leaned back against the wall. "I hate that man." She still had her hand resting on one of the bars in the gate. She felt the boy reach through the gate to hold it. His hand was rough and not much smaller than hers.

"There aren't any girls in the watchers."

"Why not?" she asked.

"Because girls aren't warriors."

"We have two women here who are warriors. They're really tough."

"Not as tough as a watcher."

"Wait until you meet them before deciding that. I think some watchers even fought one of them. Selena."

"I heard about that."

"Do you mind if I open this gate? You don't have to come to the big house. You can stay here, of course, but I think you'll be more comfortable at the house."

"Watchers don't need comfort."

"What if Mr. Edwards came for you tonight? Just a few days ago, there were some men in the woods here with a boy. Was that you?"

"No." He looked worried. "I wonder if they got another of the boys. Or maybe that was Beetle."

"The men outside would like to hear the story about the poison. And Beetle. They could help you find the rest of your group. Will you come with me to the big house?"

"No."

"You'll be safe with us."

The boy's eyes widened. He straightened as if he were about to sprint away. Wynn turned to see what he was looking at. Some of the team were headed this way. Kit, Max, and Kelan. She looked back just as the boy disappeared around the far corner of the stall.

She hurried after him. She heard a distinct "ouff" in

a man's deep voice, then before she could leave the stable, Angel came in, carrying a struggling boy. He wiggled, kicked, hit, and struggled like a wild thing. Then he leaned down and bit Angel's collarbone.

"Sonofabitch!" Angel fisted the boy's hair and pulled his face away from him.

The other men had joined them by then.

"Put the boy down," Max ordered.

"Oh, no. This little hellion will bolt," Angel said as he stepped out of the stall.

"No, he won't," Max said as he glared at Fox, who had gone still. "He'll behave like a watcher, just like Lion taught him."

Angel's face rumpled up with distaste, but he set Fox down. The little guy straightened his shoulders and returned Max's hard stare.

Max nodded. "We have Lion's sister at the house. She would like to meet you. We've all been looking for you and the other cubs."

"Why?" Fox asked.

"To protect you."

"We protect you, not the other way around."

Max gave him a nod as if he were talking to a peer. "What's your name, cub?"

"Fox."

"Will you come to the house with us?" Max asked in a polite but commanding voice. "You won't be a prisoner. You can leave anytime, though I would prefer that you stay. We're trying to find all the cubs—and Lion."

"Why?"

"To get you to safety and out of the hands of our enemies. A war's coming."

"The cubs are all headed here."

Kit exchanged glances with Max. "We thought so, but why?" he asked.

"Lion told us to."

Max nodded. "Good. Then let's go inside. Dinner is almost ready."

The boy considered him, then nodded. Kit led the small group back toward the house. Max and Kelan flanked the boy. Angel held back, staying with Wynn for a second.

She knew questions were all over her face. "Are there still other prides out there? You said Ace had found a few and turned them in, but are there more?"

"We do think there are more."

"How many of these secret populations are there in this Omni world?"

"We're still figuring that out. It's proving to be a fucking hydra. Every time we cut one head off, more replace it. I think we're close to finding the body of the monster, and when we do, we can take it out."

He picked up the cooler and started after the guys, but she caught his wrist, stopping him. "Are you part of the resistance? Or something else?"

He sighed and squinted. "I'm not sure anything in this fight is simply one thing. All I know for certain is that we're fighting the bad guys, with the blessing of the

Feds. Unfortunately, the bad guys are widespread in places where it's hard to root them out—in government, corporations, and banks...in this country and every corner of the world."

She shook her head. "How are you going to fight this?"

"We're going to reach into the hydra and rip its heart out."

THERE WAS confusion in the house when Wynn and Angel came back to the living room. She noticed Angel fussing at his collar. A red smudge marked where the boy had bitten him. That needed to be cleaned.

She slipped her hand in his and led him through the dining room and kitchen, then to the backstairs. He kept their hands tight all the way upstairs, but in the hallway to her apartment, he stopped her. "What's this about, Wynn?"

She nodded to the blood on his shirt. "Your bite needs to be cleaned."

"Yeah, it does, but I can do it." His eyes were intensely focused on her. She would have let his hand go, but he was holding hers too tightly. His knees bumped her legs when she moved. Maybe it hadn't been such a good idea to bring him up to her apartment. She had no defenses against him.

But she wanted it that way, didn't she?

"Did you mean what you said outside?" he asked.

Wynn felt heat spread upward from her neck. What he wanted and what she wanted were exact opposites— now and forever. What had she been thinking earlier to reopen this can of worms?

Truth was, she wasn't thinking. She'd only been feeling. Those feelings were her truth. And truth was perhaps the only thing that could lead them through the shadows blocking their way.

She licked her lips. "When I went home after Grams' funeral, leaving you was the hardest part. We ended before exploring what was between us. You were something I would never know, and I regretted that. I don't want us to end." *Ever*.

Angel's nostrils flared. He braced his hands on either side of her head. She was a tall woman, but his size and height made her feel petite. She liked that.

She'd always been about self-control, managing her own life so that she didn't end up like her parents, swallowed by the passion they felt for their careers. This situation she, Angel, and the others were in felt similar. It consumed them, informed their choices, and likely would end them just as the work her parents had done had ended them...or at least ended the life they knew. This was a very dangerous thing to give in to.

She knew it—she just didn't want to fight it.

Wynn wrapped her fingers around his and pulled his hand away, then kissed his palm. How she wished things were different for them. While her eyes were closed, she felt him lift her palm to his mouth...her scarred palm. She tried to pull away, but his grip was unrelenting. His mouth was warm and soft against her puckered skin, his chin hard and bristly. Shattered by the gentleness of his gesture, she looked up at him. His eyes met hers in a hypnotic gaze.

She thought he was going to kiss her. She hungered for it with every cell in her body, though she knew it would make everything so much worse. He stared into her eyes. The heat she was feeling was electrifying. Maybe it was too late. Maybe she'd already given her soul to him.

"Okay. Here's how it's going to go—" he started, but she interrupted him, reining things in before they made a big leap to a place they couldn't get back from.

"I know how it's going to go. You're going to let me clean that bite. And then we're going to stay with Fox so that he doesn't feel alone here without his friends."

Angel's face tightened. He seemed seconds away from devouring her...and she was seconds away from letting him. She ducked beneath his arm and went into her apartment, feeling as if she were walking on a tightrope.

He followed her. She went straight to the little hall bathroom that she'd been in when he came to help her after Mr. Edwards had carved the butterfly into her palm. She felt the energy shift as he followed her into the small space. She looked at his reflection in the mirror. He'd removed his shirt, and now the broad wall of his muscled chest blocked the doorway. A light covering of hair sprinkled across his pecs and continued in a narrow line down to his jeans. She must have stared too long, because he grinned at her. His white teeth made such a contrast against the olive tone of his skin.

As she turned to face him, that tightrope underneath her feet shifted. She was off balance. She reached for him, grabbing at the only thing she knew was solid. Every muscle in his chest was starkly defined. He didn't reach for her, didn't interrupt her exploration. He stood before her, absolutely still. She leaned in to touch her face to his skin. She pulled a long draw of his simple scent—soap and sunshine. His lungs expanded beneath her palms. She heard the hiss he made and looked up at him, meeting dark brown eyes that had gone black, their pupils dilated.

He caught her hair and tilted her head back. Leaning over her, he crushed his mouth to hers. His kiss wasn't gentle, and Wynn was glad. She wanted him wild and free, fierce and passionate. She wrapped her arms around his chest and held on tight, giving as he took.

He let go of her hair to slip his arms around her, crushing her against his body. The whole thing was violent and over as fast as it had begun. They were both breathing hard as he looked into her eyes.

"Tell me again how you think this is going to go," he growled.

She didn't say anything. He'd taken control of it, of her, of them. Not having an answer, she pulled free and collected the things she needed to wash the bite marks —a washcloth, disinfectant, and bandages. When she closed the big mirrored cabinet door, her eyes settled on the huge man standing behind her. He looked at her in the mirror, then wrapped an arm about her waist and pulled her back against him.

Bending close, he nuzzled her neck, his breath hot against her hair. "I never wanted to feel this for anyone." His teeth raked her earlobe. "I fought it. I didn't want to bring the woman I cared about into the dark world I live in. I didn't want to subject her to the evil of the Omnis. But it occurs to me that by denying myself joy, the Omnis win. Again."

She set her hand on his forearm, moving it over his hand.

"I don't have a future to give anyone right now." He pressed his face against the side of her hair. "But we have now. Give me now."

"I want more than that, Angel." She pulled free and ran the washcloth under warm water, then squeezed the extra moisture out. Facing him, she held it to the bite marks for a second, gently dabbed at them, then squirted the Bactine over the circle of red marks, half of which had broken the skin.

"Wow. This looks like it hurts. The poor boy must have been terrified."

Angel shook his head. "Not terrified. Instinctive. He's a feral little thing."

"Where are his parents, do you think?"

Angel gave her a regretful look. "Dead. Disaffected. Doing whatever else King wants them to do other than parenting. The boy comes from a fucked-up system."

"That's so sad. It would kill me to know my children were out in the world, living wild."

Angel's hands settled on her hips. "That's why we're looking for Lion and his cubs."

It was hard to think when surrounded by his arms and body. She could feel his heat and power. His breath was sweet. He slowly, slowly closed the distance between them. She took a chance on this thing she knew they were both feeling—and fighting—by leaning in to him ever so slightly. She breathed in his scent. No perfumes. Just Angel.

She still held the washcloth in one hand, but her other was free to flatten against his pec. She leaned her forehead against his neck on the side opposite his cut. "Angel," she whispered. His name was like an endearment in itself, but she hadn't meant it to also sound like a sigh.

"Wynnie."

That nickname was one her grandmother had used forever. She was gone now, because of the work Angel and his team did—a good reminder why she had to keep her eyes open and not take anything for granted.

She pushed free and reached for the gauze bandage and tape she'd set out. She tried to be coldly professional about what she was doing, but he was standing so close, and he smelled so good, that it was hard to keep her mind on the task.

When she finished, she stepped back and looked up at him. Tension had drawn his face taut. She frowned. "Does it hurt much?"

He shook his head. His chin was tucked in. There was an edge in his eyes as he watched her.

"What is it?"

He lowered his head to hers. When their faces were too close to focus, his gaze went to her mouth. Then his lips touched there. She shivered. She fought the urge to touch him with every ounce of willpower she had and still failed. Her hands caught his muscled waist. She returned his kiss, just that light touch at first, then opening beneath his as his tongue searched for hers. He caught her face in his hands and angled her head a little. She surrendered herself to him, taking what he gave and hungering for more.

Her arms traveled higher up his back, holding his body to hers, her nails digging into his bare skin. She didn't know if the groan she felt in her mouth came from him or her. Both, maybe. When the kiss ended, she couldn't keep herself from stroking his chest one last time. His arms went around her back. She leaned her face against his chest. For a long moment, neither of them spoke.

Angel broke the silence. "I think they may be holding dinner for us." He offered her a smile. She could tell he was as shaken as she was. She nodded and moved to the side so that he could open the door. When he walked out, she gasped, stopping him in his tracks. She held a hand to her mouth, but she couldn't hide the furious heat blooming across her neck and face.

His brows lowered as he turned to look at her.

"Don't go downstairs like that. Please."

"Why?"

She gestured toward his back. "Because I... Because you have... Oh, God. I'm so sorry. I—"

He hunched his back and looked in the mirror at the set of little red marks. He looked angry as he straightened and faced her. He walked back. Catching her chin in his hand, he leaned close. "No matter how we fight this, we aren't finished."

"We have to be, if this isn't going anywhere, because every time we're together, I lose a little bit more of me to you and you to me. Soon, there won't be anything left of me in me or you in you. Ending it then will kill us."

He dropped his hand, letting a sliver of space slip between them. "So forever or nothing."

She nodded.

He looked at her lips. "Forever doesn't exist, Wynn." His gaze lifted to her eyes. "There's only now."

"I believe in forever."

He shook his head. He pivoted and left her room.

16

W ynn went down the hall a few minutes later. The house was buzzing with animated conversations. Whatever Russ had made for supper, it smelled delicious. She stopped at the top of the stairs in the northern wing, her senses taking it all in. This huge, rambling house, with its diverse group of occupants, suddenly felt like home.

What an awful time for that to happen, when her heart felt like it was breaking. When this was all over, she was going to have to leave these people, leave Zavi and his family. Leave Angel—again. Before the panic fully took root in her chest, she saw him coming down the hallway. He frowned at her.

Scratch that. Her heart was definitely fully broken.

"Ready to go down?" he asked.

"Yes, but you don't have to go with me."

A muscle ticked in the corner of his jaw. "I told you

I believe in now. Now is when I have you within arm's reach. Now is when I can sit next to you at dinner. Now is real. Tomorrow isn't. Yesterday isn't. I am not about to fucking lose my now with you."

He held his hand out. She took it and pretended being near him didn't hurt as they walked down the stairs.

"Fox has had a bath," Angel said. "Blade's dad fetched clothes for him that Ivy borrowed from a friend. Mandy and Rocco are with him and Zavi in the kitchen. Mandy thought the watcher would be over-whelmed by all of us if we made him eat in the dining room."

"I'd like to join them."

Angel nodded. They paused outside the kitchen entrance. "She said you're welcome." He stared at her a moment. "Want me to stay with you?"

Yes. She felt guilty ditching him after hearing his "now" meant he got to sit next to her at supper. "I'm afraid you and Rocco together would scare him."

"Truthfully, I think Fox would be more comfortable with Rocco and me than he would with you ladies. The watchers have no female members and don't interact with women at all. It's you and Mandy that may scare him."

"That's odd."

"This whole thing is fucking odd. Kit wants to talk to the boy after dinner. Hopefully, we'll be able to find out more about him and what's going on with the other boys then." He kissed her forehead. "I'll be in the dining room. If you need me, if that watcher scares you, just shout."

She smiled. "He's a kid. Believe it or not, I've been professionally trained to deal with little boys." Just not big ones.

"Right." He didn't leave, just watched her with his worried eyes.

She smiled and gently pushed his chest. "Go. I'll be fine. I'm sorry about missing dinner with you."

"Me too."

She stepped into the kitchen.

"Hi, Miss Wynn," Mandy said. "Want to join us for dinner?"

"I would. Thank you." She smiled at Zavi then nodded at Fox, who gave her a dark look. He seemed just about ready to bolt. Maybe Angel had been right about the boy being feral. His borrowed clothes were just a little too big. His wet hair looked brown against the white of his tee.

Russ and Jim brought over a bowl of salad, the dressings, a basket of Italian bread, and a big dish of penne pasta. They also brought over a platter of parmesan chicken and a big bowl of marinara sauce. All of it smelled delicious. They filled two plates, then took them over to the kitchen counter to eat.

Wynn realized that they were staying in the kitchen to give Rocco backup in case something happened with the boy. She looked at the back door, wondering if it was locked.

So much precaution for one little boy. What was it about watchers that put everyone on edge?

Wynn took a seat at the kitchen table. Mandy filled her plate, as she had with everyone else at the table. An awkward silence filled the group. Rocco ate without really noticing his food, as if it was just something to get through so he could move on to the next thing. Mandy moved slowly and carefully, probably so she wouldn't spook Fox. Only Zavi seemed himself. Several times he would kneel in his chair and start a conversation with Fox, which the newcomer only half listened to. The watcher's gaze moved about the room, noting people and exits. His only ease seemed to come when his gaze settled on Mandy's two dogs.

"That's Yeller and Blue," Wynn said.

"They're my dogs," Zavi said.

"They love everyone," Mandy said. "They were runaways and had no home and no family."

Fox made the connection she was skirting. "I'm not a runaway. I have a pride for my family."

Mandy answered, "You're very fortunate for that." Wynn admired her easy grace with the boy.

Silence fell among the group again. Wynn struggled to find a topic of discussion that would ease the tension. "We've been studying shapes this week." She smiled at Zavi. "After we covered the basics—"

Zavi finished the story for her: "After we learned

them in English, Papa taught us how to say them in Spanish, Pashto, and Arabic."

"I'm getting quite the education," Wynn said, smiling at Mandy.

They talked about their lessons for a little while. Fox looked interested but didn't participate in the conversation. When they were just about finished with their meal, there was a commotion in the dining room. Rocco received some communication from his earpiece.

He nodded, then tapped it and said, "Copy." He looked at Mandy. "Sheriff Tate is coming to the front door. We'll stay put here."

Fox looked worried.

"There's nothing to fear, Fox," Wynn said.

"I'm not afraid." The boy gave her a frosty glance. Wynn wasn't convinced—he looked ready to jump out of his skin.

"No harm will come to you here," Rocco assured him.

"You'll hand me over to Mr. Edwards."

"Never," Rocco said.

Everyone went silent, straining to hear what was going on in the other room. A quick look from Rocco had Russ and Jim taking up positions by the hallway door and the patio door. Wynn was impressed with how fluid that directive was delivered and followed. Both men stood in their positions as if nothing unusual at all was happening.

ANGEL WASN'T the only one looking at his phone after the alert came through. The security app showed the sheriff and his deputy coming up the front walk.

Kit stood up. Setting his napkin on the table, he excused himself. "Angel, with me," he ordered.

They went to the foyer, opening the door before the last chimes of the doorbell ended. What they saw wasn't what Angel was expecting.

The sheriff had his hands on the shoulders of two young watchers. Another boy—a teenager—stood between him and Deputy Jerry. Kit stepped back and let them in. Tate looked pissed. Kit kept his face blank.

Goddamn, Angel wanted to hug those boys.

Took the sheriff a minute to find his words. "These boys showed up at the station. Said they were looking for Mad Dog."

"Max!" Kit bellowed. Max joined them in the foyer.

The sheriff shifted his gaze to Max. "I'm guessing that would be you."

"Yup," Max said.

"Why are they coming here if they belong to the community up the street?"

"Safe harbor," Max answered.

"Safe harbor from what?"

Kit looked at Max. "I'll take the sheriff and Deputy Jerry to the den for a chat. How about you and Angel get the boys settled?"

Jerry pulled the boys behind him. "They ain't going anywhere with you. You don't have custody over them."

A muscle ticked in Kit's jaw. "We don't. It's true. But the FBI does. Our contact is on his way now."

Sheriff Tate nodded at his deputy to let the boys go.

Kɪᴛ ʟᴇᴅ the way down the hall to the den. He closed the door behind them, then leaned against the desk. "How did you find them?" he asked. "We've been searching for them ever since finding their campsite."

"I didn't find them. They were dropped off at the station. All of them said the same thing—that they'd been freed from a trafficking group and needed to be brought to Mad Dog. Now, I didn't know no Mad Dog, but I know you've been looking for the boys. And they all had the same label sewn in their clothes with your address." Tate gave Kit a hard glare. "I'm not a fan of crazy in my town, son."

"I know. Nor am I."

"So I think I'll hang around and talk to Mr. Villalobo."

"Yeah. He'll be here shortly."

Tate's brows lifted. "You knew I was coming?" He shot his deputy a glance.

"No. We have another boy here," Kit said.

"Told you to tell me if any boys showed up."

"He just got here. Was going to call you after supper."

"Four boys. When's this gonna end?"

"I guess when another dozen or so show up."

"Goddammit," Tate snapped. "I had hoped months ago that this would be a short-term assignment for you guys."

"I wish you were right. Every time I think we're getting close, something else blows up." Tate gave him a hard look. Kit held a hand up. "Just a figure of speech."

The door opened and Lobo came in. He shook hands with the sheriff and his deputy. Kit brought him up to speed.

Lobo addressed the sheriff: "None of us are happy with this situation. Nothing about it speaks to a situation we'd expect to have happen here in Wolf Creek Bend—or anywhere in the U.S. These children are in a dangerous predicament. We will be reuniting them with their parents, where possible, or rehoming them with stable foster families in their community if their families cannot be found, just as soon as it's safe. Their community is in flux. Returning them there at this point could send them back into the danger they've just escaped from. For now, I'm going to have them fostered here."

"Here?" Kit asked, frowning.

"Yes. You have the space and the infrastructure. You've a teacher in residence, plenty of food, and the ability to protect them while we identify and notify their families." Lobo turned back to the sheriff. "How many have shown up so far?"

"Three came to us," the sheriff said. "One came here. I'm hearing there could be a lot more yet to show up."

Lobo looked at Kit. "How many were in Lion's group?"

"I'll ask Max, but I think it's a little over a dozen, not including Lion. We counted fifteen cups of poison at the campsite."

Lobo nodded. "Let's find them and get them all accounted for. I'm not comfortable with kids being out on their own. Especially knowing what we do about the organization they came from."

"And what is that, specifically?" Jerry asked.

Lobo met the deputy's curious gaze. "You don't have clearance to know."

The deputy took a step closer to him. "Don't get all high and mighty with your FBI shit. If this town, its residents, and these kids are in danger, the sheriff and I need to know."

Lobo nodded. He opened the den door and stood next to it. "Agreed. When that situation occurs, you'll be read in." He shook hands with them as they left the den.

Kit followed them into the hallway and down to the foyer. "Thanks for bringing the boys over, Sheriff. When more show up, let us know. Day or night. You have my number."

ANGEL FOLLOWED Max and the boys. They paused at the powder room in the hallway outside the kitchen. The boys were tired and looked thirsty and hungry, but generally no worse for the wear. "Wash up. Then I'll get you some dinner. You hungry?"

"Starving," one of the younger ones said.

"Are you really Mad Dog?" the oldest boy asked.

Angel considered Max, realizing he'd cleaned up some since Hope moved in—he probably looked different than he had when he was with the WKB. Max grinned as he rubbed his chin, which still had gone a few days without a razor.

"I am. Lion's sister's my girlfriend. You'll be safe here." The younger boys were in the bathroom washing their hands and faces, sucking water from the tap. The teenager waited in the hallway with them. "We have a lot of questions for you. Lion said we can trust you."

"You can."

Max and the boy exchanged stares until the little ones came out of the bathroom. The teenager took his turn, then Angel directed them toward the kitchen.

"Where are we going?" the teenager asked.

"Fox is eating dinner in here," Max said. "Thought you'd like to say hello."

"Fox is here? Where?"

"Just in the kitchen. Go ahead," Angel said, pointing the way to the kitchen.

"Fox! You made it," one of the younger boys said, laughing and smiling.

Fox jumped up from the table and hugged the new arrivals.

Wynn and Rocco began clearing the table as Mandy brought over fresh plates, silverware, and glasses for the new boys. Jim refilled the serving dishes. In no time, the table was turned over.

"Zavi," Mandy said, holding out her hand to her son, "time to go upstairs."

Zavi was standing on his seat. He tucked in his chin, as Wynn had seen Rocco do a few times. "Mom, can't I stay and talk to my new friends?"

Mandy checked Rocco, who nodded. "He can stay while they eat."

Jim told the boys to help themselves.

"They have all you can eat here." Fox set his hands on his stomach. "I've been eating all day."

Without further chatter, the boys filled their plates. Bending low over the table, they rapidly shoveled it into their mouths.

"Whoa." Mandy chuckled. "Slow down. There's plenty. And like Fox said, if we run out of dinner, we'll find something else for you to eat, if you're still hungry."

Wynn filled glasses with ice water. "Besides, eating fast will just give you the hiccups."

The boys looked up, food overfilling their mouths. They sent each other looks, but straightened and finished chewing before adding more to the mix.

Angel smiled at Wynn. She was good with children. That thought, for some odd reason, gave him a total hard-on. He crossed his arms and tried to focus on something else...anything else, which might have happened had Wynn not come to stand next to him. He became aware of the little cuts her nails had made in his back. He flexed his shoulders to try feeling the minor stings.

"What are your names, boys?" Mandy asked.

The teenager swallowed, then gulped some water. "I'm Badger. That's Coyote and that's Wren."

"Nice to meet you. I'm Mandy. This is my husband, Rocco. Zavi's our son. This is Miss Wynn, Zavi's teacher. You know Max. That's Angel."

The boys nodded at them. For the next few minutes, they were focused on eating while Zavi told them about meeting Fox in the woods, and then the hunt to find him. Fox told them about eluding the men for most of the day, until Miss Wynn tricked him into getting caught.

"I'm sorry for that, Fox," Wynn said. "We were just very worried about you. And I knew you were hungry."

Fox nodded. "I was."

The door to the kitchen from the dining room opened as everyone began to clear the big table. Casey came over to say hello to the boys. Kit flanked her. Max stepped closer, too, forcing Casey to move behind them slightly.

Casey pushed them aside, or tried to. "Dad, Uncle Max, stop. It's rude for me not to say hello."

"So say it and move along," Kit growled.

Casey waved to the boys through the narrow column of space her dad and Max allowed. "I'm Casey." She pointed a thumb at Kit. "This is my dad, Kit Bolanger. He looks mean like a bear, but he's really not."

Kit frowned. "No, I really am." He looked at his daughter. "After they finish eating, I want you to take Zavi upstairs."

She nodded.

"I'll go with you," Wynn said.

Zavi made a face. "That's fine, Miss Wynn, but can you not read to us until they come to bed, too?"

Wynn laughed. "There are plenty of books in this house. We can read more than one story tonight."

"Okay."

The kitchen grew loud as food was being put away and dishes were being done. When Casey and Zavi headed up, Wynn followed.

Angel caught her hand before she left the kitchen and leaned close. "I'll catch you up later."

She nodded. The warmth in her eyes went right to his groin.

ANGEL CAME upstairs a little while later to get Wynn. Kit was intent on getting debriefed about what had happened to the pride, and Angel didn't want Wynn to miss out on that discussion. He was glad Kit was letting the women join them. If the kids were going to be staying here, they needed to be in on the decisions that had to be made concerning their addition to the household. Hell, everything from here out was going to affect them in some way.

Zavi and Casey were both up, watching TV, already in PJs. "Wynn—mind if I borrow you for a while?"

She looked up at him and smiled. Her gentle expression arrested the breath in his chest.

"Case, do you mind staying with Zavi?"

"Sure, Uncle Angel."

"You do still have your security necklace, right?"

She frowned as worry whispered across her features. "Yeah. I got it." She lifted the beaded chain and showed him.

"Good," Wynn said, trying to offset her concern. She showed Casey her necklace. "I have mine, too. We won't be long."

"We might be a while," Angel corrected.

Wynn looked at her watch. "At eight, Zavi's to go to bed." She looked at her charge. "Understand?"

"I don't want to go to bed that early."

Wynn laughed. "That's the time you go to bed every night."

"But tonight, there are other kids here."

"Yes. And you'll be able to see them tomorrow. No arguments."

"Yes, Miss Wynn. But Casey has to go to bed then, too."

"No, Casey doesn't have to until nine. Good try."

She kissed them both, then followed Angel.

THE TENSION in Angel's face tested her nerves. "What's this about?" she asked when they were a good distance away from the kids.

"We're going to find out what's happening with the watchers, where the rest of the pride is. I wanted you to be there for that. Lobo, our FBI handler, wants them fostered here, which means you'll likely be on point to deal with them and maybe add them to your classroom."

"I'd like that. I know Zavi will as well. But if there are a dozen or so boys, I don't think our small classroom will work."

"Those are the things we need to figure out."

They walked down the main stairs. The group was gathering in the living room. The furniture had been rearranged so that all four boys sitting on the sofa were the center of attention.

Kit was pacing the length of the room as he waited for everyone to get settled. When everyone was there, he stopped next to the armchair Ivy was sitting in and faced the boys. Ivy tugged on his shirt and indicated he should perch himself on its arm. He did.

"Tell me your names and ages, please," Kit said.

"Is this a council meeting?" the oldest of the boys asked. "Are we on trial?"

"You are not on trial. And this isn't a council meeting. Consider us family." Kit sent a glance around the group. "We are all family. Lion would not have sent you to us if he didn't trust and respect us. Your names and ages, please."

From left to right, the boys sounded off. "I'm Fox. I'm nine."

"I'm Wren. I'm eight."

"I'm Coyote. I'm eleven."

"I'm Badger. I'm fifteen."

Kit nodded. He pointed around the room, calling off names. He saved Hope for last, though she was the most anxious of all of them to meet the boys. "How many boys are in your pride?"

"We have fifteen, sir," Badger said.

"There are more of you than there were at the WKB compound," Max said.

Badger nodded. "Two more joined us in the new camp."

"What happened after you left your old camp?" Max asked.

"We were taken to other camps, still in the mountains. The last one was southeast of our old home."

Angel looked the little group over. They were lean, sharp-eyed boys. Blond- and brown-haired. Fair skinned. Loyal and brave, all of them.

"We saw your camp. Looked like there was a fight. Tell us what happened," Kit said.

Badger looked at the other boys. "We'd been training to come here. The day we actually left started out like many others over the weeks we were there. We made the trek down to the highway. We were just getting back when everything happened."

Badger sent Fox a dark look. "We each had a group we were to stay with for the trip here. Each group was given a route through the woods, which we were to follow until we reached this house."

"What happened to your group?" Kit asked Fox.

"We were chased into the woods," Fox said. We had to split up. I tried to the find Vole and Spider but I couldn't, so I headed toward the highway myself. A car stopped. They seemed nice. They said they would take me to Wolf Creek Bend. So I went with them."

Max crossed his arms and tucked his hands under his armpits. He glared at Fox. "Your enemies and ours are powerful and cruel opponents, cub. You took a risk, and this time it paid off. In the future, you will not get into a stranger's car. Instead, I expect you to run like hell."

Fox nodded. "Yes, sir."

"Tell us about the fight at the camp," Kit said.

The younger boys exchanged nervous glances as Badger continued. "Mr. Edwards was in the camp when we got back. They brought two vehicles. I wondered if they were going to move us again, and I worried about all of the supplies caches we'd placed in strategic places in the woods for when the time came for us to bug out.

"Mr. Edwards came into the mess hall and walked around us, checking each of us out. One of his men brought in a tray, a stack of cups, and a drink container. He poured juice into the cups and told us to drink. Lion took the first one."

A gasp across the room caught Angel's attention. Hope had a white-knuckled grip on Max's thigh.

"Go on," Kit said.

"Lion told the man holding the cups to take a drink of it first. Mr. Edwards made his man do it. Lion watched him for a few minutes, then shouted that it was poison and told us to run." He looked at the two boys who'd been found with him. "Each of us older boys were put in charge of a couple of the younger ones. I caught my cubs as they entered the woods. I told them to wait for me at our designated rendezvous location. When I knew they were secure, I went back. I saw Lion and Hawk fighting with two of Mr. Edwards' men. And I saw Mr. Edwards drag Beetle out of the mess hall and into one of the SUVs. I don't know why he did that."

"Shit," Kit snapped. "Do you know what happened to Lion?"

"No. I waited while the vehicles drove away, then I went up to the mess hall. I saw the dead men, but not Lion or Hawk. I talked to Squirrel, who was in Hawk's group. He and Mouse were waiting for Hawk at their rendezvous spot. I tried to get them to come with us, but they refused, didn't want to change the plan."

Max exchanged glances with Kit. "There could still be boys waiting in the woods for their group leaders. We need to get out there."

Kit nodded then looked at Badger. "Do you know the other rendezvous spots?"

The cub nodded. "I can show Mad Dog."

"Head up early tomorrow so that you're there at first light. Take Val and Kelan with you."

Ivy stood up. "That's enough for now. I think it's time these boys got some rest."

"There's an empty room next to my room upstairs," Selena said, standing to go upstairs with Ivy.

The boys stood as well. Badger was as tall as Selena was. He frowned at her. "I remember you. That night in the woods."

Selena's smile was anything but nice. "It was memorable. I look forward to having Mouse under my roof."

Mandy and Remi joined the small group. "We'll get them settled, then we'll be back down," Mandy told the group. Rocco frowned and followed them up the stairs.

Wynn watched them leave the room, surprised how little the team trusted the watchers.

"FROM THE SOUNDS OF THINGS, there will be about ten other boys heading this way—eleven when we find Beetle," Kit said. "We need to figure out where we're going to put them."

Wynn looked around at the group sitting in the living room. The kids had gone to sleep more than an hour ago. It was odd to be sitting here with the team discussing this out in the open. Her old instinct to distance herself pulled at her. As if reading her thoughts, Angel perched on the arm of her chair and reached for her hand.

Heat filled her cheeks. She supposed it wouldn't surprise anyone that they were seeing each other. He grinned at her, that dirty I-would-so-much-rather-be-alone-in-your-apartment grin of his.

"The construction in the basement is almost finished," Kit said. "We could make bunkrooms down there for the boys."

"No," Ty nixed that. "You want to use that for offices or for classes during the day, fine. No boys are living down there."

"Some of them could use the extra room in our wing," Ivy offered.

"No. You guys need that for your nursery," Eden said.

"Eventually," Ivy said. "But at first, I'm sure the baby will sleep in our room."

"There are two rooms upstairs in the main corridor that we could convert to kid rooms with bunk beds," Eden said. "They're big rooms. We could put three sets of bunks in them."

"We still need a little more space. There are thirteen boys, but also Hawk and Lion," Max pointed out. "We're gonna need a third room."

"We could put some of them in the bunkroom in the bunker," Kelan suggested.

Kit shook his head. "I don't want a bunch of kids down there."

"They aren't kids, Kit," Max said. "Haven't been for a long time. They're warriors now."

"How about the basketball court?" Val asked. "Plenty of room for several prides in there."

Wynn looked around, surprised that that option was being seriously considered. "No," she said. Everyone looked at her.

"Wynn, these boys are not regular kids," Angel said. "They're warriors. Their training is the only thing that helped them survive their journey alone through dangerous terrain."

Her heart was pounding. The boys needed someone to look out for them. Little Wren was no more than eight years old. "They're not warriors. In this house, they're children—children who need to be cherished."

"You can't undo what's been done," Ty said.

"Maybe not, but we can help them move forward from this point. They aren't going to be banished to some distant wing. They can have my apartment. I'll take one of the spare rooms."

"That might work," Max said. "The boys are used to being together. Six bunks could fit in the living room area of her apartment. Hawk and Lion could take the master."

Wynn nodded.

"No," Mandy said as she came back into the room. Wynn realized that Rocco had stayed up with the kids.

261

"Wynn, more than any of us, needs space to retreat from the boys since she's going to be spending the most time with them. I think we should look at consolidating rooms."

"Now that Kelan and I are together, I don't need my old room," Fiona said. "That gets us to the three bedrooms."

"And Ty and I can give up one of our old rooms, too. That makes four open rooms." Eden looked at Fiona. "Let's plan on that anyway. We can always use those rooms for guests or new teammates or something."

Fiona nodded. "Good idea."

Ty chuckled. "Can't believe we've almost filled the twenty bedrooms in this house."

"If it's all right with everyone, I'd like to keep the extra room Greer and I have. I'm using it for a study," Remi said.

"That's fine," Eden said. "We don't need it."

"I haven't used my room for a while," Hope said, giving Max a private smile. "So that's another open one."

"And you've got my old room, too," Ace said.

"Then we're good," Kit said. "Maybe we could just consolidate the boys' rooms in the same block, in case they get scared or something. I'll call Owen's office and put in an order for furniture. Wynn, let me know what we need to order."

"I'll put a list together," she said. "We'll need clothes and other supplies, too. Sheets. Towels."

"That all sounds good," Kit said. "There's something else we need." He shot Ace a look. "You said that one of your handler's operatives took DNA from the cubs before administering their smallpox vaccines. We need those records so that we can work on matching these boys to their families. I want to return them as soon as it's safe to do so."

"I can only get that info through Jax," Ace said, "and he hasn't responded to me yet. I don't think he's returned any of the other watchers to their families. Maybe because it wasn't safe. Maybe for some other reason. I don't know. Owen needs to know that his son was taken by Edwards."

"If Jax didn't hand the boys over, what did he do with them?" Blade asked.

"I don't know," Ace replied. "I always assumed he had a safe place to shelter them. He wouldn't have harmed them. At least, I don't think he would have."

"Kit—I'm not sure handing the boys back to their families, or what's left of their families, is the best thing for them," Remi said. "Some of these boys have been in the pride longer than not. The pride's become their family. Let's just stay open about what we do with them."

"Their families deserve to know their boys are alive and well," Ty said.

"They do," Remi agreed. "This won't be easy or straightforward, but we have to put their welfare first."

17

The meeting broke up shortly after they resolved the room situation. Wynn wondered about Jax. Besides being Ace's handler, he seemed to have a bigger relationship to the group, given the way they talked about him. She asked Angel that question as he walked her to her apartment.

He sighed and swiped his hand over his head. "I've told you a lot of what's going on, but there's more."

"Like what?"

"Relationship stuff. Some of it you may know. Like the fact that Ace is Greer's sister. I told you that she was raised inside the Omni world. Hope is Lion's half-sister, which you know. But you may not know that Lion and Fiona are also half-siblings, or that Lion and his boys kidnapped Casey and Selena for a short while as a distraction to help one of our enemies infiltrate us." He shook his head. "Jax and Owen grew up together. They went into the Army together. Owen was in love with Jax's sister. Jax's father, along with Greer's grandfather and Owen's dad, were instrumental in getting the Red Team unit started in the Army."

"Wow. Those ties are intense. Not even six degrees of separation."

"And they were all hidden from us when we started. It's taken us a while to untangle them." They reached her door. He gave her a worried look. "You gonna be all right alone tonight?"

She nodded. "I'm going to work on the list of things Kit needs to order for the boys. I wish I knew the ages of the other boys who haven't gotten here yet."

"Don't stress over it. Get multiples of everything. If one boy can't use it, another will."

"Good idea. How old do you think the youngest is?"

"Beetle was six when he was taken from his mom. There was another boy about that age who died of smallpox. I guess you should assume that to be the youngest in the group. Twenty-one or so would probably be the oldest, like Lion."

"Six years old. That's horrible."

"Yeah. Ace has been looking for Beetle for the last three years. He should be nine now."

"Does Owen know his son is a watcher?"

"I'm not sure. The intel we have isn't definitive until we get the boy's DNA to compare to Owen's."

Wynn was speechless. The Omnis were a vile,

corrupt group, and until the FBI sicced Angel and his team on them, no one was doing anything about them.

Angel shoved his hands in his pockets. "Okay. So, I'm gonna take off."

"Night, Angel."

He gave her a little grin. "You were fierce down there, you know. We all look at the watchers as mini guerrilla fighters. You see them as boys. They need you. I'm glad you spoke up."

"I hope the other boys show up soon. I'm worried about them."

"We all are. Night, Wynn." He leaned over and kissed her cheek.

~

ANGEL PULLED a pair of jeans over his bare ass. His skin was still damp from his shower. He ran a hand over the bulge in the front of his jeans. He'd eased himself in the shower, but already he was burning again...for a pair of kind blue-brown eyes and lips that were soft under his.

For passion that left its mark on him.

For Wynn. *His* Wynn.

He stood sideways in the doorjamb of the bathroom. Leaning his forearm against the jamb, he dropped his head on it, trying to mentally cool himself down. Just thinking of her made his cock throb. There was no way he could go to sleep while he was in this torment. And he sure as hell couldn't bust his way into her apartment. He'd said he'd shelter her, take this slowly, but who was going to protect her from him?

He thought back to the first time he'd met her, with her big eyes and sweet face. Innocence personified. He'd known right then, right there, he was going to make her his—a visceral knowledge that had nothing to do with logic or reason or even his best intentions. It was like some gear had shifted into place, linking them as one.

Now or forever. If he were honest with himself, he'd admit he wanted more than just now; he wanted the forever that Wynn saw for them. Wanting—hell, needing—something didn't mean it was the right thing for them. Sometimes, the thing you were jonesing for was the very thing that would kill you. How could he lie to her and say he'd give her forever when he didn't believe in it? Especially when she would never be his first priority. Whatever war or battle or enemy he was fighting would always dictate his actions.

He startled as a cool hand touched his shoulder. His head shot up.

Wynn. She was here, in his room. He glared at her, his eyes burning like the rest of him.

She looked worried. "Angel? Are you all right? I knocked, but you didn't answer, and I didn't want to wake anyone, so I let myself in."

He stared down at her, aware that she'd spoken but clueless as to what she'd said. "Wynn." His voice was a dry rasp. He had to warn her away; he was too weak to resist her. He'd promise her anything, any fucking thing, if she'd just let him into her body right then.

"Wynn...*run*."

She blinked and frowned, trying to make sense of what he was saying.

He straightened. "Get the hell outta here, while you can."

Not only did she not move, she gave him one of those looks that probably worked like magic on children...but not a man on fire. "If there's anything I've learned in all of this, Angel Cordova, it's that I don't ever have to run from you."

His breath left him in a rush. He shut his eyes, willing her to leave. He had no control over himself. She deserved sweet, slow, patient lovemaking, not a savage joining, which if she stayed, was what would happen.

Please. Leave. Go. The room was silent. He opened his eyes. She was still there, watching him with concerned eyes. She couldn't know that the fire he was fighting was about to consume her too.

He closed the space between their bodies to grip the back of her head, half surprised her hair didn't burst into flames at his touch. He lowered his face to hers, feeling her sweet breath against his mouth. "I warned you."

He took her lips, turning her head to maximize contact between them as he opened his mouth and thrust his tongue between her teeth. She opened for him, giving him what he needed.

He caught her face between his hands and held his face against hers. "Wynn. Jesus. Wynn. I tried to fight this. I tried, but I can't anymore. So leave now. Or stay and become what you are: mine. Now *and* forever."

He paused the short length of breath. She didn't pull away. In fact, her hands were on his back. God, her eyes were big and innocent.

"Angel...I don't have any mittens. I can't protect you from me."

Took him a second to understand her reference. When it clicked she was talking about the marks her nails had made earlier that day, he laughed, his mouth against hers. "Fuck it all. Do your worst. I seriously won't even notice. And I kind of like those little stings in my back. Reminds me of you when we're not together."

He kissed her jaw, her chin, then took her mouth again. She hooked her hands over his shoulders, lifting herself up against him. Her kimono and silky nightgown were soft, like her skin, except the fabric was cold and her skin was hot, and the friction between the two set his nerves on edge.

He untied her kimono and pushed it from her shoulders, letting it drop to the ground. He slowly backed her up to the wall. Pulling her nightgown up in fistfuls, he finally touched her bare legs. No human should be so soft. He rubbed his hand along the side and back of her thigh. Moving his hand upward ever so slowly, he kissed the crook of her neck, burying his face in her shoulder, licking and nipping at her skin. He hadn't shaved after his shower and now worried what his rough stubble might do to her delicate skin, but she had a hand on the back of his head, holding him against her. She was gonna have a little beard rash, but she didn't seem to mind. He growled at that thought.

He moved his hand up under the skirt of her nightgown, slipping over the stretchy fabric of her panties. Her curves were luscious. Delicious. He wanted to see and taste every bit of her. He caught her hands in his, then held them up against the wall. Spreading her legs with his, he ground himself against her core.

He couldn't wait to make her sigh, make her scream, make her body weep for him. He moved both of her hands to one of his, freeing his other hand to roam her body. He kissed her as his hand moved from her hips to her ribs, then up to her big breasts.

"Wynn, do you like this nightgown?"

She opened her eyes and stared at him with some concern. "I do. Don't you?"

"I do. A lot. But I was thinking if we don't take it off soon, it's going to get ripped."

Her brows lifted. "Losing self-control?"

"I told you to run. I wasn't being dramatic."

She leaned forward and gave him a quick kiss on the lips, then pulled her hands free. She shrugged out of the thin spaghetti straps, pausing to look at him before lowering the gown.

"The count of three, I'm ripping it open." Her eyes

widened. "Three." He reached for the gown, but she'd slipped it down to her hips. He hissed as he looked at her bare breasts. After a second, he drew a long breath and braced his hands on the wall behind her. "The count's still on, Wynn, and you're not naked," he growled.

"Nor are you."

He unzipped his jeans and shoved them off his hips then kicked them aside. His cock was thick and hard, throbbing under her intense regard. "Your turn."

She pushed her nightgown over her hips and stepped out of it.

He put his hands on his hips and glared at her white undies. "Everything."

She pushed those down her legs, too. Unlike the thick, dark hair around his cock, her sex was neatly trimmed in a small triangle of tawny hair. He had to slow his roll. She deserved the best he could give, not a fast pounding but a slow seduction.

He closed his eyes and drew a long breath, then took her hand and led her over to his bed. "Wynn, do you remember when we met? That lunch on your first day?"

She nodded.

He wrapped his arms around her body and drew her close. "I knew something monumental happened then, between you and me. It was like my soul knew yours."

"I was so overwhelmed. You guys are really intimidating. But I felt that too."

He stared into her eyes. "It was like our souls hugged, though only our hands touched. You think that's possible?"

She reached up and caught his face in her hands. "I do. Make love to me, Angel."

He lifted the covers. As she was getting settled, he took a condom from his nightstand drawer and covered himself. He set a few more on top of the nightstand—in easy reach—then slipped under the covers with her. He moved over her body, settling between her legs. He braced himself on his elbows and looked into her eyes, letting his body become familiar with hers and all of its rich curves. Just the feel of her under him was nearly enough to finish him.

Leaning forward, he kissed her chin, the side of her mouth. Her lips were as soft and curvy as the rest of her. He kissed her mouth, stroking her tongue with his. He had everything he wanted right there in his arms and in his bed. He was a rich man.

He kissed her neck, then her collarbone, then made his way down to her breasts. "Oh, yeah." He caught the soft sides of them in his palms. They were far more than a handful...and he had big hands. "Fuck yeah." He put his face between her breasts and pressed them against his cheeks. He smiled up at her. "These are first rate. Just perfect."

She shook her head. "They're too big."

He nuzzled the underside of one, then repeated with the other. "Says who?"

"Me."

He gave her a horrified look. "You don't like them?"

"They don't fit in half the things I want to wear."

He chuckled. "Well, if you want to go bare-chested, that'd work for me. No dress codes here."

"Yeah, I'm sure that would work for your team, too."

"Fuck that. Okay, belay that suggestion." He tightened his hand around the base of one breast, pointing its nipple for his tongue to tease. "I could spend a week on each of these alone."

"No, you couldn't."

He looked up at her. "Why not?"

"Because there are other parts of me that need attention."

He grinned and moved back up to kiss her mouth. "Look how beautiful your eyes are."

She laughed, then touched his face. "You make me forget the bad stuff."

"I hope so." He moved back down her body, lavishing attention on her other breast. He could tell from her little gasps that she liked it when he played with them, which sure as hell worked for him.

He moved down to her ribcage, running his face down the middle of her ribs to her navel. Holy hell, her skin was soft. He swept his tongue around her belly button. He thought about the terrible bruises she'd had. She'd been brave to show the whole team, but God, that was a sight he couldn't un-see.

He pushed up to his elbows and looked up at her.

He ran his hand over the areas where her bruises had been. "How are they today?"

"You're not hurting me."

"I hope not. I never want to." He eased his thumb over one of the spots that had been purple and green. Reminded him he had a few motherfuckers to kill.

"Angel," Wynn whispered, breaking into his thoughts, "you're scaring me."

He huffed a breath, forcing those thoughts back into the shadows of his mind. "Forget it." He kissed her hip, the tender flesh south of her bellybutton. Finally, he was down to her mound. He bit his lip, wondering how best to pleasure her. He kissed her upper inner thigh, then did the same on her other thigh.

The hair in the small triangle on her mound was soft and coarse. He rubbed his face across it as he pressed his chin against her clit. Slipping his arms under her thighs, spreading them, he nuzzled the seam of her sex. Her hips jerked against him. He licked her soft flesh, then slipped his tongue inside to stroke her clit. He moved around it, purposefully avoiding the center of her pleasure, then at last stroking over it. When he sucked her aroused flesh, she cried out. Her hips reflexively arched against his face. He bent a forearm over them to hold them in place. The pressure further excited her, and when he slipped two fingers into her, she lost all control. She convulsed in little pulses and every time they seemed to be receding, he renewed his attention on her clit and the thrusts his fingers made inside her.

When at last she was limp, he kissed his way back up her body. Kneeling between her legs, he entered her. She was slick and hot and tight. The first full thrust he made almost ended everything. He went still, wanting this to last a long, long time.

He kissed her mouth, letting his tongue do what his cock couldn't yet, thrust freely inside her succulent body. She moaned and wrapped her arms around his chest. Bracing her feet on the bed, she began pushing up against him. He responded in kind, pulling almost all the way out, then thrusting into her, deeply, going fast then slow, then slower, enjoying the long slide in and the long slide out.

He knelt between her legs, lifting them as he pumped into her, enjoying the sight of her breasts moving with each thrust. That alone kept him going longer than he normally would have. When he reached down to work her clit, she instantly peaked, crying out as her small muscles gripped his cock, bringing him to his own release.

When they were both finished, he settled on top of her, still inside her body. They were both sweating. She had a warm red flush on her upper chest and neck. "Yeah. That was good," he said. "We're going to be doing this a lot for a long time. When Kit calls me down to work, I'm going to tell him to fuck off. For at least a decade or two."

She laughed.

He smiled and eased himself from her. "Don't go anywhere." He went into his bathroom to dispose of the condom. When he came back, he brought a glass of water. She took a sip, then he turned off the lights and got in bed. Gathering her up in his arms, he adjusted the pillows, stacking them comfortably.

The feel of her luscious body pressed up against his side was heaven, but after a few minutes, he realized her breathing was irregular. He rubbed her back. "Wynnie? You okay?"

She nodded and sniffled. When she lifted her head, her face was moist and again she seemed to have stopped breathing.

"Honey, are you crying?"

She nodded and squeaked.

"Why? Did I hurt you?"

She shook her head. "I just feel so close to you right now. I think our souls are hugging again."

"So these are good tears?"

"Yes."

He reached over to his nightstand for some tissues. She quietly blew her nose. He chuckled. "Well, hell, that's never happened to me before."

"Me either."

"You sure I didn't hurt you?"

She looked at him over her tissue. "You didn't."

He held her close for a long while until she settled down, slowly stroking her soft back. "You showed me tonight there's an entirely different kind of a warrior that's needed every bit as much, maybe more, than an actual fighter."

She put her head on his shoulder. "You guys would have figured out what to do with the boys."

"Maybe you should consider child psychology or sociology or victim advocacy as a focus for your masters."

She leaned up to look at him again. "I hadn't considered that."

"Remi works with a group that helps cult victims adjust to life outside the cult. You could have a chat with her. I could see you doing that kind of work. And I have a feeling there's going to be a huge need for that as we dismantle the Omni World Order."

"I will talk to her. Thank you." Her eyes watered again. "Thank you for bringing me back here. Thank you for everything."

He rolled over to his side, facing her. "Thank you for fighting for us." He swiped the moisture from her cheek with his thumb. "Stay with me tonight. The whole night. I want to wake up with you tomorrow."

"Okay."

"Good. 'Cause I couldn't let you go while you're upset."

"I'm not upset. I'm happy."

"Huh. Okay. Damnedest thing I ever saw, but I believe you."

18

———

Wynn woke before dawn. She was lying on her side, a man's heavy arm draped over her, and his whole, warm body spooned against hers. Angel. She and Angel. Together. She thought of the past night, all the ways they'd been together.

She eased herself out from his hold, trying to slip off the bed without waking him. It didn't work. He pulled her back and locked her down with a big thigh between hers. He opened his eyes, then closed them again, giving her a sleepy smile. "You're still here. I thought I was dreaming. Don't think I've ever slept so good."

Wynn giggled. "What are you talking about? We barely slept."

"You sore?"

"A little."

"I'm sorry."

"I'm not."

He grinned. "I'm not either, really." He kissed her shoulder then rolled over to his back.

"I need to get back to my room before everyone's up. It's moving day."

"I'm glad you get to keep your apartment. I want more brownies." He caught her to him and rolled over, holding her on top of him. He adjusted her position, then slipped himself inside her. She shivered at the way he filled her. She rose up and slipped down him. Leaning over him, her hair spilled forward. His eyes were locked on hers.

"This is divine," she said, "but you aren't covered."

"Shit." He pulled out and reached for the last packet on his nightstand. "I need more," he said as he slipped the condom on. He held her as he sat up then pushed her back to the mattress with him on top this time. He entered her. She stared into his eyes as he moved over her, taking her in slow, luxurious strokes. She moved her hands over his wide shoulders and sculpted arms.

This was heaven.

It was a chaotic morning. Ace, Fiona, and Hope cleared their things out of their old rooms and moved them into their guys' rooms. Greer, Max, and Val were already situated in rooms on the upper floor of the southern bedroom wing. Angel and Kelan already had rooms in the wing south of the bridge over the living room. Selena, Ty, and Eden moved into that section. Remi kept her office in the north section of bedrooms. In no time, three rooms were emptied for the watchers.

The boys and the team took all the furniture out of the two watchers' rooms, where the bunk beds were going, and loaded it into a trailer. Then they brought up the bunk beds from the bunker and put three in one room and two in the other. The team had decided to redo the bunkroom in the bunker as a living room/bedroom studio, since it was used more often by the civilians in the house to wait out problems than it was for the guys on the team to crash. They still needed to order two more sets of bunk beds and replacement furniture for the bunkroom, but it was coming together pretty seamlessly, Wynn thought. Lion and Hawk would have the third room with the two double beds.

The watchers helped with the reorganization. The guys brought up the lockers that were in the bunker and moved them into the two rooms the youngest boys would have. It all looked Spartan to Wynn, but the watchers seemed pleased.

"What do you think?" Kit asked after inspecting the three rooms.

Wynn was surprised Angel's team lead stopped to talk to her—and cared about her opinion. "Looks great. It was terrific that you thought to bring up the bunks from downstairs—lets us get them settled faster. I hope the rest of the boys show up soon."

"I do too. I put that order in for the supplies you requested. Should be here in a couple of days."

Wynn nodded. "The only issue I see is that I don't think we'll all fit in the current classroom."

Kit considered that. "The basement isn't ready for use yet. Should be finished in a few weeks. We can set up classrooms down there. Until then, how about we set up a few tables and partitions in the gym? Will that work?"

"Perfectly. I'm assuming Casey will be joining us in the gym."

"Nope."

"Why not?" Wynn asked. Ivy came into the room then. She was curious about Kit's answer as well.

"Because the watchers have never been around females. I don't want them exploring their curiosity with my daughter."

Ivy laughed. "I think your daughter knows how to take care of herself. She and Selena have been continuing their training. And it would be good for her to be around other children—it'll make the shift to home-schooling much easier."

Kit and Ivy exchanged heated glances. "They aren't children, Iv. They're watchers." Just when Wynn thought Ivy was going to lose the argument, Kit said, "If Casey is comfortable with the boys, we'll give it a try. But I want Selena, Ace, or one of the guys on hand every day."

Ivy said, "At least until Lion shows up. He'll keep his

cubs in line."

"If that's a go, then there's a little more furniture we'll need to order," Wynn said.

Kit nodded. "Give me that list."

When Kit stepped away, Ivy asked, "Are you up for this shift? The boys could be a challenge."

"All kids are a challenge," Wynn said. "I'm looking forward to learning more about them and assessing their scholastic achievements."

Ivy slipped her arm through Wynn's. "I'm so glad you're here. We'd be lost without you. I could feed and clothe the boys, but teaching them is not my strength."

"I'm surprised to say this, but I'm glad I'm here, too."

"And Angel? How are things going with the two of you?"

Wynn felt a wash of heat warm her face. "I don't want to jinx it, but I'm really crazy about him."

Ivy laughed. "That makes me very happy. I knew you were perfect for each other."

They both startled as they heard the doorbell ring. They went down the hall to the bridge over the foyer. Kit opened the front door, then stepped back as four boys came inside. One was as tall as Kit, but super lanky. Wynn looked at Ivy to see if she knew them. The look on her face showed she didn't.

Hope came running down the hall and hurried into the foyer. She looked at their faces expectantly. "Lion?" she asked the tallest boy.

"Haven't seen him, ma'am. Not since we left. Which cubs are here?"

Before Hope could answer, Fox, Wren, Coyote, and Badger joined them in the foyer. They all exchanged hugs. The tall newcomer introduced himself and the boys he was with. "I'm Hawk. This is Mouse, Squirrel, and Robin."

Hope smiled at them. "Welcome, boys. We're just getting your rooms situated. Want to come upstairs? We can get you settled and cleaned up, then find something for you to eat."

"Wait," Max said as he joined them. "You're Hawk?"

"Yes. You're Mad Dog?"

"Yeah, that's my WKB handle. They call me Max here. Lion told me you're second-in-command."

"I am."

"Where were you? We've been searching the area around your latest camp, driving the highway, over and over."

"Our job is to see and not be seen."

"I'm heading out for another search. Want to come with?"

Hope shook her head. "These boys need to eat, hydrate, and rest."

Max's face hardened. "So feed them. Then Hawk comes with me."

Wynn could feel the tension in the foyer escalating. She went down the main stairs, stepping in to bring the energy down a notch before things hit a tipping point.

"Max," she said, "I'll take the new boys to wash up while Ivy finds them something to eat."

"Wait," Hawk said. "Is Mr. Edwards here?"

Max frowned. "No. Fuck no. Why would you think that?"

Hawk nodded toward the front door. "The black vehicles outside. He drove ones like that when he came to our camp and took Beetle."

Max looked dumbfounded. He shot Hope a stunned glance. "I've been taking the SUVs on my hunts for the boys. That's why they stay hidden; I look the same as Mr. Edwards or his thugs."

Hope laughed. "Take my truck."

"I can't. There are still six more boys. I need a bigger vehicle."

"Then I'll see if Remi will loan you hers. She's working here today."

"Do it."

~

ACE WENT into the ops room, looking for an escape from the chaos upstairs. Greer was alone. He looked up at her and smiled. "Hey, sis."

That was weird. Sure as hell was going to take some getting used to being a sibling.

"How's your arm doing?"

"It hurts."

"I bet."

She sat down next to him. "I came to ask you for some help."

"Ask away."

"I need help changing my name to Dawson." He grinned, and she shook her head at him. "Don't be weird."

"Your name was never legally changed to Myers. You never stopped being a Dawson. Fuckin' A, sis, this'll make Mom and Dad happy. What we do need to over-turn is your death certificate."

"How do we do that?"

"I'll look into it. If it's something that will bring our parents to the interest of the Omnis, we're going to have to hold off for a little while."

"Agreed."

He gave her a long look. "Hey. There's something I've been wanting to ask you."

"What?"

"I was thinking of taking Remi to meet Mom and Dad around the holidays. Was wondering if you and Val wanted to come with?"

"I'll pass."

"Well, you can't, really."

"Why not?"

"Tradition. When someone brings their future spouse in to meet the family, the whole family has to be there. You have two sisters you still have to meet. And I bet they'd like to meet Val, too."

"What are your sisters like?"

"*Our* sisters. They're nice. Not like us, but nice. They're regular people. Absolutely unaware of the world we deal with. They're both married and have a bunch of kids between them."

She shook her head. "Yeah, Greer, I think I'm not a fit for that."

"They're your family too. We broke the ice letting Mom and Dad meet you before Remi. Tina and Nancy have been hounding me to bring you back into town. You aren't the only one with wounds that need healing from that time. We all were injured."

She made a dismissive huff. "Your hearts were broken. But I was fucking steamrolled. I'm not the sister you lost."

"You are. And that you survived what you did makes you a hero to all of us. It's time you fully joined the family."

"No. I'm gonna mess something up, screw up the whole visit for Remi. Mixing me and family is not a good idea."

"Family can be tough. For sure. But not our family. Val and I—and Remi—we'll have your back. It'll be fun."

She shook her head and walked into the weapons room, finding a couple of knives that needed sharpening. "'It'll be fun,' he said. 'What could go wrong?' he asked," she whined, loud enough for him to hear.

"Jesus, Ace. Never figured you for a drama queen."

She came to the door between the two rooms, holding a machete. "I'm not. We're driving, right? I'll feel better if I have a whole bunch of weapons with me."

"I'll see if Owen will let us use his jet. If we ever hear from him again."

⁓

MAX STARTED another search that afternoon, with Hawk riding shotgun. Six cubs were still on the loose, fending for themselves. He worried about how their supplies were holding out. Every day they weren't recovered now put them in greater jeopardy. The days were getting colder, the nights bitterer.

His hand tightened on the wheel of Remi's Forester. "I don't want to think this, but it's possible that Mr. Edwards has gotten to the boys before us."

"No." Hawk actually laughed. "Lion would never be taken."

Max ground his teeth, stopping himself from pushing his fear onto Hawk. There was still time to find the boys alive. He forced himself to focus on that outcome.

Hawk leaned forward, looking at something in the side mirror. "Stop. Max, stop!"

Max hit the brakes. He hadn't been going fast since this was the stretch of road they were most likely to encounter the stragglers. He could see a tall, lanky blond in his rearview mirror, standing in the road, waving his arms at them.

Lion.

Max laughed as he turned around and went back to him. When he pulled over on the wayside, two more boys slipped out of the woods. Hawk was the first out of the car, jumping out before it was even in park. The cubs ran to him. They looked scruffy, filthy, and relieved.

Max got out and walked up to Lion. He hooked thumbs with him, then pulled him close for a shoulder bump. "Your sister is going to be so happy when she sees you."

"I couldn't leave until I knew all cubs were accounted for. These two missed their cache pickup, so I knew they were off track. Take them to the house. I have another group I need to find."

"Whoa." Max stopped Lion before he could head off into the woods. "I can't let you go. We've been looking for you for months. Your sister is beside herself with worry. Come back to the house. Get some food. Give her a hug, then you, Hawk, and I will come back for the last group."

"Which cubs got to the house?" Lion asked.

Hawk called off their names. "So we're missing Vole, Jay, and Owl." He looked at Max. "Mr. Edwards has Beetle."

"We heard."

"I memorized the license plates of his vehicles."

Max smiled. He set a hand on Lion's shoulder. "Well done. Let's give that info to Greer when we get back. Who are these two?"

"Spider and Crow."

Lion looked to the woods. "The others can't be far from here. They knew where to go. At least that group did pick up their cached supplies. I'll go with you. But we have to come back today."

"We will."

On the ride back, Max listened to Hawk and Lion catch each other up on what had happened since fleeing the camp. He didn't call ahead to Hope—he wanted to see her expression when Lion got out of the car.

It was epic.

Hope saw them pull up outside the garage. Max saw her weary eyes brighten. She straightened. The rag she was wiping her hands on fell to the ground as she ran forward. Lion jumped out of the car and grabbed her. She buried her face in his shoulder and wept. Max was never so proud of Lion as he was then, holding his sister while she cried all over him.

Eventually, Hope stepped back. Others had come out of the house. The cubs surrounded the newest arrivals. Max came over and pulled Hope against his side as he smiled down at her.

She wrapped her arms around him. "Thank you."

"We're still missing three boys. Lion, Hawk and I are going back up there. I wish I'd known about taking the big SUVs. I might have found them sooner."

"We didn't know. They've been through so much. I'm just glad they knew what to be careful of."

The big group made their way into the house. In the living room, Kit came over to greet Lion, who looked wary as hell. Kit reached a hand out to shake, then pulled him into a hug. "Don't know how you did it, but we got them all."

"No. We're missing Vole, Jay, and Owl."

KIT SHOOK HIS HEAD. "They showed up just before you did. Everyone's here."

Lion laughed as three boys came down the main stairs, jumping the last few steps when they saw Lion and the boys he'd brought to the house. The cubs took the newest arrivals upstairs to see their rooms.

Lion looked over at Kit. "Thank you."

Kit put his hand on Lion's shoulder. "You did good. I wish we could have gotten to you sooner. I'm proud of you."

"We have to get Beetle from Mr. Edwards."

"You bet. It's our number one priority now. Get settled. We'll rustle up some food for you."

Max handed Lion a pad of paper and pen. "He memorized Edwards' plates," he told Kit. "We'll plug them into the system." Lion jotted them down.

Kit was just about to take the boys upstairs when Casey shouted his name. He watched his daughter run to greet Lion, who caught her up in a big hug.

"Hi, sweet pea." He smiled as he set her back on her feet.

She frowned at him. "I'm not a vegetable."

"You're not very sweet, either." He gave her a lopsided grin. "And...it's a flower. Some of the Friends grow them in their gardens."

"Huh." She crossed her arms. "I was worried about you."

Lion nodded. "I was worried about us too."

Kit didn't like the blush that came over Casey's face as she talked to Lion. He may have growled, though he wasn't entirely sure he'd made that sound out loud until his daughter sent him a quelling look.

"Case, let the boys get settled. Go help Russ and Jim with some food for them."

"Yes, Dad." She gave Lion a little wave and the tiniest feminine smile Kit had ever seen.

Shit. He was going to have to have Ivy set some ground rules for Casey. And fast.

Hope knocked on Lion's door. It was late; everyone was gathering downstairs for a nightcap. Her brother's dark-haired lieutenant opened their door. "Hi. Is Lion here?"

He nodded and stepped back to let her in. Lion was sitting on the edge of his bed, facing the other bed. He only wore a pair of loose pajama bottoms. The lamp on the stand between the beds cast yellow light over him. He had no hair on his chest or his face. The ink tattoos of his brows looked stark against his pale skin and blond hair.

He was lean but had filled out quite a bit since she last saw him. Or maybe it was that she'd never seen him without his shirt.

"Hi," she said. She sent a quick look between him and Hawk. "Am I interrupting?"

"No," Lion said.

She sat on the end of Lion's bed and folded her legs as she reached for his hand. "I'm so glad you're here. I've been worried sick about the cubs. I don't know if you want to talk about what happened after you were taken, but I'm here, and so is Max, if you do."

Lion gave her a closed-lip smile. "Nothing happened. We camped for a while, then took a hike and came here."

Hope looked at Hawk. He'd returned to his bed and was sitting facing them. His expression was blank. If Hope had learned anything from Max and the guys, it was to beware when their faces gave nothing away.

"You're safe here, you know," she said to Hawk.

Lion pulled his hand free. "One of our cubs is still in terrible danger. Until we have him back, none of us are safe."

"Mr. Edwards is no friend of ours. Beetle is very much in danger. The guys will work with you to get him back. They think Beetle is Owen's son."

"If Beetle is Owen's son, then his mom has to be an Omni," Lion said.

"She is." Hope spent the next hour bring them up to speed on Ace and Adelaide, on Fiona and Kelan, on the status of the smallpox quarantine at the Friendship Community, and on Rocco and Mandy's wedding. So much had happened in the time they'd been apart.

J afaar tore another piece from the cheap American bread and tossed it to the ducks in the pond. The bread was so insubstantial that it was difficult to toss it very far. Lately, everything had been difficult.

He'd thought, having curried the favor of King, the Omni World Order's leader, that he was in a good position to advance the goals of his own employer, Abdul Baseer al Jahni. At least until that raid on King's hidden underground palace.

He'd even believed the fact that the Syadne people had come to him when they needed to have Mrs. Vaughn moved into their care confirmed he was in favor. Then all of a sudden, for no reason he could ascertain, he'd been shut out.

The work Syadne was doing was the cornerstone of the OWO Armageddon. His master, al Jahni, did not want to be cut out of the most important event in human history. It was what made al Jahni decide to have Vaughn terminated.

He'd tried to use the girl, Vaughn's granddaughter, to feed him secrets from the Feds—both to strengthen his position with the Omnis and King, and to bolster his knowledge of what was really happening. It hadn't worked. It surprised him that for such a meek creature, Miss Ratcliff had a substantial backbone. She'd been virtually incapable of providing him with anything very useful. He did discover that Ace, a whore who'd come from the OWO, was related to one of the Feds. That was mostly it.

Edwards had happened to be at the house that day Miss Ratcliff had come to visit her grandmother. Enraged at Jafaar's failure to deliver useful intel, he'd cut Ratcliff up. King's man had known the Feds would come for Vaughn after that; Edwards had essentially burned him.

Ah, but Jafaar was the one with the last laugh. He'd rigged Vaughn's bed with enough explosives to leave a crater in that tattered neighborhood. If the explosion happened to take place while the Feds were working to free her, even better.

Yet even that hadn't gone as he'd wanted, which turned out to be a blessing. His employer wanted samples from Vaughn's flesh. If they couldn't get in the front door with Syadne, then they'd get in through the back door. They could reverse-engineer what Syadne had done to the old woman without ever having to partner with an organization that had proved its fickle nature.

The only fly in that ointment was that Jafaar needed the geneticists who'd engineered the change in Vaughn...and they'd gone missing.

Now, everything that happened mattered. Every step could easily be a misstep that would end all options for al Jahni...and Jafaar. Such a failure would come with a terrible price, one he did not wish to pay.

It was fortuitous that the WKB had fulfilled his order to kill Vaughn; they didn't know he'd been burned. Communication between King and the WKB had to be suffering...a situation that Jafaar tucked in the back of his head for future use. Pete, the current president of the White Kingdom Brotherhood, was weak. He could prove useful.

Jafaar tossed more bread into the pond. Things perhaps weren't as bleak as he first thought. He had Vaughn's body in cold storage. And her daughter and son-in-law were on the lam, away from Syadne. He just had to find them. Ratcliff would make a good enticement to bring the scientists out of the woods...if he could just evade the Feds long enough to put his plans in motion.

Those fools had their fingers in all of this, from meddling with the Friendship Community, interfering with the watchers, and leading the charge against King's hidden palace. They'd probably infiltrated the White Kingdom Brotherhood, too.

He wondered now if Pete knew he'd likely been played. He thought he had a good idea who one—or more—of the Feds might be. It was something that had been bothering him since the raid on King's Warren.

Khalid and his female bodyguard. They were newcomers to the scene—at least Amir hadn't warned him about them, nor had he vouched for them. Khalid had gotten him safely out of the grasp of the Feds when they raided the warren, but he'd disappeared in the melee of their escape. Some of the guards who were captured later described a man who looked like Khalid helping the Feds tear the palace apart.

Somehow, King had must have put those pieces together before him. And that had to be why Jafaar had been cut out of all interactions with the Omnis. They'd given him a last chance to prove his value to them by using Ratcliff to gather intel, but that had been an abysmal failure. It rankled. It was why he'd wanted so very much to deal them a terrible blow by killing Ratcliff's grandmother in such a spectacular way.

But as it turned out, Allah had found an even better use for Vaughn's remains, and Jafaar had won after all—despite his lack of foresight. This game was deadly, and far more complex than he'd first realized. He had to get out in front of it quickly, before al Jahni found a replacement for him.

And that was why he was meeting Deputy Sheriff Jerry Whitcomb here in this scrappy park. The lawman had been on al Jahni's payroll for a while. It was time for him to earn his keep. He'd done excellent work hitting the now Mrs. Silas' therapeutic riding center in its early stages. His work had successfully brought in the fighters of Tremaine Industries, gathering them in one place, right where King wanted them. A single target was always easier to destroy than a distributed one. The attempts on the Tremaine fighters had been less than glorious so far. But Jafaar had plans to remedy that with an attack that would put him and al Jahni back in the game. His boss had been of service to King too long and too loyally to be cut out of the final act.

But first, he had to learn what he didn't know. And for that, he needed the deputy. Jafaar had selected their rendezvous site because it was one of the older, less used parks...and because it had no security cameras. For all anyone knew, the deputy now strolling over to him was just making a friendly visit.

They greeted each other. Jafaar offered the deputy a few slices of bread to tear for the ducks and geese in the pond, but he declined.

"I'm glad you could take the time from your busy schedule to meet with me."

The deputy faced the pond. "The less time this takes, the better, Jafaar."

"Indeed." It had been a smart move of Amir to put the deputy on al Jahni's payroll, especially now, when it appeared opportunities were closing for him to further al Jahni's interests through other venues. "Have you any news for me?"

"I do. Apparently some of the boys who were watching King's gold at the White Kingdom Brotherhood's compound have escaped. Looks as if they're heading into town."

That was interesting information. Jafaar wasn't certain how he could use it, but you just never knew when a little arcane fact could play in your favor. "How many of them are there?"

"A dozen or so."

"How many have shown up?"

"I don't know. Not all of them. Four, maybe. They have weird animal names. They're a bunch of little freaks."

"What's bringing them into town?"

"A man named Mad Dog seems to have offered them shelter...at the Feds' headquarters." The deputy smiled as he watched Jafaar's reaction. "They met Mad Dog when they were at the WKB. He's one of the Feds."

So Jafaar was right. The WKB had been infiltrated. "Interesting. So if these boys are no longer watching King's gold, who is?"

The deputy looked irritated, as if Jafaar had missed the point. "I don't know. I don't care. And I don't intend to find out. The point is, the WKB's been compromised by one of the Feds."

"Of course. Does Pete know?"

The deputy shrugged. "I'll leave that to you to find

out. No way I can get on to that compound to find out and stay alive. They know me." He narrowed his eyes at Jafaar. "And you still need me where I am."

"I do. And I imagine you still enjoy the benefit of working for me."

The deputy gave a curt nod.

"I do have one more question for you." Jafaar lifted his phone and brought up a picture of Khalid. "Do you recognize this man?"

"Yeah. That's Rocco Silas. He married Mandy. My girl." The deputy gritted his teeth. "If I had a chance to put a bullet in him, I would gladly do it."

"You may well get that chance. And how about this woman?"

"That's Selena. She's a Fed. Seen her around town. She bodyguards the Feds' women."

"That is all I need for the moment." Jafaar resumed feeding the birds as the deputy walked away. So. It was true about Khalid. He wondered now if Yusef knew as well. Something Jafaar would need to find out.

And even more interesting was the fact that King had enough gold under the WKB compound that it needed guarding. Jafaar smiled. Those boys knew where that gold was. All he needed was to find one of them to show him. With that gold in al Jahni's possession, not only would Jafaar redeem himself in the eyes of his employer, but it would vitally shift the balance of power in this game.

JAFAAR STOOD in Yusef's living room in front of the window that overlooked the parking lot and wide road beyond it. He kept his back to the room while Mrs. Sayed brought them coffee. She seemed to want to stay, but Yusef asked her to go manage the motel front desk. Yusef was nervous. Jafaar could hear the tension in his voice. His wife poured their coffee, then silently left.

It was a warm autumn day, but sun filtered down through a deck of thin clouds, making everything look dreary. It was a good day to oust a traitor, praise Allah.

"Please, Jafaar, come sit. Your coffee is getting cold," Yusef said.

Jafaar took his seat and accepted the coffee Yusef handed him. He took a sip. "Did you know that Khalid works for the American government?"

Yusef's cup stopped halfway to his mouth. He shifted his eyes over to Jafaar. "No. I did not know."

"Hm-mm. He is an enemy of our benefactor, Abdul Baseer al Jahni."

"Jafaar, I did not know. What do you intend to do with him?"

"I think I shall use him, as he has used us." Jafaar sipped his coffee, looking at Yusef over the rim. "You know, I've long wondered how your motel, seedy as it is, could support two boys in college. I found out that our master was footing the bill for their education, but I also learned that that changed recently, before the start of this semester. You've found another patron for their studies. Am I right in suspecting it was Khalid?"

Yusef set his coffee down. "I am a simple man, Jafaar. I only want security for my family. It's all I ever wanted. Khalid came to me with the right credentials. When you met him, you didn't call him out as a spy. I trusted you, and because of that, I trusted him. He said Amir was an enemy of al Jahni's. He offered me a different arrangement for my boys' education, one where he paid for it in advance. All of it. Completely paid for."

"And what did he want in exchange?"

"Nothing. He asked nothing of me. I thought he was working for al Jahni's security interests and was just fine-tuning our agreement. I did not know he was an American agent. How could I have known? He spoke Pashto perfectly. He could have been any man from my village."

Jafaar set his cup down and leaned back in his seat. "Well, now you know. I have not yet told al Jahni that you are working against his interests. And I will not, provided you reaffirm your allegiance to me."

"I am loyal to you."

"To me. Above your family. Above your love for your sons."

"Of course."

Jafaar glared at Yusef, waiting for him to waver. He didn't. "Swear your loyalty to me."

Yusef went to his knees in front of Jafaar. "On

penalty of my life, I swear my loyalty to you, Jafaar Majid."

"Good. After our coffee, you will call Khalid. Tell him you have seen me here, that I am staying with you for a little while. Make it sound as if you feel I am up to something." Jafaar smiled. "Because, after all, I am, so you won't be lying. And, of course, I will want to meet him."

Rocco listened to the recording twice, glad he'd put bugs in Yusef's living room. Jafaar and Yusef spoke in Pashto, so Max couldn't understand much of what they said. Rocco leaned back in his seat, digesting what he'd heard.

"I'm not getting younger, Rocco," Max growled.

"Jafaar has learned who I am. He just told Yusef and demanded he swear allegiance to him anew."

"So you've been outed, and Yusef has been compromised."

"We'll see. Jafaar ordered Yusef to call me. We'll know for sure if Yusef follows that up with another call to me without Jafaar."

Max walked into the team conference room in the bunker. He looked at the group, then gave them one of his big, crazy-ass smiles that Angel always knew meant trouble.

"Spill, Max," Kit said.

"Guess who just hunkered down in Amir's old digs in Cheyenne?"

"Who?" Angel asked.

"Jafaar." Max's grin widened.

Anger poured like molten rage through Angel's veins. "I want him."

Kit twisted his jaw then shook his head. "No. Not yet. Yusef has left our bugs in place. We're perfectly set up to watch him."

"That either means Yusef really is on our side, or he just hasn't found the bugs," Blade said, sending Rocco a glance.

Rocco took a seat at the table. "We'll find out soon. Jafaar told Yusef to call Khalid. What will be most telling is if he calls again when Jafaar is not watching him."

"And if he doesn't?" Angel asked.

Rocco tilted his head. "Then Khalid will make a visit to him."

"Does Jafaar have a security detail?" Kit asked.

"Not consistently," Rocco said. "He's often alone. A detail would attract too much attention."

"He had one when we went down to Fiona's initiation in the tunnels," Selena reminded them.

"And he had a guy with him when he visited the

WKB," Max said. "Maybe just depends on whether he feels at risk."

Kit looked at Rocco. "I want to wait to give Yusef a chance to come forward. When he does, or when you call him, find out if Jafaar has men with him. If he does, I want eyes on them."

"How long are we waiting?" Rocco asked.

"A day," Kit said. He frowned when he looked at Blade. "What?"

"Jafaar is a man who likes his creature comforts. He's in thick with the Omnis. Why would he stay at a crummy motel?" Blade asked.

"Maybe he's got an op in play and wants to be nearby," Rocco said. "I'll find out when I talk to Yusef."

Kit shifted his focus to Ace. "Any chance you're a skater?"

"Yeah," Ace said. "How'd you know? Started when I got out of the OWO. Gave me something to do between assignments."

"Got your board?"

"At my stash house. What do you have in mind?"

"Your board will be your cover. You'll plant a tracker on Jafaar's vehicle while you're there. Val can shadow you."

"Yes!" Ace smiled. She waved her cast around. "This'll be a good prop."

"Yeah. Until you fall on it and break it all over again. She can't do it," Val said. "Her arm's not healed."

"Val, I'm going crazy hanging around here, doing nothing to further the cause. I can do this."

"What if he sees you? What if it goes south? What if his detail spots you?" Val shook his head.

"You worry too much," Ace said. "We have to go get my board. I can't show up there with a new one; wouldn't be authentic. And if we just picked up a used one somewhere, I'll take a couple falls while I get used to it, anyway. Let's take a drive." She got up and kissed the top of Val's head, then started for the stairs to the den. "I'm going to get ready. Bring the tracker and meet me upstairs." She stopped at the door and looked back at everyone. "I've been wanting to see if my handler dropped off a new phone for this week. Might help with the hunt for Owen."

"Good," Kit said. "Do it. When Rocco goes to meet Jafaar, be ready to tag the bastard's car."

Max's phone rang. "It's Yusef." He passed the call over to Rocco. The room went quiet. Rocco exchanged greetings with Yusef.

"You asked that I tell you when Jafaar is here."

"I did. I like to meet up with him when he's in town."

There was a long silence, then, *"There is something else."*

"What is it?"

"I don't know, but it seems Jafaar is working on a secret plan."

"A secret plan," Rocco said with a chuckle. "He is

an enemy actor in a foreign nation representing the office of an international criminal. He is himself a secret."

"Yes. It is true. But something about him is different. It would be good if you could come and talk to him. Our employer would not be pleased if his interests were exposed."

"Very true. I will make a visit. How long did he say he would be there?"

"He didn't. But I expect it will be a couple of days."

"Then I will see you in the morning. Be at peace, my friend." Rocco disconnected the call. Rocco looked around the room. None of the team had happy faces on, but Angel's was the worst.

"I repeat my claim that Jafaar is mine," Angel said, staring at Kit.

"Not yet he's not," Kit said. "We need him to lead us to King."

Yusef did make a second call to Khalid. It came in early the next morning. The number wasn't one Rocco recognized. He got out of bed, hurrying into the bathroom so that he wouldn't disturb Mandy's sleep. Knowing Max was automatically recording it, he accepted the call but didn't speak until he heard Yusef's voice on the other end.

"Hello? Khalid?"

"Good morning, Yusef."

"You must be very careful today when you visit Jafaar. He said you are working for the U.S. government. Is that true?"

"Yes."

There were some garbled words on the other end. *"Am I in trouble? I have done everything you asked."*

"You have been very helpful. I consider you a trusted ally in our fight against terrorism. Peace is what we all desire, no?"

"Yes. Peace. For my boys. My wife. Our country. I am an American, you know."

"I do know. As is your whole family."

"Yes."

"How many men does Jafaar have with him?"

"None. He came alone."

"Thank you for warning me."

The line went dead.

Mandy was leaning on one elbow, watching the bathroom as he came out. Even in the gray light of the early morning, he could see the worry on her face. He smiled at her. She didn't smile back. He sat on the bed and faced her, letting her read him. After a minute, he smoothed a lock of her copper hair from her shoulder. "I will be fine."

"Rocco—"

"I think I'll kick some ass today."

"You enjoy this."

He shook his head. "No. I enjoy *ending* this. It's been a long journey for us." He set his hand on her growing belly. "I think I'd like peace for our new son."

"Or daughter."

"Mm-mm. But you're having a boy." He leaned over and kissed her belly, then slipped back under the covers and pulled her against his side.

Yusef's wife was at the front desk when Rocco got to the motel. He greeted her, then went up the stairs to the couple's private apartment. Yusef was not upstairs, but Jafaar was, standing by the window. He turned his back to it, throwing his features into stark relief against the bright light.

"It is good to see you again, my friend," Rocco said in Pashto.

"Is it?" Jafaar said. "I wonder. I called the company you work for to reconfirm your credentials. They said they have no record of you. For some reason, they felt they'd been hacked recently."

"Hackers are a problem everywhere."

"Can you explain your absence from their systems?"

"I have no need to explain it. Of course, my employer wishes to shield my identity. Why does this concern you?"

"Because you lied to me?"

"Did I?"

"You are a federal agent."

"Is that so?"

"Yes, it is, Rocco Silas."

Rocco smiled. Since the ruse was over, he switched to English so that the guys listening from Blade's could understand him. Outside he heard the noisy roar of a skateboard, heard the crack it made as the board was dropped at the start of another run. He took a seat near where he'd placed one of the bugs weeks ago, drawing Jafaar's attention from the window. "How did you find out?"

"I have my sources."

"Now would be a good time to turn yourself in."

Jafaar gave him a cool smile as he sat in a nearby chair. "I think not. I think, instead, we might make an exchange."

"Oh?"

"I have three little boys. They have unusual names. I believe they are Toad, Skunk, and Robin, if I'm remembering correctly."

Rocco instantly knew he was lying. All the boys were accounted for, and there wouldn't be two Robins in a pride. But it was uncanny that he'd said the boys' animal names. How had he known about the watchers? "What is it you want in exchange?"

"Miss Ratcliff."

Rocco laughed. "You had your shot at her and blew it."

"I am not finished with her. Surely the lives of three boys more than equal one girl's?"

"They don't." Rocco stood, disgusted by this convo.

"You can't take him in yet," Kit said via the comm unit in Rocco's ear. *"Ask him who King is."*

"Do what you want with the boys," Rocco said to Jafaar. "They are a troublesome handful. My team might be more inclined to make an exchange for something we actually want."

"And that is?"

"Tell us who King is."

Jafaar chuckled as he got to his feet. "I do know who he is. And you should as well. He is quite close to you."

Rocco grunted. "Riddles are insufficient for a trade." He walked to the stairs. "Tell me what I want to know, and I will consider putting Miss Ratcliff at your disposal."

"And why would you, supposedly a man of such honor, surrender one of your dependents to me?"

"It is for the greater good, no?"

"Indeed. When you call me with her coordinates. When I pick her up, I will give you King's name."

20

Rocco called in to the team after he left Jafaar. *"Why does Jafaar want Wynn?"*

Angel looked around the conference table. Only Blade seemed to have an idea. "Straight speculation says he's got a lead on Wynn's parents and wants her as a carrot," he said.

"That's what I was thinking, which is a new development, else he wouldn't have let her go before."

"True that. We'll have to table this for now. Val and Ace are finished with the tracker," Kit said. "Meet up with them and head over to the airport. Val's dad's library should be landing in a couple of hours. I'll send some of the team down. We're out." He looked at the group. "Angel, Kelan, head down there. Don't want those documents vulnerable to Omni thugs. If you aren't there when it lands, they will be."

"Who's staying with the watchers?" Angel asked.

"Blade, Greer, and I are taking shifts," Selena said.

THE TEAM WAS WAITING in Owen's private hangar when his plane pulled in. The pilot opened the door as the stairs were rolled over. Val wasn't expecting the first person out of the plane to be his father. In fact, he wasn't expecting his father at all. He glared at his aging parent—it had been years since he saw him.

His father's expression was blank as he walked toward Val, an emptiness Val mirrored. "Thanks for bringing the library out. We'll get it unloaded, then you can be on your way back."

"I'm not going back."

"Yes, you are. You aren't welcome here."

"William's dead."

Despite feeling certain that the family's longtime butler was an Omni plant, Val still felt saddened by the news. "William? How?"

"He drank a lethal cocktail of pain meds and blood pressure pills."

"You knew he was working for the Omnis?"

"Not until I did the library reconstruction."

"That's a long time to live with a spy."

"It is. But had I fired him, his replacement would have been younger, savvier and harder to hide from. Did you check out your sisters' staff?"

"They're clear."

"Good. 'Cause William's death is the beginning of the end."

"Yo, Val," Kelan shouted from the top of the steps. "We brought you for muscle, not your looks. The plane's loaded. Give us a hand."

"End of what?" Val asked his dad as he headed toward the steps.

"Life as we know it. I can't go back."

Shit. Val jogged up the stairs and into the plane. Kelan and Angel were picking up boxes.

"My dad's staying for a while," Val said. "I'll have to find someplace he can hang."

"Why not at the house?" Angel asked.

"Because for all we know, he's one of them."

"Keep your friends close and your enemies closer," Kelan said. "If he is one of them, we can pick his brain."

Val shook his head. "Don't. He has nothing but evil in there."

"Maybe he can stay at Mandy's place. Or in Ace's old apartment," Rocco suggested.

Kelan set a big hand on Val's shoulder. "We'll figure it out, man. Maybe he knows something of what Owen and Wendell are up to. Whatever, we got your back." He frowned as he looked around at the boxes. "If he's staying, where's his luggage?"

Val looked around. "I don't know. I'll ask him. He rides back with one of you guys. I can't deal with him yet."

"We'll take good care of him, though it may be a rough ride back to Blade's." Angel grinned.

Val grabbed a couple of boxes and headed down the steps. When the big SUVs were loaded, he waved Ace back. Since she couldn't move boxes with her broken arm, she'd been fooling around with her skateboard outside the hangar. She looked happy. That wouldn't last long once she met his dad. He'd break the news to her on the way back that the bastard was going to be with them for a while. He texted Kit an update.

AT THE HOUSE, Val couldn't put off the inevitable any longer. He asked Ace to stay with his dad until they could figure out what to do with him.

"Dad, this is my girlfriend, Ace." Val nervously looked from his dad to her and back again. "Don't insult her. In fact, don't look at her, don't talk to her, don't try to interact with her at all. For your own safety."

When she was alone with Mr. Parker in the living room, Ace walked around him in a close circle, sizing him up like a puma to her prey.

"So you're with my son," he said.

Ace stopped in front of him. "I'm not 'with' your son. Nor is he 'with' me." She stared into Mr. Parker's eyes. "We are one being. You hurt him, you hurt me." She smiled. "And I no longer tolerate being hurt by anyone."

Jason didn't flinch. "You're a fighter."

"Sometimes I fight. Sometimes I just kill. I'm moody like that."

Jason smiled. "Thank God my son found you."

Ace blinked, surprised by his announcement—and by how similar his eyes looked compared to Val's when he teased her. "Which side are you on, Mr. Parker?"

"Jason, please. I'm on my son's. Always my son's."

"It wasn't like that when he was growing up."

"Yes, it was, only I chose the weakest of all ways to show it."

Her eyes narrowed. "And now you expect forgiveness?"

"No. I don't. I wouldn't forgive me. I don't expect my son to."

"Then why are you here?"

"This is where I need to be."

"Why?"

"It's time for me to be here, that's all."

"What's coming now?"

"End days."

"Shit." *Shit. Shit. That can't be good.*

Ace looked up as Val and Kit came down the hall. Kit shook hands with Jason. Had to be one of the coldest handshakes she'd ever seen. Good. At least they were all on the same page.

"Mr. Parker—" Kit began.

"Jason, please."

"Jason. I understand that you're here for the foreseeable future. Val will show you to your room." He looked at Val. "Let's put him in Grams' old room."

"You're letting him stay?" Val didn't hide his shock.

"I am. He can help unpack and organize his library."

"Yeah, and he can set it all on fire, too," Val grumbled.

Jason gave Val a scolding look. "I'm not going to destroy my life's work, son—no matter what you think of me."

"I don't think a whole helluva lot of you."

Ace moved to Val's side and slipped her hand in his. If she had to keep cool, he better as well.

"Your room's this way." Val started down the southern hall. Kit and Ace followed them.

"Jason, I'd like you to wear this while you're with us," Kit said, handing him a security necklace. "If you encounter trouble, something odd, anything that makes you feel uncomfortable, press the alarm. It will summon us. You're also not to leave the grounds unescorted. And you're not to be in the den or down in the bunker unless one of us is with you. Understood?"

"Loud and clear."

Ace noticed that Jason didn't seem surprised to hear there was a bunker under the house. Most civilians would have been endlessly curious about that.

"You may, of course, make yourself at home." Kit looked at Val. "I'll let Russ know he's here." He nodded at Jason. "I'll leave you to get settled. Dinner will be at seven this evening in the dining room."

KIT WALKED OUT. Ace followed, but Val stayed behind. He wanted to set some parameters for his dad's visit. "I don't like this. I don't like you. I don't trust you. And if it were up to me, I would just feed you to the fucking Omnis."

"I wouldn't expect anything else from you. It's what I've earned."

"Yes, it is."

"Is Owen here?"

"No."

"Where is he?"

"That's need-to-know. Why didn't you bring any luggage? Did you decide mid-flight you were gonna stay?"

Jason sat on the bed. "Did you ever play hide-n-seek when you were a kid?"

"You know I didn't. I wasn't allowed friends over."

"Hmmm." His dad didn't take the bait. "Well, when kids are out in the field and the game's over, the boy who's 'it' shouts 'Olly olly oxen free' or some equivalent. It varies by region, but the meaning's the same." He looked up from his suitcase. "It's a call to all who are hiding that the game's up. That call's gone out."

"What the fuck are you talking about?"

"The jig's up, son. Time to return to home base. Guess where home base is?"

Val shook his head. "Don't do this."

Jason smiled. "Yup. It's right here."

"Jesus. I fucking don't want you to bring it here."

"This thing is bigger than you. Bigger than me or us or anything. I could no more stop it than I could a tsunami. God knows I tried. So did Nick. You boys are the last line we're holding and our only hope."

Val couldn't take much more of his dad's cryptic shit. "You got something to say, say it."

Jason straightened and faced Val. "I will. Gather the team. Everyone should hear this."

Val glared at his dad, then stalked out of the room and slammed the door behind him. Ace was there. "Don't let him out of that room. And if you see an opportunity to kill him, take it. Fuck it all. Just kill him and put me out of my misery." He activated his comm unit. "Kit, you read me?"

"Like you're standing next to me."

"My dad seems to have a story he wants to tell us."

"Right. I'll call everyone together. Give me fifteen. I'm running out to pick up Ivy from the diner."

"You want him in the conference room or the den?"

"Conference room."

"Copy." Val sighed and looked over at Ace, who, even with her broken arm, wasn't going to let his dad move an inch.

"Val—"

"What?"

"Sit down." She gestured toward a bench fitted into the hallway's outside wall.

"Why?"

"Because I can't reach your head with my broken arm."

"You gonna hit me with that thing?"

"No. I want to kiss you. You need to calm down. Your bastard father may have good intel for us. We have to get that out of him before we kill him."

Val slumped onto the bench. She held his face and kissed his forehead. He caught her hips and pulled her between his legs, settling her on his thigh. "He said it's a game. That this is all a game. Same thing Santo said." He pulled her close for a kiss. Somehow, his tongue in her mouth completely grounded him. "I love you, Ace."

She smiled. "I know." She forked the fingers of her good hand through his hair. "I love you too."

He stood, putting her on her feet. She didn't move back, so he hugged her. "I gotta tell you, I'm afraid of what he's going to say."

Her face hardened. "Yeah. You aren't alone, Val, but we got this together. All of us."

They fetched Jason and took the elevator down. Val had the weird thought that he should have restrained his dad.

His dad looked at Ace then back at him. "You did good with your choice, son."

Val watched the front wall of the cab. "You lost your right to have an opinion on that."

Jason tilted his head and gave him a half-smile. "I guess I did."

Angel had a bad feeling about what was coming. Something about Val's dad set his teeth on edge. He was glad the women had been recalled to the house...he couldn't shake the sense that something was up. He passed Kelan on the stairs to the den as he took Fiona up, giving her a break from the scanning and logging of historical Omni documents she'd been doing for the team. Selena was staying upstairs with the women. Rocco had all the kids in the gym shooting hoops. Angel was glad the watchers weren't anywhere near Parker.

He sent a quick glance around the bunker confer-ence room. The documents on the table were covered. The big smart screen showed Greer's digital model of the charts that had been in Jason Parker's secret room in his library.

The guys looked as tense as he was. Only Val's dad looked at peace. No, not peace. He looked like a felon who'd just had his case dismissed due to a technicality. The sneaky, sneaky bastard. What was he up to?

"You got a nice setup down here," Jason said. "Much better use of the space than Bladen's layout."

Angel tensed and shot a look over to Val, checking his reaction. There was nothing to see. His face was utterly without emotion—not even a hint of curiosity. "So you were here when Bladen was alive," Angel said.

"Mm-hmm. I was." Jason took a seat at the head of

the table and made himself comfortable by leaning back until his chair balanced on its two hind legs. "I visited once while you were in the service, Ty."

Well, that at least answered the question of whether he'd been here when Blade had been caged in the basement, Angel thought. But it opened a whole heck of a lot more questions. When Blade was in the service, Jefferson Holbrook was building a relationship with Amir Hadad—Jafaar Majid's predecessor. Had Jason just admitted to being on the wrong side of this Omni hell?

Kit walked into the room. He'd been listening to their convo through his comm unit. "What were you doing here at that point, Jason? Amir had his boys bunked here...all of them were enemies of the state."

Jason leaned forward, dropping his chair back into place. His eyes were bright as he looked up at Kit. "It's been a fabulous game, hasn't it?"

The room went silent.

"Has it been a game?" Blade asked.

"Yes!" Jason laughed, though no one else did. "Yes, it has. We had a good run. I thought it would only amuse me for a few months, but it's been decades of fun."

Val started to rise, but Kit set a hand on his shoulder.

"Go on," Kit said.

Jason nodded to Val. "You were to be my game piece, son."

Val's face turned to ice. "You killed my mother."

"No, you did. I had my girls. No one was going to

touch them. No one even knew the game had begun. But I still needed a boy. Once I had you, I was finished with her. You were her death sentence."

"You killed her," Val repeated.

Jason waved his hand. "I took her off the board. You didn't even know you were in the game, and still you thwarted me at every turn. I made sure you were taught martial arts, archery, marksmanship, but did you ever go hunting with me? No, you preferred to stay home with your sisters. I saw to it that you got into West Point, but you didn't want to be a soldier, you wanted to be a *barber*. You aren't a man—you're the creature your sisters made you. Your cousin, on the other hand, was born a warrior, that Owen was. I wanted one like him. I had to try again. And so there was Fiona. Lucky for her, I suppose, that she was a female. She got to stay with her mom, at least until it was time to take on her duties as an Omni princess." He glared at Kelan. "She could have been a queen had you not played the War Bringer and fouled things up."

"Whoa, there sparky." Kit held up his hand. "You aren't Fiona's father. We ran her DNA."

Jason chuckled and glanced at both Greer and Max. "You think you're the only one who can hack a database? I knew you'd come looking for some answers. I had Val's and my records switched out for another father/son pair. Of course you didn't see it." He looked around at the group. "But I still needed another son. Had to have the right game piece. Hope's mom was a good fuck." He sighed. "The way she fought me, I knew she'd give me what I wanted. A true warrior. She gave me Lion."

Angel went cold. "So, you're King?"

Jason smiled, glad someone was keeping up with him. "You think I'm King?" He laughed. "That's rich. You guys still don't get it, do you?"

"Enlighten us," Blade said.

"I wish I could, but that would violate the rules of the game."

"And what game is this, specifically?" Kit asked.

"One I made up. I was bored. My father and grandfather had already sown such a thick harvest of sins and secrets, it was easy to take up the reins of their operation. My tastes always ran a little darker than theirs. They were in it for power and money. I like rituals and sex." Jason bit his bottom lip, then smiled. "I was careless in those early days. But no one stopped me. Anything I said, they did. It was so much fun that my friends were begging to join me. So we made a game of it. Owen was Nick's game piece. Senator Whiddon had his son, Roy. Old Myers had his granddaughter, but only because he refused to use his grandson in the game." He shot a glance over to Ace. "He did cheat, though. He entered the game himself so he could train you. Senator Jacobs had his son, Wendell. Bladen had his little Ty, although he should have been disqualified, shouldn't he, since you're not his flesh and blood." Jason smiled at Blade. "And I...well, I cheated, too. I had two game pieces in play." He looked at Val. "One of whom I didn't care if I lost."

"A game, huh?" Blade said in a calm voice. "Who was the winner?"

"Oh, it's not over. But the winner will be the player whose game piece is the last one standing."

"So who is King?" Kit asked.

"Who is King?" Jason tapped his chin. "Who the fuck is King?" He laughed. "*I* can cheat, since I created the game, but you can't. You're going to have to figure that out yourself."

"Why come forward now?" Blade asked. "You could have played to the very end, possibly without us ever knowing what you were doing."

The humor left Jason's face. He looked at Val and then the others. "Because someone's hijacked *my* game. They're changing the rules, changing the players, mucking everything up. They're ruining everything I've built."

"Who's this new player?" Kit asked.

"I don't know. I'm relying on you to find that out."

Kit stared at Jason a long moment before nodding. "All right. Rocco, Kelan—take him to the bunkroom and lock him up. I want Lobo here before we go any further."

Jason stood. "I will give you a clue. Don't say I didn't help you. What's Syadne spelled backward?"

The letters rolled through Angel's mind. He cursed, which made Parker laugh as the guys led him away.

Before he disappeared into the hallway, he looked at Val over his shoulder, giving him a victorious smile. Val kept his cool, which told Angel just how pissed off he was.

"Syadne backward is endays...the fucking end days we've been hearing about," Angel growled.

The room went silent as Rocco and Kelan rejoined them. This thing—this game—had been in play a long, long time.

"If we can believe him, then Armageddon's coming from Syadne," Kit said.

"Yeah, and that nonsense about this being a game fits with what Greer discovered about his grandfather," Val said.

"Blade—get Eddie and Tank and go check out everything that Jason brought into the house, everywhere he was, including the boxes from his library," Kit ordered.

"On it." Blade left the room.

Greer tossed his spider chart up to the smart screen. He highlighted Jason, Nick, Whiddon, Bladen, Myers, and Jacobs. "Six monsters." He glanced around the table. "Could they have started this whole thing?"

"No. It started before them, early last century," Angel said. "But I do think they used whatever was already in play as a platform for their game."

"It's sickening they call it a game," Kelan said.

"Whatever it is," Rocco said, "it's gone beyond the destruction of our individual families and has spilled out to the world at large."

"And it's coming to a head," Val said. "Before he came down here, he said the call had gone out for all the players to come in. He said this was home base. I suppose because he thinks the game's been infiltrated."

"Armageddon's about to break loose," Angel whispered.

21

"**K**it, we got a visitor coming to the front door," Max said.

"What kind of visitor?" Kit asked.

"Don't recognize him...but he's got the sheriff and his deputy with him."

Kit went upstairs into the den, Angel and Val trailing him. The doorbell sounded down the long hall to the foyer. He opened the door.

"We got an issue, son," the sheriff said. He pointed a thumb toward the stranger. "This here's Walter Prescott, Jason Parker's lawyer. He's claiming you're holding Mr. Parker against his will."

"Nope. We're holding him in the interests of national security."

"You don't have the authority to do that," Deputy Jerry said.

Kit laughed. "We sure as fuck do. When Lobo gets here, we'll hand him over."

It was interesting that Jason's lawyer showed up now, Angel thought. Jason hadn't made any calls from the house. So this was all part of the bastard's elaborate plan. Another step in his fucking game.

"You have neither the authority nor the jurisdiction to hold him," the suit said. "If you don't release him immediately, the sheriff will arrest you."

Kit shook his head. "Can't do it. He's admitted to being involved in one murder and has implicated himself in two others. And we've only begun our interrogation."

The suit glared at the sheriff. "This is unacceptable. This extralegal procedure violates at least a dozen federal laws. None of the information will be valid in court, given the irregular circumstances under which it was collected. I demand Mr. Parker's immediate release."

"Does Lobo know about Mr. Parker?" the sheriff asked.

"I haven't called him yet," Kit replied.

"Then release Mr. Parker into my custody. I'll hold him until Lobo can take him," the sheriff said.

Kit shook his head. "He's an extreme flight risk. You have no understanding of the damage he can cause if he gets away from us. It is a matter of national security."

"Is this how the law works in your town, Sheriff?" the suit asked. "Anyone can violate anyone's constitu-

329

tional rights with impunity? Maybe I need to call the governor. Or the president."

"Call Lobo," the sheriff said to Kit. "The FBI has jurisdiction over this," he said to the suit.

"Go, Kit," Lobo said when he picked up the call.

Kit filled him in.

Lobo cursed. *"Hand him over to the sheriff. I'll be up there in a couple of hours. I'll take custody then."*

"I want to be part of his questioning."

"Not a problem."

WYNN WENT to answer the knock on her door. It was almost nine o'clock in the evening. Angel was there, leaning against the jamb. He wore a black cashmere V-neck sweater over a white tee and a pair of jeans that were tight on his thighs. The sweater fit him like a velvety second skin. There was a tension in his face that even his smile couldn't hide. She'd heard about Val's dad's visit earlier that day. It had to have been a shock for the whole team.

"Hi," he said.

"Hi." She caught her lip between her teeth. *Now and forever.* Did it mean to him what it did to her? She leaned against the opposite doorjamb and watched him. "Heard you guys had a tough day. Sorry about that."

"Seriously. And it's not over yet. We're waiting to hear from Lobo that he picked the bastard up. I feel awful for Val. And Fiona and Lion. Looks as if Val's dad may have been responsible for their mothers' deaths—if he didn't do the deed himself, then he ordered it done. All his life, Val was told he killed his mom, when it was his own father who'd killed her." He looked at her a long moment. "You feel like getting a drink or something?"

"Is it safe for us to do that?"

He gave her a wry grin. "It's safe. We're just going downstairs."

She looked down at herself. She was wearing a loose teal cotton sweater over jeans—and slippers. She'd been just about to change into pajamas before he came.

"You look perfect. Slippers are allowed in the billiards room. This is your house, after all."

She shook her head. Leaving the door open, she went down the hall to her room and switched her slippers for a pair of flats. She smiled at him when she came back into the living room. Was it wrong of her to want to be near him all the time? Because whatever that feeling was, it sure wasn't getting any better.

He caught her hand and threaded his fingers through hers. The contact felt amazing. In the billiards room, she was pleased to see they had the space to themselves. He used his phone to call up a playlist that he ran through the room's sound system. It was an instrumental piece from an artist she didn't recognize.

"Keaton Henson," he said when she asked whose music it was.

"It's nice."

"Make yourself comfortable. What would you like to drink?"

"Do you have any wines?"

"I'm sure we do." He went behind the bar. "There's an open bottle of Shiraz in the fridge. Then we have whites, rosés, and red wines. Any of those suit?"

"The Shiraz."

"Shiraz it is." He poured a glass, then grabbed a beer. He handed her the glass and sat next to her on the leather sofa. "Looks as if we'll be having the boys here for a little while. You really okay taking on their education?"

"I am. I'll need to do an assessment to get a feel for where they are with their schooling. Their conversational skills are well developed. We'll see where they're at for reading comprehension and math."

"Max said Lion took their education seriously, that he always had them studying some topic or other. Mostly war skills and military history."

"Interesting. I'll need a little time to put together a course of studies for them." She smiled at him. "It'll be a challenge—one I'll enjoy."

"Can they use the same online class system that Casey's doing?"

"Eventually, maybe. For now, I think they need human interaction even more than straight academics." She sipped her wine. "Do you think you'll be able to find their parents?"

"We'll try. The Omnis are a tough nut to crack. They

take secretive to a whole other level. They may not want to be found. And even if we do find them, they may not want their boys back for fear of retribution from the cult leaders. I think Remi was right about the need to preserve the pride, at least until the younger ones age out."

"I hope you find Beetle soon. Do you think Owen even knows he's missing?"

"We've had no communication with him, so it's hard to say. He may already be looking for him. I can't wait for the two of them to meet each other."

"How do you think he'll take it?"

Angel grinned. "Honestly, I bet he'll think he hit the lottery. Setting eyes on his son will be the best thing that ever happened to him. Owen's no different from any of us. He's just trying to find his place in the world."

"Why does he make me so nervous?"

Angel lifted a brow. "He's a hard-ass. Maybe you have an issue with them?"

She laughed. "Maybe."

Angel took her glass and set it with his on the coffee table, then took her hand and stood up. "Do you dance, Wynn?"

She smiled, feeling self-conscious. "Yes. Some."

He led her over to an area where the floor was bare wood. He drew her hands up to his shoulders and put his hands on her waist. The music had changed to another soulful tune. Wynn closed her eyes, letting herself be carried away by the feel of Angel's body against hers, the heat and scent of him. She laid her head against his chest.

How long they moved like that, she wasn't sure, but she startled when she heard other voices in the room. She looked over to see Kelan and Fiona and Rocco and Mandy also slow-dancing. She looked up at Angel, wondering if he'd been surprised by them as well.

"They've been here a while," he said.

When the music switched to a new song, Angel led Wynn back to the sofa and their drinks. Val and Ace came in, neither looking especially happy. Val poured two whiskeys, then the two of them joined Angel and Wynn. Over the course of the next few songs, all the rest of the team and their women came into the room. Fiona and Ace sat on Kelan and Val's laps so there was space for everyone in the circle.

The atmosphere in the room was heavy, as the guys were waiting for the other shoe to drop. Wynn broke the ice. "I'm sorry to hear about your dad, Val."

Val shrugged. "I guess I'm not completely shocked about him. What gets me is that we thought we were after a network of terrorists, but all along, it's been my dad playing us." He looked around the group. "My own flesh and blood's a danger to all of you. That's what I don't like."

"There's not much difference between a terrorist and a psychopathic serial killer," Ty said. "Maybe just a difference of politics."

"We need to find Owen. And Beetle," Kit said. "If

this game's nearly over, I don't like having them out in the wind."

"Don't forget Adelaide," Ace said. "She's been at the mercy of the Omnis a long time."

"Right," Kit said, nodding.

"What's her story?" Wynn asked. She remembered Owen's explosive behavior at Rocco and Mandy's wedding, but never really understood it.

"Owen had a thing for Jax's—Wendell Jacobs'—sister all of his life," Val said. "She was quite a bit younger than him, so she was always a little separate from them growing up. She graduated a year early from college. Owen and Jax went to celebrate her graduation. That's when she and Owen got together. Before they could announce their relationship, she was killed in a train accident."

"Oh, God. That's terrible," Wynn said.

"Yeah. Except it never happened," Val said. "It was staged. The Omnis faked her death and sucked her into their world. And now, after what Santo and my dad revealed, I wonder whether the senator colluded with them to surrender his daughter into 'the game.' Like Myers did with Ace."

Kit held up a hand. "We don't know for certain Myers did that."

Val shook his head. "Doesn't matter. He either put Ace in play or left her there. There's little difference."

"But didn't the senator start the Red Team?" Mandy asked, looking from Val to Rocco.

"He did," Angel said. "But we've discovered nothing is as it seems. Until we capture King, we won't know the whole truth."

"King is the leader of the Omnis?" Wynn asked.

"Yeah."

"Do you think my father's King?" Val asked the group. "I know he laughed it off, but..."

"That thought occurred to me," Ty said. "Could be there's more than one King. Maybe King is a consortium. Maybe the six men he mentioned are together acting as King."

IT WAS MUCH LATER when Angel walked Wynn back to her apartment. The group had stayed and talked for hours while they waited for Lobo to get there. Angel came inside to make sure everything was secure and no boogeymen were hiding in closets or under the bed. Wynn had to admit to herself that she always felt more comfortable once he'd cleared the space.

"I'm sorry I can't stay with you. Lobo should be here any minute."

"Go. I understand." He kissed her, then started for her door. She stopped him. "Angel—I get it now. Your war. You don't have a choice but to do your part."

He studied her for a long, silent moment. "Where does that leave us?"

She smiled. "Right where we need to be. Your team is lucky to have you. And so am I."

He slowly smiled. "Night, Wynn."

❧

IT WAS after midnight before Lobo got to the house. Kit let him in. He was alone. "Where's Parker?" Kit asked.

"His lawyer pulled some strings, got him released," Lobo said.

"I knew we shouldn't have turned him over to the sheriff."

"That wasn't your call to make."

Val went behind the small bar in the living room to pour himself a Balcones. "He never planned to stay. He didn't bring luggage. And his lawyer showed up without any communication from him. We were just a scheduled stop on his bullshit tour."

Lobo nodded. "I listened to the recording of your convo before his lawyer showed up. That's some fucked-up stuff. You believe him? He could still be playing you...acting a role, for some reason."

"It's that 'for some reason' part that's the kicker," Blade said.

"We've sent in fresh DNA swabs from Val, Lion, and Fiona. We'll see if the results corroborate his story," Kit said.

Lobo took the beer Greer handed him. "I'll visit his lawyer tomorrow. You guys believe this was all a game?"

Val set his glass on the bar top with an audible bang. "What does that even mean? People are dying. Families are being destroyed. Lives are being wrecked. This is no game."

"To him it is," Blade said. "And he's been playing it a long time."

"You crashing here tonight?" Kit asked Lobo.

"You got room? The watchers are here, no?"

"We have room. And even if we didn't, you could bunk in Owen's room," Kit said.

Lobo laughed. "I'd take the couch over his room... even without him in it."

22

———

"Miss Wynn! Look at this one!" Zavi called out excitedly.

Angel smiled as he watched Wynn hurry over to Zavi, glad she finally got her time to go hunting for leaves.

She looked at orange aspen leaf from both sides. "It's beautiful,"

He put it in his brown paper bag. "It's the only orange one I found."

Wynn glanced around them. "Maybe it blew from over there." She pointed toward a small grove of aspens where some had turned reddish-orange instead of yellow. "Let's see if we can find others like it."

They spread a few feet apart, wending their way toward that grove. Angel wondered how it was possible for him to fall deeper in love with Wynn with everything she said or did. She was able to keep Zavi's attention without much effort, but it was a little harder to get buy-in from the younger pride boys. Hunting for leaves was way below their skill level. Nonetheless, the activity helped all of them have some semblance of normal...even if normal came with a few heavily armed bodyguards like him, Selena, and Ace.

As for the watchers, Angel couldn't blame them for their flagging interest. They'd already spent weeks, months, or years, depending on when they joined Lion's pride, learning far more significant activities, like foraging for food, hunting, field-dressing game, cooking, celestial navigation, and so many other lifesaving skills that hunting for leaves in an autumn forest was like learning to walk all over again—when you never forgot it in the first place.

Wynn was working on introducing the boys to their childhood, using low-stress activities to tune their psyches to simple and fun activities. He hoped like hell it eventually worked. Clearly, it was an uphill battle. The three boys with them fell below the cutoff that Hawk had set for which boys joined which activities. Those who were thirteen or older went with Val and Kit to the gun range. They were well versed in all weaponry other than firearms and needed to modernize their education.

The older boys were likely never getting out of this world they'd grown up in, but the team hoped the younger boys might one day be returned to their families. Lion was a helluva leader. He'd kept his pride alive for a long time. That bond of loyalty became familial quickly, and breaking it was like losing your whole family all over again. In truth, Angel wasn't sure the boys could survive away from the pride—even if they reconnected with their original family.

Angel crossed his arms as he considered the possibility that they might need another plan for the watchers. A word carved on a tree trunk caught his attention. BEETLE. The hairs lifted on his neck. The team had missed it earlier when they searched the woods after the kidnapping attempt on Wynn.

"Spider, come here." The boy came over. Angel pointed to the tree. "Did you or one of the boys do that recently?"

"No, sir." Spider went over to touch and sniff the letters. They were about the height of a nine-year-old boy's chin. "Was Beetle here?"

"Possibly. A few days ago, some men used a boy to bait Miss Wynn to come into the woods. We don't know who the kid was. Given that Beetle's the only one missing—and now seeing this—I guess we have our answer." He took a picture of the carving and made a mental note to update the guys.

Ace distracted him from the tree. She was swatting at some bug that had a persistent interest in her. After a minute, the insect flew over to Wynn. He frowned and headed over to her. Nothing was going to wreck this day for his woman. God knew, she and the boys deserved this simple afternoon fun in the outdoors.

"Ouch!" Wynn slapped at her arm, then rubbed it as

she looked around her for the insect she'd just flattened. She took a few more steps toward the little aspen grove where Zavi's colorful leaf had come from, but collapsed before she reached it.

Angel ran the last few steps. So did Lion's boys, Zavi, Selena, and Ace. She was out cold. Christ, was she allergic to whatever had just stung her?

Angel pointed at Ace. She knew immediately what she needed to do. On their comms, she ordered an ambulance. "Have it come down the dirt road behind the forest. We're near the edge of the woods. I don't know if Wynn is breathing or not. She got stung by a bumblebee."

Angel heard Max's brief response. Wynn was pale, but not bluish. She had a good pulse. He put his cheek near her mouth and felt the warm flow of breath. What had happened to her? This didn't look like anaphylactic shock.

"Get the boys back in the house," he ordered Ace.

Ace nodded and grabbed Zavi's shoulder. She waved to the three pride boys, but they weren't moving.

"Go with her," Angel ordered. Normally, when he used that tone of voice, the people he was speaking to complied. Fast. Not so now.

The boys shook their heads. "No. We'll help guard your woman," Spider said, taking the lead as the eldest of the three watchers in the group.

"No need, boys. Get inside." Between the time Angel issued that order and when he looked up from

Wynn, they'd disappeared into the woods. He glared at Ace. She shook her head and hurried off with Zavi.

He lifted Wynn over his shoulder and brought her closer to the edge of the woods. He could hear the distant sound of sirens. The five-minute wait for the ambulance felt like a week and a half. He leaned against a tree and settled Wynn in his lap. She seemed sound asleep. He brushed the hair from her face, shocked that his beautiful princess had been felled by a dumb bug. She'd never mentioned any allergies to insect venom.

Blade and Rocco joined him. Rocco tested her pulse again. "She's breathing, Angel," Rocco said. "I don't know why she reacted the way she did."

"See if you can find the bug that did this," Angel asked them.

Both guys stood and glanced around the woods. "Angel...that's looking for a needle in a haystack," Blade growled.

"Fucking do it, Blade."

"I'll show them where we were," Selena said.

"Watchers," Angel shouted, "help us find the bug."

The boys slipped out of their hiding places and went deeper into the woods with Selena and the guys. Angel could hear branches and pinecones breaking under their feet as they moved around. The sirens got louder, then stopped as the paramedics pulled onto the dirt road and parked near Angel.

They donned gloves and grabbed their gurney, then hurried to him. They checked Wynn over. Her vitals appeared normal. There was nothing they could do without getting her to the clinic. Angel helped lift Wynn onto the gurney, then followed her over to the ambulance.

One paramedic got inside the back of the ambulance. The other waited to secure the doors.

Angel held up a hand. "Hold on. I'm coming with her."

The paramedic blocked him. "No, sir. That's against our policy. You can follow in your own vehicle."

Angel stepped back and glared at him, but quickly realized he was only drawing this out, delaying Wynn getting the medical attention she needed. "Fine."

He jogged through the woods, calling out to the guys, "I'm following her to the hospital." He ran across the lower and upper yards to the back parking lot below the garage. He charged inside the house, lunging for the basket of keys to the team's vehicles. He found the vehicle that went with the keys and popped the back hatch so he could stow his weapons in the secret container under the cargo area.

He'd just shut the hatch when he saw Ace, Blade, Rocco, Vole, and Spider running toward him.

"Wait, Angel!" Ace called. She pointed to something Rocco held. "You have to see this."

Angel frowned, resenting the further delay. He noticed only Vole and Spider came with them. "Where's Owl?"

"He followed the ambulance."

Angel had a bad feeling about that. "Why? He can't keep up with the it."

Rocco shoved something in Angel's face, distracting him from the loose cub. He held the bug between a couple of leaves. "It wasn't a bumblebee that stung her, Angel. This is a drone."

"Oh, shit."

Selena dipped into the garage and came out now with an old jar, which Hope had used for small screws or nuts and bolts. "Put it in here."

Angel grabbed the jar and got in the SUV. Blade was already in the passenger side. He backed out of the parking lot and flew down the drive. He saw Owl was on his way back to the group. That was a relief; Angel didn't want to worry about him when Wynn was foremost on his mind. The boy waved to them, but Angel was in too much of a hurry to stop.

Blade punched his arm. "Stop! Something's not right."

"No shit."

"I mean it. The boy wasn't waving. He was signaling us. Go back."

Angel hit the brakes, then reversed. Owl ran to Blade's side. "The ambulance went west, not east. They didn't take her to town."

Goddammit. "Max, where is she?"

There was a brief pause. *"She's headed toward the highway."*

The boy saw the ambulance go west. But she had to

have passed town to be headed toward the highway.
"I'm following her. Send someone after the ambulance.
And get everyone safe. Don't want this distraction to be
a smoke screen."

"Copy."

Angel sped down the driveway and turned toward
town. He looked in the rearview mirror and saw
another of the team's vehicles pull out in the opposite
direction. He had to slow to a crawl as he went through
town.

"North or south, Max?" Angel asked as he
approached the highway.

"South."

Angel took the access ramp and floored it. There
wasn't much traffic, but he weaved his way in and out of
both lanes as he tried to gain on the vehicle with Wynn.

"She's about a half mile ahead of you," Max said.

VAL PULLED an SUV out of the small parking lot and
paused long enough for Rocco to get in. They had a bit
of a straight run before the road took on some hellish
curves. About a mile into the Medicine Bow Mountains,
they caught up with some flashing lights. The ambulance was pulled over, but not fully on the wayside. A
sheriff's vehicle was behind it, partially blocking
the lane.

Val pulled around them and parked in front of the
ambulance. He slammed his door as he rushed back to

the back of the ambulance. Max had said she was headed in the opposite direction, but maybe that was just because whoever had taken her had separated her from her security necklace.

His body had turned to ice as another thought occurred to him: they might have killed her and left her body for Angel. He swung around the corner and looked into the open, empty cavity of the ambulance.

"Shoulda known this had something to do with you," Deputy Jerry said.

Rocco came toward the deputy like a bull to a rodeo clown. Stopping him with an arm in front of his chest, Val snapped, "What happened?"

"How would I know? I just got here. A call came in to dispatch that an ambulance had been hijacked and two paramedics had been dumped in the woods. What do you know about that?"

Val stepped toward the deputy, who dropped his foot from the ambulance bumper and straightened. "I know my friend's girlfriend collapsed. I know we called for an ambulance. I know she was kidnapped."

"Then you know a helluva lot more than I do. Like the sheriff said, you guys have been bad news from the beginning, bringing this shit to town."

Rocco was looking around the dirt wayside, checking for footprints or tire tracks. "Look." He pointed to the ground by the driver's side. "We got a footprint." He took a picture, then followed it around to the back. "They took the gurney out here." He pointed to where the narrow cot's tires hit the ground. The tracks were partially concealed by the deputy's car. "Great job, Deputy. You've obscured evidence."

The deputy's eyes twitched. "Didn't see that when I pulled up."

Rocco walked across the road to see if there were any tracks there. There were none. "There's no way to tell which direction they took her. But whichever it was, she was still on the gurney."

Val jumped into the ambulance and looked around. "She still has her security necklace. Least, it's not here." He looked at Rocco. "Let's head out after Angel."

"Max, you got the house locked down?" Rocco asked via his comm unit.

"Yup. The bunkroom's got a full house."

Val flew to the edge of town, then slowed.

"Dammit. We lost Wynn's signal," Max said. *"Angel, you're almost on top of her. Look around."*

"Val, you said they took the gurney, too?" Angel asked. *"There's no vehicle around me big enough to hold it. Get your ass up here. We're takin' over the road."*

Val grinned at Rocco as they turned onto the highway. "Whatever the fuck that means, I'm in."

ANGEL CONTINUED to pull ahead of cars. If he'd been close to Wynn—or at least the vehicle that had her security necklace—it had to be one of these, but none of them moved in an evasive way from his aggressive driving. "Today, Val," he said into his comms.

"I'm on your six, dude."

"Take the right lane and follow my lead."

"Uh, no. Really, I prefer leading, especially if the dance is complicated."

"Val...I swear I'ma fuck you over. I got one shot to get Wynn. Don't mess it up." Angel slowed down in the fast lane. Val followed suit in the slow lane. With the highway only two lanes wide, they clogged the road. Angel slowed then stopped, fully blocking the left lane and a good part of the wayside. Val did the same with the right lane.

All traffic stopped behind them. There were no barriers on either side of the road. People could have crossed the median or the wayside to get away from the shit going down, but no one did. Nor did he expect them to. Most civilians never comfortably violated rules, even to save their lives.

Angel popped the rear hatch. He took a Remington pump-action shotgun out of the weapons compartment, along with ammo, then closed the hatch. From another compartment, he grabbed a few cell phone jammers. He tossed one to Rocco.

"Let them go through as we clear them," he said to Blade and Val. "Tell Kit what we're doing. We're gonna need Lobo to smooth this over."

Moving in sync, Angel and Rocco cleared the first two vehicles. The car Angel faced had a mom and a carload of kids, all of them terrified. "Open your trunk, ma'am." Her hand shook as she complied. The trunk was full of groceries. He came back to her window. "Thank you." He nodded over to Blade, who waved the woman on over the shoulder. He repeated that search with car after car. The line slowly shifted forward. Thirty cars later, they still hadn't found Wynn. Twenty more cars, and Angel knew he'd lost her. Somehow, she'd gotten away. Maybe she'd never come this way.

He stomped back to his SUV. "We're done here." He got into the driver's side and pounded the dashboard. He pulled in front of Val, then both of them drove off over the grassy hillside that bordered the highway and headed back in the direction of town.

ANGEL STORMED INTO THE CLINIC. He held the bumblebee drone in the glass jar. He asked for Doc Beck at the front desk, but was told the doctor was seeing a patient. Angel went down the hall to the waiting room outside Doc Beck's section of rooms. He stood there for a long while, more than he could spare —every second was taking Wynn farther from him.

He wasn't in a waiting frame of mind.

He went into the hall and started banging on doors, shouting for Doc Beck. As he got to the third door, Beck came out in the hallway. Before the doctor could shut him down, Angel leaned down to his face and said, "I need you."

"So do my patients."

"They can wait." He held out the jar. "Tell me what poison was in this drone."

That piqued the doctor's interest. "What makes you think there was poison in it?"

"Because it stung Wynn and she collapsed."

"Where is she?"

"She was kidnapped by a couple of ambulance hijackers."

"Damn. Okay." Doc Beck took the jar and walked down the hall to a lab area. Angel followed him. The doc pulled a pair of gloves on, then emptied the jar into a glass petri dish. He stared at it, then looked at Angel. "This really is a drone."

"No shit. What can you tell me about the poison it carried?"

Beck put it under a microscope. "Not much. The stinger is gone. There's no visible evidence that its contents spilled on the remaining mechanism. I can test it, but it's not going to be a fast process. And I'll have to destroy this drone to do it."

"Never mind. Put it back in the jar. I'll send it to my lab."

"I hope you find Wynn, and that she's fine when you do."

———————

23

Wynn felt the pain of lying on a hard cement floor first. Her mind scrambled to identify where she was. The basement of Ty's house? She'd never been down there, but with all the construction that was intermittently progressing, she didn't think it would have the musty smell this one did.

She pushed herself to a sitting position. The room was completely black except for a thin line of dim light that came from the closed door. She reached for her emergency necklace, but it was gone. She patted her chest and legs, relieved that she was still wearing the same outfit she'd had on when she was hunting for leaves with the boys in the woods.

How long ago had that been? Hours? Days? She was thirsty, but not hungry. What had happened to her? The last thing she remembered was being in the woods behind Ty's house. Her arm was sore. She rubbed it, then remembered the bumblebee that had stung her, but everything after that until waking up here was a blank.

She got to her feet—her bare feet—then wobbled as the world spun around her. Had she been drugged? She didn't feel ill, but she didn't feel right, either. Why had they taken her shoes? To keep her from running? When her legs were steady, she made her way over to the door. Just as she was about to reach for the knob, she heard voices on the other side.

"Why are you doing this?" a woman asked. Hearing her, Wynn got gooseflesh. She tried to place that voice, but couldn't, and yet...she knew it.

Wynn turned the knob. The door was locked. The floor was cold. Her feet were freezing. She had to find a way out of there.

"It is nothing personal, you understand," came a voice she knew all too well. Jafaar Majid. But who was he talking to? "Your employers want something from me—you two. And I want something from them. I'm sure we'll be able to make an exchange soon."

No way was she ever going to let Jafaar control her fate. She felt around for a light switch near the door and flipped it on. She was in some kind of storage area for large mechanical parts. She couldn't leave the light on long for fear the people in the other room would see it and know she was awake. She did notice there was a window on the opposite side of the room covered with cardboard.

"What is it that you want?" another man said. His voice was oddly familiar as well. "We have some leverage with them. Perhaps we can help you get it."

Wynn made her way over to the window and ripped off the cardboard. It was small, and high, but if she climbed on the stacked clutter, she might be able to get out. She tested it to see if it would take her weight.

"There is some merit to your suggestion," Jafaar said. "If you go back to Syadne willingly, then I believe we could make a deal."

Wynn gasped, frozen in place as she listened to their conversation. Did Jafaar have her parents? Or was this some kind of act being played out for her benefit?

"No," the woman said. "We're never going back. We've given everything there is to give to them. I'm not going to let them get their hands on our daughter. I've already lost my mother."

"And that was unfortunate," Jafaar said. "I do apologize for having to take that extreme action. Syadne double-crossed me, reneging on a deal we'd made for the Middle Eastern franchise of the"—he paused —"human enhancement treatment you've developed."

"You killed her?" the man asked.

"No. I wouldn't do such a heinous act. Not after having hosted your lovely mother in my home. I did hire her killers, however." Wynn could hear the sneer in Jafaar's voice. He answered as if he believed Grams truly was related to the couple. "That fortuitous action not only severed the hold Syadne had over you, but King now must wonder if the alliance he made with the White Kingdom Brotherhood is as solid as he thought."

"We created that treatment," the man said. "You don't need Syadne to get it; you need us. Let our daughter go, and we'll give it to you."

There was suspicion in Jafaar's voice when he said, "That program was developed in a lab full of scientists."

"Yes. A lab we ran using procedures we developed," the man said. "We'll work for you, but you have to let our daughter go. You have no other option. Returning us to curry favor with Syadne will not get you what you want. They aren't going to share the technology. In fact, they're killing off everyone who worked in our lab rather than risk it leaking out. It's why we left. Handing us over to them will just get us killed. It won't get you the cut you want."

"Prove you can do what you say."

"That will take time," the man said. "We'll need a lab with specialized equipment, which isn't easy to source."

"Cut our daughter loose," the woman ordered. "If you don't, the men she's living with will not stop coming after you...and us."

"Perhaps I will kill her," Jafaar said.

That threat lit a fire under Wynn. She managed to get the window open, but it was still too high up for her to go through. She needed to make the debris pile higher. She climbed back down. The uncovered window let a little more light into the room. She searched around the area, looking for something she could add to the heap.

"Yes. Do that. And then you can kill us, because you'll get nothing from us," the man said.

Wynn leaned her forehead against a cold pipe. Did they know they were having this conversation within earshot of her? Was this staged? Were those people really her parents? They were putting her safety before their own, as only parents would. But it could all be an act. This terrible experience had taught her not to be fooled by such trickery.

"Let us retrieve your daughter," Jafaar said. "We will resume this discussion in a more comfortable situation."

Wynn just had time to dash behind a tumbled shelving unit and a big engine of some kind before the light flashed on and Jafaar and the couple came into the room. She wasn't able to see them until they stopped in front of the window. The man and woman were taller than Jafaar. Though she still couldn't see their faces, she could tell they were slim and youthful looking—far too young to be her parents.

So it had been a bit of acting. It might have worked, had she never seen them.

"She's gone." Jafaar muttered something in a language she couldn't understand. He turned and sent a look around the room. Wynn held her breath, hoping they would continue to believe she'd gotten out the window and not give the room a once-over.

"We have to leave. Now," Jafaar ordered.

"Not without our daughter," the man said.

"She isn't here. We will look for her outside, but we can't stay here. Just as I discovered where you were, others will too. We must leave."

The room went silent. And dark. Were they gone? Or merely trying to flush her out? She waited the length of a breath, then counted out another minute before easing away from her hiding place. Cold air blew in from the window she'd opened. The door to the other room was open. She peeked into the next room. It looked like a ship's engine room. Big, rusted boilers and thick pipes stood forgotten. All kinds of metal debris covered the floor. Pigeons flew about, unhindered by the broken windows. No one was around. She didn't want to call out for fear someone might have been left to guard her. If Jafaar was right and others were coming, then she couldn't stay there either.

She had no idea where she was, other than in an abandoned warehouse of some sort. She was barefoot. She had no phone and no money to make a call. And she didn't know Angel's number. She'd never bothered to memorize it because her phone was always with her... until now, when she needed it the most.

She walked, very gingerly, toward a wide-open, hangar-sized door. The floor shifted beneath her feet. A sharp piece of metal cut her big toe. Wynn cried out, then slapped her hand over her mouth. She couldn't risk alerting someone this close to getting out.

Perhaps I will kill her. Jafaar's words slipped through her mind.

Her hands shook as she used the same sharp piece of metal that cut her foot to cut off a bit of her sweater sleeve so that she could tie it around her toe. She had to get out of the warehouse before anyone else came.

She peeked around the corner of the yawning warehouse entry. All she could see was a whole lot of nothing. Junkyards overgrown with grass and weeds. Closed businesses. And yet she could hear the sounds of the city tantalizingly close. But what city? The mountains looked the same as those near Cheyenne. She walked out of the warehouse, into the gravel parking lot, the borders of which had been obscured by a heavy growth of weeds.

She walked out to the dirt road. There was so much flat land around that she could see she was well east of the mountains, but beyond that, she couldn't find any identifying landmarks. As she walked in the direction of the city sounds, she passed a burned-down house, a few more empty warehouses—these were steel buildings, more recent than the brick one she'd just come from. There was an abandoned gas station. The gas tanks had all been removed. A minor miracle was hanging on the wall...an old pay phone. She hoped it was still in service as she jogged over to it.

She picked up the phone from its cradle. Her knees

went limp with relief when she heard the dial tone. She hit zero for the operator.

"Operator. How may I help you?"

"Yes. I need to make a collect call, but I don't have the number. Can you look it up for me?"

"Yes, ma'am. Who are you trying to reach and in what city?"

"Mandy Silas, Wolf Creek Bend, Wyoming."

"And your name, please?"

"Wynn Ratcliff."

"One moment." Pause. *"I have that number. I'll attempt to put the collect call through. Just a moment."*

"Thank you." *Please hurry,* she silently urged. She looked around herself, making sure there was still no one around. Her teeth were starting to chatter. Her feet were freezing.

She heard a phone ringing. *Pick up, Mandy. Pick up.*

"Hello?"

"This is the AT&T operator with a collect call from Wynn Ratcliff. Will you accept the charge?"

"Yes! Yes, I will."

"You're all set, Ms. Ratcliff."

"Thank you." There was a click on the line.

"Wynn! Where are you? Are you safe? Angel's losing his mind."

Relief tangled with her anxiety, making it difficult to speak. "I'm fine. Well, I cut my toe and it's bleeding. Is he there? I really need—"

"Wynn!" Angel's deep voice came over the line.

"Angel." Wynn choked on a sob. "I'm scared."

"Baby, where are you?"

"I don't know. Near some abandoned buildings. I'm calling from an old gas station. Near Cheyenne, I think."

"Are you alone?"

"Yeah. Jafaar had a couple pretending to be my parents. They couldn't have been them—they were way too young."

"Keep talking. Max is getting your coordinates. Are you hurt?"

"Just my toe. I cut it on something. Angel, I'm scared. I don't know if they're coming back."

"Max, text the info, we're heading toward her now."

She didn't hear Max's response, but she could tell Angel was hurrying someplace. Maybe coming up from the bunker. She never thought she'd miss that place, but she wished she was back there right now.

"Wynn, can you find a safe place to hide? Someplace you can see us when we come for you?"

"Yes. I will."

"Go do that now."

"Okay."

"Wynn—babe, I love you."

She drew a shaky breath. "I love you too, Angel."

"I wanted to say that to you in person the first time, not over the phone. I've loved you forever."

"Come find me."

"Done. We'll be there fast. Don't call the police. I'm afraid

the Omnis have infiltrated them. They've infiltrated everything."

"I won't. Hurry."

"We're not even an hour away now. Go hide."

"I will. Bye." She was reluctant to hang up.

"Bye, sweetheart." The line went dead.

She stood there, feeling the emptiness of her without him. *Go hide,* his voice whispered in her mind. She looked around, wondering where she could go. The grass was tall, and she was barefoot. She didn't want to get hurt again if there was broken glass or other sharp things she couldn't see. She hurried down the rough road to a fence on the opposite side of the road. No one was around. She wasn't certain if that was comforting or disturbing. Either way, she was on edge.

She crouched down for a long wait. She didn't have a watch or her phone, so she had no idea how much time passed. Her legs were cramping from being kept in the same position for a long time. She distracted herself by replaying in her mind the conversation she'd overheard between Jafaar and the couple.

Had they been her parents? She leaned forward, resting her forehead on her knees. Was that even possible? Maybe they were older than they'd looked. She hadn't seen their faces, after all.

Another thought struck her. When they had come into the storage room where she was hiding, they seemed to believe she'd gotten out through the window.

And still they had continued acting like her parents. Why would they have done that if they weren't?

More than ever, she wished Grams was still around so that she could ask her all the questions she had. If her parents were alive, had Grams known they faked their deaths?

She had to accept that she was never going to have some of the answers she needed. It was time to quit looking backward and start looking forward. Angel's face slipped into her mind, a welcome sight. He was always looking out for her—he had even before they were together.

How had she, in the middle of all this chaos, found such a solid guy?

After a long while, she heard the engines of a couple large vehicles coming down her street. She crawled forward to see if they were the team's SUVs. Sure enough, two black Suburbans drove past her.

She laughed with relief. This horrible night was over. She could go home and be with Angel. He *loved* her. What a wonderful feeling it was to love someone who loved you. She hopped up out of her hiding place and hurried down the street after the SUVs. They pulled into the parking lot of the big brick warehouse.

As she approached, three men got out of one vehicle and four out of the other. That number was the first thing that set off alarms. Why would the team send so many for her? It left everyone at Ty's house with little protection.

She knew the answer as soon as she thought the question: they wouldn't.

She came to a stop, then turned and ran. Too late. They'd spotted her. Two men ran after her. Another was calling off orders to search the warehouse. A man caught her from behind and lifted her off her feet. She kicked at his shins, kicked at the air, tried to throw him off balance. She threw her head back, but connected with his chin instead of his nose. She hooked her feet around the guy's knees, causing him to stumble and drop her.

Another of the men hurried over to help. He had some sort of big automatic rifle, which he pointed at her. "Get in the SUV."

"No."

He lifted his gun, butt first. Before he could hit her with it, she cringed and shouted, "Okay. Okay."

The guy opened the back passenger door on the driver's side and shoved her inside. He and three other guys got in. "Get us out of here," the guy riding shotgun shouted.

"What about the others?"

"They'll follow."

Before they could go far, their car was rammed from behind, sending them into a spin. Wynn looked out the rear window and saw a third SUV. The guy beside her on the back seat opened his door and leaned out, peppering rapid fire at it. Wynn kicked him out of the car.

After that, everything happened fast. She saw Angel rush for the newly emptied seat, but the driver shot at him, so he had to fall back. Wynn screamed and kicked the back of the driver's seat to stop him from shooting.

"Hold her, dammit!" the driver shouted to the man who was sitting next to her. She struggled with him, until she felt the cold metal of a gun barrel pushed into the side of her neck.

There was a sound on the roof of the SUV. Someone was up there. The guy in the front passenger seat started shooting into the roof. Wynn could do nothing to help Angel. If she lost him now, she doubted she'd ever recover.

The window next to the driver shattered. The front passenger fired more shots into the roof as the driver slipped his arm out and fired haphazardly at something above him. All of a sudden, his door was yanked open and the driver was jerked from the vehicle.

Angel slipped into the driver's seat, shooting the front passenger as he did so. The man holding Wynn tightened his grip on her. The way he was holding the gun against her throat hurt, and his arm around her ribs was cutting off her air.

Angel parked the SUV, grabbed the dead passenger's weapon and tossed it in the back seat. Wynn lunged for it. When she did, Angel shot her captor.

It was over. In mere seconds, all four of her captors had been decommissioned. Angel grabbed her hand and pulled her out of the SUV, rushing her back to the team's vehicle. As soon as they got in, Val and Max jumped in. They turned around and headed back toward the main portion of town.

"What about the others?" Wynn asked. "There are more guys in the warehouse."

"Yeah. Max put trackers on their vehicles. We'll let them run to ground, see where they go." He reached into the third-row seat and grabbed a blanket, which he wrapped around her. "Are you hurt? Besides your toe?"

"No. What happened, Angel? How did they get me?"

"You were stung by a drone. They poisoned you or gave you a sedative. We're taking you right to the clinic to find out what it was. And to have your toe stitched up."

"But you were with me. I couldn't have been safer."

"The ambulance we called had drivers working for Jafaar. The real drivers were found while we were looking for you. They said their hijackers spoke to each other in a Middle Eastern language."

He moved closer and wrapped his arms around her. "I can't believe how easy it was for them to get you. It could have happened to any of us. You must have been terrified."

"I was. But now I'm just mad. I overheard Jafaar talking to a man and woman. He said they were my parents, but I don't know that I believe that. When I saw them, they seemed too young to be my parents."

"What did he say?"

"Jafaar was who ordered the hit on Grams. And he said he wanted to exchange my parents for some kind of drug that Syadne had. He called it a 'human enhancement treatment.' My parents, if that's who those people really were, bargained with him, offering to go with him and give him the medication in exchange for my freedom. I guess it worked, because he took them but left me. Who were those guys you fought?"

"I think they were more Omni trackers, probably looking for your parents."

"The man—my dad—said they needed a lab and specialized equipment. It sounded like they had the formula for whatever it is that Jafaar was after."

Max looked back at them. "The Syadne labs in the missile silo tunnels are empty...or were when we were last there. And there may be room in their labs under the WKB complex."

"I don't think Jafaar would risk going there," Wynn said. "He wouldn't risk exposing my parents to being recaptured by the Syadne people. Or the Omnis."

Angel's hold around her tightened. "We need to find them before they give Jafaar the technology they developed—and before Syadne terminates them."

Wynn nodded. "My father said Syadne was killing off its scientists to keep whatever it was they developed locked down. If Syadne finds them, they're dead."

24

W
ynn watched the early morning fog move through the woods in back of the team's house. November mornings were often moody. She couldn't tell if it was going to burn off and be a brilliant autumn day or if it was going to stay gray and socked in the whole day.

Angel had gone for a run a little while ago, even though neither of them had gotten much sleep the night before. It had been the middle of the night before they got home from the clinic, and then almost morning before she finished debriefing the team. The rest of the night, Angel had just held her. She must have dozed off, because she never heard him get up.

The morning sun was just starting to filter through the fog, spreading light on a continuum that played through all the yellows and oranges that nature knew. It was mesmerizing. Wynn opened her kitchen door so she could go out and stand in the damp, colored air.

As she watched, something moved in the fog. Something big. A man. She gasped and was just about to rush back inside when she recognized who it was.

Angel.

He was damp from head to foot. His nose was slightly pink. He looked up at her. He changed directions. Stepping out of the fog tendrils, he came toward her. Helpless to step away, she watched him come up the steps, fast at first, then slow for the last few treads.

He came onto the landing. She moved back, making room for him on the small deck. He caught her face. For a long minute, they simply stared into each other's eyes. Wynn had the oddest feeling that he was all she ever needed. His gaze lowered to her lips, and his mouth followed, pressing against hers. She caught his waist, then moved her hands up his back, tightening the contact of their bodies as he worked her mouth. Her nails found the shallow valley of his spine. She ran her fingertips as far up his back as she could reach, then back down again.

Waves of heat rolled off him. He smelled sweet, like mountain snow and the pine forest he'd been running through. He reached behind her and opened her kitchen door, then closed it behind them. He kissed her as he moved her backward through the kitchen, down the hall, and into her bedroom—a long and sexy walk to her bed. She wasn't certain her feet hit the floor once.

He pushed her kimono off her shoulders, baring her lacy peach bra and panty set. She'd been getting ready to finish her morning routine when she stopped to watch the morning fog. She'd brushed her teeth, but hadn't put her makeup on yet. And her hair—she'd just dried it and was getting ready to use the curling iron, but it was a frizzy mess. She put her hands up to her head.

"Angel. I'm a wreck. I don't even have my face on."

He chuckled, looking thoroughly unconvinced. He ripped his fleece pullover and tee over his head. "No, sweet knees. What you are is a feast I'm about to dive into." A wolfish grin followed his words as he cupped her breasts, lifting their heavy weight as he bent to kiss the soft flesh above her bra. He kissed his way up to her neck, her jaw, her mouth. One of his hands went around her back, down the small of her back, and over her boy briefs to palm her ass.

She reached to unclasp her bra, but he stopped her. "Not yet." He bit his lower lip. He stepped away from her, his eyes devouring her body. He kicked off his running shoes, then backed into one of the armchairs so he could take his socks off. He stood and pushed his jogging pants and briefs down his hips and kicked them off, all while letting his eyes devour her.

Looking at his rigid erection, Wynn felt the strength leave her legs. She sat on the bed. Angel's eyes, usually a dark coffee brown, had now gone black. Gooseflesh covered her arms and back as she anticipated the feel of his body on hers.

He covered himself from the stash of condoms he'd put in her nightstand. Grinning at her, he took a dive onto the bed. Neither of them expected the mattress to crash to the floor at that end.

Wynn yelped as she rolled down the bed toward him. He caught her and rolled her under him. "Oh my God. You broke the bed!"

"Yeah, didn't think that through." He laughed.

"Do you suppose they heard that downstairs?"

"Probably." He laughed again.

"You're going to get in trouble."

That just made him laugh harder. "No, I won't. I'll tell them you did it."

Wynn gasped, but couldn't be too angry. She'd never seen Angel's whole face so filled with humor. He was too beautiful to be human. Nonetheless, she squealed and wiggled out from under him to crawl her way up to the top of the bed, which was still standing.

He hissed. On her hands and knees, she looked behind her. He met her eyes, then roared as he caught her ankles. The bed shifted as he came after her. She squeaked and tried to get away. He lifted her hips up, making her kneel again. He moved her panties aside and pushed into her. She pulled a sharp breath as he filled her. Her body shivered. He leaned down over her, covering her.

"God, I love your body."

No guy she'd ever been with had said that to her. In fact, none of them had ever even given her an orgasm. Angel moved her hair to one side and kissed her shoulder. The bristles of his beard were nearly her undoing. He reached under her and caught her breast, flattening her other one with his forearm. He held her as he thrust in her, his rhythm fitting perfectly with hers.

"You were right," he whispered in her ear.

"About what?" What had they been talking about? She couldn't think with fire licking her skin and his hard body filling her.

"You said our souls bonded the moment we met. You were right. I'm sorry it's taken so long to follow what they already knew." He moved his hand down to her core. His expert touch found just the spot to massage. She cried out, peaking instantly.

As soon as her orgasm eased, he pulled out of her to turn her over. She whimpered in complaint. He pulled her panties off and entered her again. The brief break in contact had only hardened him. He spread his legs wide, forcing hers farther apart. He reached up to grip the edge of the mattress, using it to deepen his thrusts. The tension in his face tightened with each thrust. She loved the look of his passion, the way it hardened the planes of his face. He freed a hand and pushed her bra up over her breasts. It was uncomfortably tight, but the pressure on her breasts was exquisite.

He dipped his head, and his hot mouth latched onto a breast as his hand squeezed it, tightening and releasing in pulses. She touched herself as he pounded into her. Another violent orgasm racked her body. She dug her heels into the slanted mattress and pushed up, meeting his thrusts. He went deep, banging at the back wall of her vagina. One peak rolled into another.

He grunted, then did a final thrust. She felt his body stiffen as he peaked. Her string of orgasms hadn't yet subsided. He licked and sucked her breasts as her body slowly, slowly calmed. He kissed his way up to her mouth, which he leisurely made love to.

She wrapped her arms around his shoulders. He looked down at her, deeply into her eyes as he moved the hair from her face. He gave her a warm smile. "So, this is love, huh?"

She nodded. It had to be. It felt wonderful. Warm, from her toes to the ends of her hair. It felt complete. Perfect. She set her hands on his cheeks. "I love you, Angel."

"I love you." The warmth left his face, leaving behind the mask of a warrior. "I'm never giving you up. Now *and* forever, that's what I want."

She smiled at his fierce words. "I like that."

He got up, then reached for her hands to help her up. He stretched a leg across the bed and kicked the headboard. The bed banged to the floor. His jaw clenched as he looked back at her. He picked the footboard up and leaned it against the wall, then came back and caught her hand. "Didn't want to slow us down later. How about a shower?"

"I just took one."

"I'm not done with you." Not taking no for an answer, he led her into the bathroom. He turned the shower on to warm up, then covered himself with a new condom.

"You're not finished?" She smiled as she said it, surprised he was ready to go again, but that was clearly the case.

He faced her. "No. I will never be finished with you."

AN HOUR LATER, they went down to breakfast. Wynn's body and mind were humming. Angel never let go of her hand as they stepped up into the dining room.

Max was at the buffet, filling a plate. He sent them a look over his shoulder. "Sounded like a wrecking ball in your room. Hope thought you were both coming through the ceiling."

Wynn gasped. She'd already forgotten about the bed.

"Sorry about that. Wynn broke the bed."

She gasped. "I did not. You did."

Angel laughed, as did the rest of the guys. "So I did." He got serious. "I intend to break a whole bunch more beds, too."

She leaned closer to him and used her stern teacher's voice to scold him. "Angel, there are children here."

He grabbed her and buried her in his arms. "Wynn's agreed to marry me," he told the room.

She pushed free of him. "Maybe I will, if you ever asked me properly."

Angel dropped to one knee, still holding her hand. "I don't have a ring yet. I wasn't anticipating we'd move this quickly. And besides, you should probably pick it out, since you're going to wear it the rest of your life. But I do have this." He fished in one of the pockets of his cargo pants, then pulled out a little brown velvet box, which he opened.

Inside were the earrings she fell in love with in Cheyenne but couldn't afford to buy. "You remembered. I love them."

"Wynn, will you marry me? Will you complete my life and give me a future worth living?"

The breath left Wynn's chest. She pulled her hand free from his and held both hands against her cheeks. She felt a little dizzy.

"Jesus, don't say no," Angel whispered.

When she shook her head, dread filled his face. She hit her knees and reached out to him. "Yes. Yes, I'll marry you."

He huffed a breath, then pulled her into a big hug. "Yeah?"

She laughed. And cried. "Yeah."

"So I get to break all your beds?"

She chuckled through her tears. "I think we may need to work on that behavior."

He kissed her forehead, her cheek, her mouth. The room erupted into cheers as everyone surrounded them. He helped her to her feet. She switched out her earrings for the ones he'd given her. He looked down into her eyes, and the silence of that moment wove them together, almost as if she could feel their souls talking. She threw her arms around his neck. He squeezed her tight. When he pulled back, he wiped the back of his hand across his eyes.

Wynn had no time to react to that as the chaos of the room ended their moment. Mandy and Eddie were giving her hugs. She looked over at Angel, surrounded by his friends and smiled at him. His gaze was so intense, his face so hard, he seemed unable to smile back at her. God, she loved him.

25

———

"Whom shall I say is calling?" the butler asked Owen. His self-effacing manner was little cover for his alert eyes. Was he part of King's world? A plant, like the Jacksons had been?

"Tell her I'm a friend of her brother's."

The butler admitted him into the foyer. Owen's heart beat so hard his ribs felt bruised. He took a few controlled breaths to calm himself. He didn't know what he felt more—excitement, relief, or anger. All were rangy emotions that jumbled his attempts to calm himself.

He walked around the grand entryway, looking at the art. This house was like a British palace that had been transported across the ocean to sit in this place, right down to the buttery marble and portraits that made the foyer look like a gallery.

Helluva place to hole-up in.

There was a whisper of fabric on the stairs. He looked up to see a woman coming down the curving staircase, her graceful, long-nailed hand holding tight to the ornate banister. Adelaide. She was as slim as he remembered. Her white silk shirt was tucked into the front of her skinny jeans. Her golden hair was loose and long, spilling about her shoulders, straighter than he remembered it.

When their eyes met, she stopped. Midway down the stairs, she looked as if she wanted to run back upstairs. If she did, he'd follow. He'd goddamned earned that right. She continued down the stairs. Owen didn't move, didn't take his eyes from her, didn't do anything to make this meeting easier on either of them. She stepped off the last step, but kept close to the stairs. She stared at him. So many emotions flashed through her eyes that it was like watching a movie played on the fastest speed.

Eventually, she walked into one of the large parlors off the entryway. He followed her. She moved deep into the room, so composed and silent that he wouldn't have known anyone was there, were his eyes shut. Except the faint scent of her lingered in the air, teasing his memory, reminding him of what never was.

They stared at each other for a long moment. There seemed no need for words the way their eyes exchanged all the injuries of the years since she'd faked her death. Owen was the first to lower his gaze. What the fuck was he doing there? He had only useless things to say to her, things that were only stating the obvious. *So you aren't dead, as I'd believed all these years. So we had a son together, whom you never saw fit to tell me about. So I'm nothing to you, if it was so easy to walk away from me, away from us. So I see you survived the hell of life in the Omni royalty.*

His mind told him to leave the room, fast, like the walls were on fire.

His soul told him to touch her. Just fucking touch her.

His feet broke the tug of war. He walked up to her. Her shoulders were squared. Her gaze was unapologetic. Only inches of air separated them. *Touch her. Touch her, you goddamned coward.* He lifted his hand as her eyes bored into his. His palm touched her face. A shiver sliced through him.

"Laidy." His voice broke on the nickname he'd given her decades ago, a play on her name that he'd used when he'd pretended to be her knight in shining armor. He caught her face in both hands. His nostrils flared. "My Laidy." His voice was a hoarse whisper. Tears filled her eyes. Her long fingers wrapped around his wrists then stretched over his hands.

He wanted to kiss her, yearned to feel her lips against his, hungered to feel the curves of her body with his, but he knew he wouldn't survive losing her a second time. And she wasn't his to take. She was married to some Omni bastard.

There was nothing he felt inside. Nothing. Just a great, empty warehouse where his soul should have been. He dropped his hands. His lungs locked up, refusing to service his body. He wavered on his feet, then walked out of the gilded room, out of the marble entryway, out of her fucking palace. He slammed the door behind him, listening with satisfaction as the sound reverberated in the hollow space of the marble foyer.

Wendell was sitting on the front steps. Owen stormed past him.

"Done already? I thought you'd be longer."

"I got nothing to say to her." Nothing...and everything.

"So you're running like a coward."

"Quit fucking playing me, Jax."

Jax stood up. "Go back in there and talk to her."

Owen spun back around. "Well, that's a turnabout for you, isn't it?" They were face to face now. "You couldn't stand to see my affection for her. Before. Not once."

"I grew up." The corners of Wendell's cheeks bunched and relaxed and bunched again.

"Yeah?" Owen coughed out that snarl. He punched Wendell's chest. "When did that happen? Yesterday? The day before?"

Wendell was stoic. "A long time ago."

"That a fact?" Rage exploded inside Owen. He

shoved Wendell, then came after him again, fisting his tee and fleece pullover as he dragged him close. "You couldn't have told me she was still alive? That I have a child?"

Jax didn't push free. "I didn't know if it was the truth—until the DNA sample. I couldn't believe it myself. I thought the Omnis were screwing with us."

It was an exquisite torture, one the Omnis would have used if they'd known it would have brought Owen instantly to heel. That thought made him ease his grip on Jax on long enough for his friend to pull him into an embrace. A broken breath cut free from Owen.

Wendell wrapped his arms around Owen's neck and dipped his forehead to Owen's. "Please. I beg you. Don't abandon my sister."

Owen let out a ragged sigh. "I never did. She abandoned me."

"You don't know the story."

"I can't live it again."

"Hear her out." Wendell looked at him. "Did you see her hair? Beautiful, wasn't it?"

Owen nodded.

"It's a wig."

Owen frowned. Blood was rushing through his veins like a spring runoff. He had to take a couple of breaths to slow it down. What was Jax implying?

"Our only hope is that we can stop your father from his aggressive attack on the neo-Omnis. It's making them clean house. They're getting rid of all of their researchers, any one of whom might have engineered the disease that Adelaide's fighting. We don't have a lot of time." Wendell stared into his eyes. "She's dying, Owen."

OTHER BOOKS BY ELAINE LEVINE

MEN OF DEFIANCE SERIES

(This series may be read in any order)

ABOUT THE AUTHOR

Elaine Levine lives in the mountains of Colorado with her husband and a rescued pit bull/bull mastiff mix. In addition to writing the Red Team romantic suspense series, she's the author of several books in the historical western romance series Men of Defiance. She also has a novel in the multi-author series, Sleeper SEALs.

Be sure to sign up for her new release announcements at http://geni.us/GAlUjx.

If you enjoyed this book, please consider leaving a review at your favorite online retailer to help other readers find it.

Get social! Connect with Elaine online:
    Reader Group: http://geni.us/2w5d
    Website: https://www.ElaineLevine.com
    email: elevine@elainelevine.com

Made in the USA
Monee, IL
20 November 2019

17158671R00223